Acclaim for

Tatyana Tolstaya's

Sleepwalker in a Fog

"An impressive display of imagination and prose virtuosity."
—*Philadelphia Inquirer*

"Tolstaya creates a special richness....She makes her tales extraordinarily charming for all their sadness." —*Wall Street Journal*

"The stories are held together by the bubbling energy of the prose, sympathetic characterizations, and Tolstaya's rueful humor...but it is [her] willingness to charge her language...that also results in the haunting lyricism of her art." —*Boston Globe*

"[Tolstaya] observes the turbulent battlefield of Russian life with an acute eye, a ready wit and...a compelling way with words."
—*Chicago Sun-Times*

"[Tolstaya's] elegant, musical prose, her imagistic virtuosity and the apparent timelessness of her themes evoke a bygone age and attitude." —*Times Literary Supplement* (London)

Tatyana Tolstaya

Sleepwalker in a Fog

Tatyana Tolstaya lives in Moscow with her husband and two sons.
She was born in Leningrad in 1951, and graduated from Leningrad
University in 1974. She has taught in the United States at the
University of Richmond in Virginia and at the University of
Texas, and has lectured widely throughout the United States. Her
stories have appeared in *Neva, Novyi Mir, Oktyabr, Aurora,*
Sintaksis, The New Yorker, and *The Paris Review.* Her first
collection, *On the Golden Porch,* was published by Knopf in 1989.
Tolstaya is a distant relative of Leo Tolstoy and a granddaughter
of the writer Alexei Tolstoy.

INTERNATIONAL

Also by Tatyana Tolstaya

On the Golden Porch (1989)

Sleepwalker in a Fog

Sleepwalker
in a Fog

Tatyana Tolstaya

Translated from the Russian

by Jamey Gambrell

Vintage International
Vintage Books
A Division of Random House, Inc.
New York

FIRST VINTAGE INTERNATIONAL EDITION, APRIL 1993

Copyright © 1991 by Jamey Gambrell

Library of Congress Cataloging-in-Publication Data
Tolstaia, Tatiana, 1951–
    [Selections. English. 1993]
    Sleepwalker in a fog / Tatyana Tolstaya; translated from the Russian
by Jamey Gambrell. — 1st Vintage international ed.
        p.   cm.
    ISBN 0-679-73063-X
    1. Tolstaia, Tatiana, 1951–   —Translations into English.
I. Title.
    [PG3476.T58A24   1993]
    891.73'44—dc20   92-50613
                        CIP

Author photograph © Jerry Bauer

Book design by Anthea Lingeman

Manufactured in the United States of America
10 9 8 7 6 5 4 3 2 1

Contents

Sleepwalker
in a Fog

Sleepwalker
in a Fog

Having made it halfway through his earthly life, Denisov grew pensive. He started thinking about life, about its meaning, about the fleetingness of his half-spent existence, about his nighttime fears, about the vermin of the earth, about the beautiful Lora and several other women, about the fact that summers were humid nowadays, and about distant countries, in whose existence, truth be told, he found it hard to believe.

Australia aroused special doubt. He was prepared to believe in New Guinea, in the squeaky snap of its fleshy greenery, in the muggy swamps and black crocodiles: a strange place, but, all right. He conceded the existence of the tiny, colorful Philippines, he was ready to grant the light blue stopper of Antarctica—it hung right over his head, threatening to dislodge and shower him with stinging iceberg chips. Stretching out on a sofa with stiff, antediluvian bolsters and worn-out springs, smoking, Denisov glanced at the map of the hemispheres and disapproved of the continents' placement. The top part's not bad, reasonable enough: Landmasses here, water there, it'll do. Another couple of seas in Siberia wouldn't hurt. Africa could be lower. India's all right. But down below everything's badly laid out: the continents narrow down to nothing, islands are strewn about with no rhyme or reason, there are all kinds of troughs and trenches. . . . And Australia is obviously neither here nor there: anyone can see that logically there should be water in its place, but just look what you've got! Denisov blew smoke at Australia and scanned the water-stained ceiling: on the floor above him lived a seafaring captain, as white, gold, and magnificent as a dream, as ephemeral as smoke, as unreal as the dark blue southern seas. Once or twice a year he materialized, showed up at home, took a bath, and drenched Denisov's apartment along with everything in it, though there wasn't anything in it other than the sofa and Denisov. Well, a refrigerator stood in the kitchen. A tactful man, Denisov couldn't bring himself to ask: What's the matter?—especially since no later than the morning following the cataclysm the splendid captain would ring the doorbell, hand him an envelope with a couple of hundred rubles—for repairs—and depart with a firm stride. He was off on a new voyage.

Denisov reflected on Australia irritatedly; on his fiancée, Lora, distractedly. Everything had already been pretty much decided; sooner or later he intended to become her fourth husband, not because she lit up the world, as the saying goes, but because with her no light was needed. In the light she talked incessantly, saying whatever came into her head.

"An awful lot of women," said Lora, "dream of having a tail. Think about it yourself. First of all, wouldn't it be pretty—a thick fluffy tail, it could be striped, black and white, for example—that would look good on me—and you know, on Pushkin Square I saw a little fur coat that would have been just the thing for that kind of tail. Short, with wide sleeves, and a shawl collar. It would go with a black skirt like the one that Katerina Ivanna made for Ruzanna, but Ruzanna wants to sell, so just imagine—if you had a tail, you could get by in a coat without a collar. Wrap it around your neck—and you're all warm. Then, say you're going to the theater. A simple open dress, and over it—your own fur. Fabulous! Second, it would be convenient. In the metro you could hold on to the straps with it; if it's too hot—you've got a fan; and if someone gets fresh—slap him with your tail! Wouldn't you like me to have a tail? . . . What do you mean, you don't care?"

"Ah, my beauty, I should have your worries," Denisov said morosely.

But Denisov knew that he himself was no prize—with his smoke-stale jacket, his ponderous thoughts, his nocturnal heart palpitations, his predawn fear of dying and being forgotten, being erased from human memory, vanishing without a trace in the air.

Half of his earthly life was behind him, ahead lay the second half, the bad half. At this rate Denisov would just whir over the earth and depart, and no one would have reason to remember him! Petrovs and Ivanovs die every day, their simple names are carved in marble. Why couldn't Denisov linger on some memorial plaque, why couldn't his profile grace the neighborhood of Orekhovo-Borisovo? "In this house I dwell. . . ." Now he was going to marry Lora and die—she wouldn't have it in her to make an appeal to the place where these things are decided, whether or not to immortalize. . . . "Comrades, immortalize my fourth husband, okay? Comrades, pleeease." "Ho-ho-ho . . ." Who was he anyway, in point of fact? He hadn't composed anything, or sung anything, or shot anyone. He hadn't discovered anything new and named it after himself. And for that matter, everything had already been discovered, enumerated, denominated; everything alive and dead, from cockroaches to comets, from cheese mold to the spiral arms of abstruse nebulae. Take some old virus—swill, worthless rubbish, couldn't make a chicken sneeze, but no, it's already been grabbed, named, and adopted by a couple of your scholarly Germans—just have a look at today's paper. If you think about it—how do they share it? They probably found the useless bit of scum in some unwashed glass and fainted from happiness—then the shoving and shouting started: "Mine!" "No, mine!" They smashed eyeglasses, ripped suspenders, gave each other a thrashing, puffed and panted, then sat down with the glass on the sofa and embraced: "Hey, pal, let's go fifty-fifty!" "All right, what can I do with you? . . ."

People assert themselves, sink their hooks in, refuse to go —it's only natural! Take the recording of a concert, for example. A hush falls over the hall, the piano thunders, the keys flash like lozenges gone berserk, lickety-split, hand over fist, wilder and wilder; the sweet tornado swirls, the heart can't stand it, it'll pop right out, it quivers on the last strand, and suddenly: ahem. Ahe he kherr hem. Khu khu khu. Someone coughed. A real solid, throaty cough. And that's that. The concert is branded from birth with a juicy, influenza stamp, multiplied on millions of black suns, dispersed in all possible directions. The heavenly bodies will burn out, the earth will become crusted in ice, and the planet will move along inscrutable stellar paths like a frozen lump for all time, but that smart aleck's cough won't be erased, it won't disappear, it will be forever inscribed on the diamond tablets of immortal music —after all, music is immortal, isn't it?—like a rusty nail hammered into eternity; the resourceful fellow asserted himself, scribbled his name in oil paint on the cupola, splashed sulfuric acid on the divine features.

Hmmm.

Denisov had tried inventing things—nothing got invented. He had tried writing poems—they wouldn't be written. He started a treatise on the impossibility of Australia's existence: He made himself a pot of strong coffee and sat at the table all night. He worked well, with élan, but in the morning he reread what he had written, tore it up, cried without shedding tears, and went to sleep in his socks. It was soon after this that he met Lora and was nourished, listened to, and comforted many a time, both at his place in Orekhovo-Borisovo, where the captain of course drenched them in a golden rain, draining his Kingston valves again, as well as in her messy little apartment, where something rustled in the hallway all night.

"What is that," asked Denisov, alarmed, "not mice?"

"No, no, go to sleep, Denisov, it's something else. I'll tell you later. Sleep!"

What was there to do? He slept, dreamt nasty dreams, woke up, thought over what he'd dreamt, and dozed off again, and in the morning he drank coffee in the kitchen with the sweet-smelling Lora and her widower father, a retired zoologist, a most gentle old man, blue-eyed, a bit on the strange side— but who isn't a bit strange? Papa's beard was whiter than salt, his eyes clearer than spring; he was quiet, quick to shed tears of joy, a lover of caramels, raisins, rolls with jam; he bore no resemblance to the noisy, excitable Lora, all gold and black. "You know, Denisov, my papa's wonderful, a real dove of peace, but I've got problems with him, I'll tell you about it later. He's so sensitive, intelligent, knowing, he could go on working and working, but he's retired—some ill-wishers schemed against him. He gave a paper in his institute on the kinship of birds and reptiles or crocodiles or something—you know what I mean, right?—the ones that run and bite. But the research director's last name is Bird, so he took it person-ally. These zoologists are always on the lookout for ideological rot, because they haven't decided yet whether man is actually a monkey or if it just seems that way. So they sacked poor Papa, bless his heart, now he stays at home, cries, eats, and popularizes. He writes those, you know, notes of a phenologist, for magazines, well, you know what I mean. On the seasons, on toads, why the cock crows, and what it is that makes ele-phants so cute. He writes really well, none of that wishy-washy

puffery, but like an educated person, plus he's lyrical. Pop-
pykins, I tell him, you're my Turgenev—and he cries. Love
him, Denisov, he deserves it."

His head lowered, sad and humble, Lora's snow-white papa
listened to her monologues, dabbed the corners of his eyes
with a handkerchief, and shuffled off to his study with little
steps. "Shhhhh," whispered Lora, "quiet now . . . he's gone
to popularize." The study is silent, desolate, the shelves are
cracking, the encyclopedias, reference books, yellowed jour-
nals, and packets with reprints of someone's articles are all
gathering dust—everything is unneeded, disintegrating, grown
cold. In a corner of the necropolis, like a solitary grave, stands
Papa's desk, a pile of papers, copies of a children's magazine:
Papa writes for children; Papa squeezes his many years of
knowledge into the undeveloped heads of Young Pioneers;
Papa adapts, squats, gets down on all fours; noise, exclama-
tions, sobs, and the crackle of ripping paper issue from the
study. Lora sweeps up the scraps, it's all right, he'll calm down
now, now everything will work out. Papa's on the wolf today,
he's tackling the wolf, he's bending him, breaking, squeezing
him into the proper framework. Denisov looked distractedly
at the swept-up scraps:

"The Wolf. *Canis lupus.* Diet."

"The wolf's diet is varied."

"The wolf has a varied diet: rodents, domesticated livestock."

"Varied is the diet of the gray one: here you have both
rodents and domesticated livestock."

"How varied is the diet of the wolfling cub—our little gray
dumpling tub: you'll find both bitty baby rabbits and curly
little lambs. . . ."

Don't worry, don't worry, Papa, my darling, write on; everything will pass. Everything will be fine. Denisov is the one
destroyed by doubts, worm-eaten thoughts, cast-iron dreams.
Denisov is the one who suffers, as if from heartburn, who

kisses Lora on the top of the head, rides home, collapses on the sofa under the map of the hemispheres, his socks toward Tierra del Fuego, his head beneath the Philippines. It's Denisov who sets an ashtray on his chest and envelops the cold mountains of Antarctica in smoke—after all, someone is sitting there right now, digging in the snow in the mighty name of science; here's some smoke for you, guys—warm yourselves up; it's Denisov who denies the existence of Australia, nature's mistake, who feebly dreams of the captain—time for another drenching, the money's run out—and whose thoughts again turn to fame, memory, immortality. . . .

He had a dream. He bought some bread, it seems—the usual: one loaf, round, and a dozen bagels. And he's taking it somewhere. He's in some sort of house. Maybe an office building—there are hallways, staircases. Suddenly three people, a man, a woman, and an old man, who had just been talking with him calmly—one was explaining something, one was giving him advice about how to get somewhere—saw the bread and sort of jerked, as if they were about to attack him but immediately refrained. And the woman says: "Excuse me, is that bread you have there?" "Yes, I bought it—" "Won't you give it to us?" He looks and suddenly sees: Why, they're siege victims. They're hungry. Their eyes are very strange. And he immediately understands: Aha, they're victims of the siege of Leningrad, that means I'm one too. That means there's nothing to eat. Greed instantly overwhelms him. Only a minute ago bread was a trifle, nothing special, he bought it just like he always does, and now suddenly he begrudges it. And he says: "We-ell, I don't know. I need it myself. I don't know. I don't know." They say nothing and look him straight in the eyes. The woman is trembling. Then he takes one bagel, the one with the fewest poppy seeds, breaks it into pieces, and hands it out; but he takes one piece for himself all the same, he holds it back. He crooks his hand strangely—in real life you couldn't bend it that way—and keeps the piece of bagel.

He doesn't know why, well, simply . . . so as not to give everything away at once. . . . And he leaves posthaste, leaves these people with their outstretched hands, and suddenly he's back at home and he understands: What the devil kind of siege? There is no siege. We're living in Moscow anyway, seven hundred kilometers away—what is this all of a sudden? The refrigerator is full, and I'm full, and out the window people are walking around contented, smiling. . . . And he is instantly ashamed, and feels an unpleasant queasiness around his heart, and that plump loaf oppresses him, and the remaining bagels are like the links of a broken chain, and he thinks: So there, I shouldn't have been so greedy! Why was I? What a swine . . . And he rushes back: Where are they, those hungry people? But they aren't anywhere to be found, that's it, too late, my friend, you blew it, go look your heart out, all the doors are locked, time has opened and slammed shut, go on then, live, live, you're allowed! But let me in! . . . Open up! It all happened so fast, I didn't even have time to be horrified, I wasn't pre-pared. But I simply wasn't prepared! He knocks at a door, bangs on it with his foot, kicks it with his heel. The door opens wide and there is a cafeteria, a café of some sort; tranquil diners are coming out, wiping well-fed mouths, macaroni and meat patties lie picked apart on the plates. . . . Those three passed by like shades lost in time; they dissolved, disintegrated, they're gone, gone, and will never come back. The branches of a naked tree sway, reflected in the water, there's a low sky, the burning stripe of the sunset, farewell.

Farewell! And he surfaces on his bed, on the sofa, he's surfaced, the sheets are all tangled around his legs, he doesn't understand anything. What nonsense, really, what is all this? If he would just fall asleep again immediately, everything would pass and by morning it would be forgotten, erased, like words written on sand, on the sea's sonorous shore—but no, unset-tled by what he had seen, he got up for some reason, went to the kitchen, and, staring senselessly straight ahead, ate a meat-patty sandwich.

A dark July dawn was just breaking, the birds weren't even singing yet, no one was walking on the street—just the right sort of time for shades, visions, succubi, and phantoms.

How did they put it? "Give it to us"—was that it? The more he thought about them, the clearer the details became. As alive as you and me, honestly. No, worse than alive. The old man's neck, for example, materialized and persisted, stubbornly incarnating itself, a wrinkled, congealed brown neck, as dark as the skin of a smoked salmon. The collar of a whitish, faded blue shirt. And a bone button, broken in half. The face was indistinct—an old man's face, that's all. But the neck, the collar, and the button stayed before his eyes. The woman, metamorphosing, pulsating this way and that, took the shape of a thin, tired blonde. She looked a little like his deceased Aunt Rita.

But the other man was fat.

No, no, they behaved improperly. That woman, how did she ask: "What've you got there, bread?" As if it weren't obvious! Yes, bread! He shouldn't have carried it in his string bag, but in a plastic bag, or at least wrapped in paper. And what was this: "Give it to us"? Now what kind of thing is that to say? What if he had a family, children? Maybe he has ten children? Maybe he was bringing it to his children, how do they know? So what if he doesn't have any children, that's his business, after all. He bought the bread, therefore he needed it. He was walking along minding his own business. And suddenly: "Give it to us!" How's that for a declaration?

Why did they pester him? Yes, he did begrudge the bread, he did have that reflex, it's true, but he gave them a bagel, and a flavorful, expensive, rosy bagel, by the way, is better, more valuable than black bread, if you come right down to it. That's for starters. Second, he immediately came to his senses and rushed back, he wanted to set things right, but everything had moved, changed, warped—what could he do? He looked for them—honestly, clearly, with full awareness of his guilt; he banged on doors, what could he do if they decided not to wait and vanished? They should have stayed put, held on to the railings—there were railings—and waited quietly until he ran back to help them. They just couldn't be patient for ten seconds, how do you like that? No, not ten, not seconds, everything's different there, space slips away, and time collapses sideways like a ragged wave, and everything spins, spins like a top: there, one second is huge, slow, and resonant, like an abandoned cathedral, another is tiny, sharp, fast—you strike a match and burn up a thousand millennia; a step to the side—and you're in another universe. . . .

And that man, come to think of it, was the most unpleasant of them all. For one thing, he was very stout, sloppily stout. He held himself a bit apart, and although he was aloof, he looked on with displeasure. And he didn't try to explain the way to Denisov either, he didn't take part in the conversation at all, but he did take the bagel. Ha, he took the bagel, he pushed himself ahead of the others. He even elbowed the old man. And him, fatter than everyone. And his hand was so white, like a child's, stretched taut and covered with freckles like spilt millet, and he had a hook nose and a head like an egg, and those glasses. A nasty sort all round, and you couldn't even figure out what he was doing there, in that company. He obviously wasn't with them, he had simply run up and hung around, saw that something was being given out—so, why not. . . . The woman, Aunt Rita . . . She seemed the hungriest of the three. . . . But I gave her a bagel, after all! It's a real luxury in their situation—a fresh, rosy morsel like that. . . . Oh God, what a situation! Who am I justifying myself to? They don't exist, they don't. Not here, not there, nowhere. A murky, fleeting, nighttime vision, a trickle of water on glass, a momentary spasm in some deep dead end of the brain; some worthless, useless capillary burst, a hormone gurgled, something skipped a beat in the cerebellum or the hippocampus— what do they call them, those neglected side streets? Neglected side streets, paved thoroughfares, dead houses, night, a streetlamp sways, a shadow flits by—was it a bat, a night-flying bird, or simply an autumn leaf falling? Suddenly everything trembles, dampens, floats, and stops again—a short, cold rain had fallen and vanished.

Where was I?

Aunt Rita. Strange traveling companions Aunt Rita had chosen for herself. If, of course, it was her.

No, it wasn't her. No. Aunt Rita was young, she had a different hairdo: a roll of bangs on her forehead, fair, wispy hair. She would whirl in front of the mirror, trying on a sash and singing. What else? Why, nothing else. She just sang.

She must have been planning to get married.

And she disappeared, and Denisov's mother ordered him never to ask about her again. To forget. Denisov obeyed and forgot. Her perfume flacon, all that remained of her, a glass one with an atomizer and a dark blue silk tassel, he traded in the courtyard for a penknife and his mother hit him and cried that night—he heard her. Thirty-five years had passed. Why torment him? . . .

What does the siege have to do with it, I'd like to know. The siege was already long past by then. That's what comes of reading all sorts of things at bedtime. . . .

I wonder who those people are. The old man looks like the farmer-fisherman type. How did he get in there? . . . And the fat guy—what, is he dead too? Oh, how he must have hated dying, his kind are afraid of dying. What squealing there must have been. And his children probably shouted, Papa, Papa! . . . Why did he die?

But comrades, why visit me? What do I have to do with it?

What did I do, murder someone? These aren't my dreams, I
don't have anything to do with it, it's not my fault. Go away,
comrades. Please, go away.

Lord, how sick I make myself!

Better to think about Lora. A pretty woman. And one good
thing about her—although she shows all signs of really loving
Denisov, she doesn't pester him, doesn't demand uninter-
rupted attention, hasn't set her sights on changing his way of
life, but entertains herself, goes to the theater, to underground
art openings, to saunas, while Denisov, thinking arduously,
wastes away on his sofa and searches for the path to immortality. What problems could she be having with her father?
He's a good, quiet papa, just what the doctor ordered, he
keeps himself busy. He sits in his study, doesn't meddle in
anything, nibbles on chocolates, writes articles that he puts by
for winter: "The master of the woodlands loves a tasty treat
of dry, fleshy multicarpels and dry indehiscents. . . . But as
soon as the north wind blows, as soon as foul weather begins
to sport and play, the Bruin's overall metabolism slows ab-
ruptly, the tone of the gastrointestinal tract lowers, and we
observe a corresponding growth of the lipid layer. But the
minus range doesn't frighten our friend Mikhailo Ivanych: a
first-rate scalp and a splendid epidermis. . . ." Oh, to crawl
into a cave like a bear, to burrow into the snow, close your
eyes tight, grow deaf, depart into sleep, pass through the dead
city along the fortress wall from gate to gate, along the paved
streets, counting the windows, losing count: this one's dark,
that one's dark, and this one too, and that one will never light
up—and there are only owls, and the moon, and dust grown
cold, and the squeak of a door on rusty hinges . . . but where
have they all gone? Aunt Rita, now there's a nice little house,
tiny windows, a staircase to the second floor, flowers on the
windowsill, an apron and a broom, a candle, a sash, and a
round mirror, why don't you live here? Why don't you look
out the window in the morning? The old man in the blue shirt

is sitting on a bench, resting from his long life, the freckled fat man is bringing greens from the marketplace, he'll smile and wave; here the knife grinder sharpens scissors, and over there they're beating rugs. . . . And there's Lora's papa riding a bicycle, turning the pedals, dogs are following him, they get in the way of the wheels.

Lora! I'm sick, my thoughts oppress me. Lora, come on over, say something. Lora? Hello!

But Lora doesn't have the strength to come all the way out to Orekhovo-Borisovo, Lora's terribly tired today, I'm sorry, Denisov, Lora went to see Ruzanna, something's wrong with Ruzanna's leg, it's a real nightmare. She showed the doctor, but the doctor doesn't have a clue—as usual—but there's a woman named Viktoria Kirillovna, she took one look and immediately said: You've been *jinxed*, Ruzannochka. And when they put the hex on you, it always affects the legs. And you could probably find out who put this spell on you, Viktoria said, but that is a secondary question because there are thousands of witches in Moscow, and right now the main thing is to try and lift the spell. First off you have to fumigate the apartment with onion stalks, all the corners. So we went and fumigated, and then Viktoria Kirillovna checked out all the potted plants and said: These are all right, you can keep them, but this one—what, are you crazy, keeping this in the house? Throw it out immediately. Ruzanna said that she knows who's out to get her, it's the women at work. She bought herself a third fur coat, went to work, and right away she felt the atmosphere tense up. It's just plain envy, and it's not even clear why they have such base feelings; after all, like Ruzanna says, it's not like she bought the fur coat for herself, she really bought it for others, to raise the aesthetic level of the landscape. Ruzanna herself can't see anything from inside the coat anyway, but it makes things more interesting for everyone on the outside, there's more variety for the soul. And for free too. I mean, it's almost like an art show, like the *Mona Lisa* or Glazunov;

for that they push and shove and wait in humongous lines for five hours and have to pay their own hard-earned rubles to boot. But here Ruzanna spends her own money and presto—art delivered to your door. And then they're unhappy about it. It's just crass ignorance. And Viktoria Kirillovna agreed: That's right, it's crass ignorance, and instructed Ruzanna to lie on the bed with her head to the east. Ruzanna showed her a photo of the dacha that she and Armen have on the Black Sea so that Viktoria could tell her whether everything was all right there, and Viktoria looked at it carefully and said: No, not everything. The house is heavy. A very heavy house. And Ruzanna got upset, because so much money's been put into that dacha, would they really have to redo everything? But Viktoria reassured her; she said she'd find some time and visit the dacha with her husband—he possesses amazing abilities too—she'd stay there awhile and see what could be done to help. She asked Ruzanna whether the beach and the market were nearby, because they are sources of negative energy. It turned out that they're very close, so Ruzanna got even more upset and asked Viktoria to help right away. She begged her to fly to the Caucasus immediately and do everything possible to screen out these sources. So Viktoria—she's really got a heart of gold—is taking a photograph of Ruzanna's leg with her so she can work on healing her down south.

And Viktoria told Lora that her energy core had become completely unfocused, her spinal cord was polluted, and her yin was constantly sparking, which could mean serious trouble. It's because we live near the TV tower and Papa's and my fields are incredibly warped. And as for Papa's case—I'm having some problems with Papa—Viktoria said it's beyond her capabilities, but there's an absolutely amazing guru visiting Moscow now, with some unpronounceable name, Pafnuty Epaminondovich, or something like that; he cures people who believe in him, with his spittle. A wonderful, totally uneducated old fellow with a beard to his knees and piercing, piercing eyes. He doesn't believe in blood circulation and has already convinced a lot of people that it doesn't exist—even a woman doctor from the departmental clinic, a big fan of his, is completely convinced that he's basically right. Pafnuty teaches that there's no such thing as blood circulation, only the appearance of it, but juices, on the other hand, do exist, that's certain. If a person's juices have stagnated—he gets sick; if they've coagulated—he'll be disabled; but if they've gone to hell and completely dried up, then it's curtains for the poor guy. Pafnuty won't treat everybody, only those who believe in his teachings. And he demands humility, you have to fall at his feet and beg—"Grandfather, help me, poor, wretched worm that I am"—and if you do it just right, then he spits in your mouth and they say you feel better instantly, it's as if you've seen the light and your soul has been uplifted. The healing takes two weeks, and you can't smoke or drink tea, or even take a drop of milk, God forbid—you can only drink unboiled water through your nose. Well, the academicians are furious, of course. You see, all their scientific work is shot, and their graduate students are beginning to look elsewhere, but they can't touch him because he cured some bigwig. They say that firm from Switzerland came—what's it called, Sandoz or something—anyway, they took his saliva to analyze—those guys won't do anything without chemistry, they've got no spirituality, it's just awful—so, well, the results are top secret, but supposedly they found levomycitin, tetracycline, and some sort of psi factor in the old man's saliva. And back in Basel they're building two factories for the production of this factor, and that journalist Postrelov, you know, the famous one, he's writing a very polemical article about how we shouldn't stand for bureaucratic red tape and the squandering of our national saliva, or else we'll end up having to buy back our own resources for foreign currency. Yes, I'm sure of this, and just yesterday I was in that shop called Natasha, waiting in line for Peruvian tops—not bad, only the collars were pretty crude—

and I started talking to a woman who knows this Pafnuty and can arrange a meeting with him while he's still in Moscow, or else he'll leave and go back to his Bodaibo in the Far East again. Are you listening to me? . . . Hello!

Silly woman, she, too, ambles along haphazardly, her arms outstretched, groping at ledges and fissures, tripping in the fog; she shudders and twitches in her sleep, reaches for will-o'-the-wisps, her graceless fingers grasp at the reflection of candles; she grabs ripples on the water's surface, lunges after smoke shadows; she leans her head to one side, listens to the swish of wind and dust, smiles a distracted smile, and looks around: something flickered by just now—where has it gone?

Something bubbled, rippled, tripped, skipped, snapped—pay attention!—behind, up above, upside down, it's vanished, it's gone!

The ocean is empty, the ocean rages, mountains of black water crowned by wedding wreaths of seething foam move with a roar: These watery mountains can run far and free—there are no obstacles, nothing to limit the gale-force turmoil. Denisov abolished Australia, tore it out with a crackling rip like a molar. He dug one foot into Africa—the tip broke off—and then dug in more firmly: good. He pressed the other foot into Antarctica—the cliffs jabbed him and snow got into his boot—steady now. He grasped the erroneous continent more firmly and swayed back and forth. Australia was staunchly moored in its maritime nest; his fingers slipped in the slimy seaweed, coral reefs scratched his knuckles. Come on now! One more time . . . there we go! He ripped it out, broke into a sweat, held it with both hands, wiped his brow on his forearm; Australia was dripping at the root, sand flaked from the top —a regular desert. The sides were cold and slippery, the slime had grown fairly thick. Well, and where to put it now? In the Northern Hemisphere? Is there any room there? Denisov stood with Australia in his hands, the sun shone on the nape of his neck, evening was coming on, he could see far into the distance.

His arm itched under the flannel shirt—yikes, there are bugs or something crawling on it. They're biting! Damn! He flopped the heavy stump back—spray shot up—it gurgled, listed, sank. Ehh . . . That's not the way he wanted to . . . But something had bitten him. He squatted and disappointedly ran his hand through the murky water. To hell with Australia. It doesn't matter. The population there is uninteresting. A bunch of ex-convicts. He only wanted what was best. But he did feel sorry for Aunt Rita. . . . Denisov turned on the sofa, knocking over the ashtray; he bit his pillow and howled.

Deep in the night he nurtured the thought that it would be fine to lead some small, pure movement. For honesty, say. Or against theft, for example. To purify himself and call on others to follow. For starters he'd return all borrowed books. Not filch any more matches and pens. Not steal toilet paper from offices and trains. Then greater and greater things—before you knew it, people would follow. He'd nip evil in the bud, wherever he encountered it. Before you knew it, people would remember you with a kind word.

The very next evening, standing in line for meat, Denisov noticed that the shop assistant was cheating, and he decided to expose him immediately in word and deed. He loudly informed his fellow citizens of his observations and proposed that everyone whose meat had already been weighed and who was waiting in line to pay, return to the counter and demand that it be reweighed and the price recalculated. There are the control scales right over there. How long, O compatriots, will we tolerate falsehood and injury? How long will the greedy beasts, those insatiable leeches, flout the sweat of our labor and mock our dovelike timidity? You, old grandfather, reweigh your brisket. I swear on my honor that there's twenty kopecks' worth of paper there.

The line grew agitated. But the old man to whom Denisov's righteous appeal had been directed cheered up immediately and said that he had cut down counterrevolutionaries like

Denisov on the southern and southeastern fronts, that he had fought against Denikin, that as a participant in the Great Patriotic War he now received his bit of caviar on holidays, an iron-shaped tin of ham made in the Federal Republic of Yugoslavia, and even two packets of yeast, which testified to the government's unconditional trust in him, a participant of the GPW, in the sense that he wouldn't use the yeast improperly and make moonshine. He said that now, in response to the government's trust, he was trying to stamp out sexual dissolution in their Black Swan cooperative and he wouldn't allow any lowlifes in Japanese jackets to lead a revolt against our Soviet butchers, that a correctly oriented person should understand that the meat shortage was due to the fact that certain individuals had gotten an expensive breed of dog inaccessible to simple people, and the dogs had eaten all the meat; and so what if there's no butter—that means there won't be any war, because all the money from butter has gone into defense, and those who wear Adidas shoes will betray our motherland. When he had spoken his piece, the old man left contented.

Having listened to the old-timer's speech, a few people grew serious and vigilantly examined Denisov's clothes and feet, but the majority willingly made a fuss, and returned their meat to be weighed. Convinced that they had indeed been variously cheated, they grew joyfully irate and, pleased with their just cause, crowded toward the manager's office in the basement. Denisov led the masses, and it was as though church banners were waving in the air and the unseen sun of Bloody Sunday were rising, and in the back rows some people apparently even began singing. But then the manager's door flew open and out of the dim storeroom, laden with bursting bags—women's bags, quilted ones with flowers—emerged the famous actor, the handsome Rykushin, who just that week had frowned manfully and smoked meaningfully into the face of each and every one of them from the television screen. The rebellion fell apart instantly; the recognition was joyous, if not mutually so. The

women formed a ring around Rykushin, the curly-headed manager beamed, fraternization ensued, a few people shed tears,
unacquainted people embraced one another, one stout woman
who couldn't see what was going on climbed onto a small
barrel of herring and delivered such an impassioned speech
that it was decided then and there to direct a note of collective
gratitude to the central trading organization, and to ask Rykushin to take on the creative leadership of Nursery School
No. 238, with an annual appearance as Santa Claus. Rykushin
riffled a notebook, tore off pages with autographs, and sent
them wafting over the waves of heads; new admirers poured
in from the store up above; they led a four-time award-winning
schoolteacher who had gone blind with excitement, and Pioneer scouts and schoolchildren slid whistling down the shaky
banister, plopping into the cabbage bins. Denisov kept talking
hoarsely about truth. No one listened to him. He took a risk,
bent down, lifted the edge of Rykushin's bag, and picked at
the paper. There were tongues of beef in there. So that's who
eats them. Squatting, he glanced up into the cold eyes of the
gourmand and received an answering look: Yes. That's how
it goes. Put it back. The people are with me.

Denisov acknowledged his accuracy, apologized, and took
off against the stream.

The view of a serenely existing Australia infuriated him. Take
that! He yanked at the map and tore off the fifth continent
plus New Zealand. The Philippines cracked in the bargain.

The ceiling oozed during the night. The captain was back.
There'd be some money. Why not write a story about the
captain? Who he is and where he comes from. Where he sails.
Why he drips. Why does he drip, anyway? Can't do without
water, is that it?

Maybe his pipes have rusted.

Or he's drunk.

Or maybe he goes into the bathroom, lays his head on the
edge of the sink and cries, cries like Denisov, cries and mourns

his meaningless life, the emptiness of the seas, the deceptive beauty of lilac islands, human vice, feminine silliness, mourns the drowned, the perished, the forgotten, the betrayed, the unneeded; tears overflow the soiled ceramic glaze of the sink, pour onto the floor, they're already up to the ankles, now they've risen to the knees, ripples, circles, wind, storm. After all, isn't there a saying: The heart of the wise is in the house of mourning, but the heart of fools is in the house of mirth.

Aunt Rita, where are you? In what spaces does your weightless spirit wander, is peace known to you? Do you sweep like a wan breeze across the meadows of the dead, where hollyhocks and asphodels grow, do you howl like a winter storm, pushing your way through the cracks of warm human dwellings, is it you singing in the sounds of the piano, living and dying with the music? Maybe you whimper like a homeless dog, run across the night road like a hurrying hedgehog, curl up under a damp stone like an eyeless worm? You must be in a bad way wherever you are now, otherwise why infiltrate our dreams, reach out your hand, ask for alms—bread, or, perhaps, simply memory? And who are these people you've taken up with, you, so pretty, with your fair hair and colored sash? Or are the roads that all of you take so dangerous, the forests where you spend the night so cold and deserted, that you band together, press close to one another, and hold hands as you fly over our lighted houses at night? . . .

Can it really be that this is what lies in store for me as well: to wander, whimper, pound on doors—remember, remember! . . . The predawn clatter of hooves on cobblestone, the dull thud of an apple in an orchard gone to seed, the splash of a wave in the autumn sea—someone is beseeching, scratching, someone wants to return, but the gates are closed, the locks have rusted, the key has been thrown away, the caretaker has died, and no one has come back.

No one, do you hear, no one has come back! Do you hear? I'm going to scream!!! Aaaaaaaa! No one! No one! And we are all pulled that way, an invincible force pushes at our backs, our legs slip on the crumbling incline, our hands clutch at clumps of grass, at least give me time to collect myself, to catch my breath. What will remain of us? What will remain of us? Don't touch me! Lora! Lora! For heaven's sake, Lora!!!

. . . And she arose from the dark, from the damp fog, arose and moved toward him, unhurried—clip-clop, slip-slop—in some sort of outrageous, slit-open gold boots, in brazen, wantonly short boots; her thin, orphaned ankles creaked, wobbling in the gold leather, higher up a flamboyant raincoat furled and rustled in the black beads of the night fog, buckles clinked and clanked, higher still her smile played, the lunar rainbows of streetlamps set her rosy teeth ablaze; above the smile hung her heavy eyes, and all this rustling, all this effrontery and finery, triumph and abomination, the entire living, swirling maelstrom was topped off with a tragic man's hat. Lord almighty, Father in heaven, it was with her that he would share his bed, his table, and his dreams. What dreams? It doesn't matter. All sorts. A beautiful woman, a garrulous woman, a head full of rubbish, but a beautiful woman.

"Well, hello there, Denisov, I haven't seen you in ages."

"What are those puttees you're wearing, my lovely?" Denisov asked disapprovingly as Lora kissed him.

She was surprised and looked down at her boots, at their dead, gold cuffs, rolled inside out like the pale flesh of poisonous mushrooms. What's that supposed to mean? What's with him? She'd been wearing them for a whole year already, had he forgotten? Of course, it was definitely time to buy new ones, but she wasn't up to it at the moment, because while he had been off keeping himself in seclusion, she'd had a horrific misfortune. She got out to the theater only once in a blue moon, and she wanted to take a little break from Papa and live like a human being, so she sent Papa to the country and asked Zoya Trofimovna to keep an eye on him. Zoya Trofimovna couldn't stand it more than three days—well, no one

could, but that's beside the point—so anyway, while she was
cooling out in one of those basement theaters—a very fash-
ionable little theater and very hard to get tickets to—where
the whole decor is only matting and thumbtacks, where the
ceiling drips, but there's a lofty spirit, where there's always a
draft on your legs, but as soon as you enter you have this
instant catharsis, there's so much enthusiasm and the tears are
so divine that you want to burst. So anyway, while she was
hanging out there and lapping it all up, hoodlums cleaned out
their apartment. They took everything, literally everything:
candlesticks, brassieres, an entire subscription set of Molière,
a poisonous pink Filimonovsky clay toy in the shape of a man
with a book—it was a gift from one of those village writers,
a born genius, they won't publish him, but he came on foot
from the backwoods, he spends the night with kind people
and he doesn't bathe on principle; on principle, because he
knows the Fundamental Truth and hates tile with a fierce
hatred, he simply turns purple if he sees glazed or brick tile
somewhere, he even has a cycle of anti-tile poems—powerful
lines with the strength of timber, all full of "Hail!" this and
"Hail!" that, and about magical singing zithers, something
really profound—so anyway, his present disappeared and so
did that Vietnamese bamboo curtain, and whatever they
couldn't carry off they either moved somewhere else or piled
up. What kind of people are these, tell me, I just don't know;
naturally, she had reported it to the police, but of course
nothing would come of it, because they have such awful bul-
letin boards there—missing children, women they haven't been
able to find for years—so how could they be expected to rush
out and comb Moscow for a bunch of brassieres? It was good
that they didn't throw out Papa's manuscripts, only scattered
them. Anyway, she was terribly depressed about all this, and
she was also depressed because she went to a reunion of her
former classmates—they graduated from school fifteen years
ago—and everyone had changed so much that you simply

couldn't recognize them, it was a nightmare, total strangers. But that's not the main thing, the main thing is that there were these guys, Makov and Sysoev, they used to sit at a desk in the back row and shoot spitballs, they brought sparrows to school, and on the whole were thick as thieves. So anyway, Makov died in the mountains—and remained there—that was four years ago, and no one knew, just think, a real hero, nothing less, while Sysoev had become fat and happy—he arrived in a black car with a chauffeur and ordered the chauffeur to wait, and the fellow actually slept in the car the whole evening, but when the guys found out that Sysoev was so important and such a big shot, and that Makov was lying somewhere in a crevice under the snow and couldn't come, and that swine Sysoev was too lazy to walk over on his own two feet and rolled up in an official car just to show off—there was a scuffle and a rumble, and instead of warm embraces and beautiful memories they boycotted Sysoev, as if there were nothing else to talk about! As if it were his fault that Makov had climbed those mountains. And everyone became simply beastly, it was all so sad, and one boy—of course, he's completely bald now, Kolya Pishchalsky—picked all the crabs out of the salad and threw them right in Sysoev's face and shouted: Go on, eat them, you're used to it, but we're just simple people. And everyone thought that Sysoev would kill him for it, but no, he got terribly embarrassed and tried to be friendly, but everyone gave him the cold shoulder, and he walked around completely flustered, offering antifog headlights to anyone who wanted to buy them. And then he sort of slipped out, and the girls began to feel sorry for him and started screaming at the others: You aren't human! What did he do to you? So everybody left hostile and angry, and nothing came of the evening. So there you have it, Denisov, why are you being so quiet, I've missed you. Let's go to my place, it's completely ransacked, but I've managed to make everything more or less presentable.

Lora's gold boots squeaked, her raincoat rustled, her eyes

shone from beneath the hat, her eyebrows smelled of roses and rain . . . while at home, in the stale smoky room, under the wet ceiling, squeezed between dislocated layers of time, Aunt Rita and her comrades thrash about; she perished, the sash tore, the perfume spilled, and the fair hair rotted; she didn't accomplish anything during her short life, only sang in front of the mirror, and now, lifeless, old, hungry, and frightened, she rushes about in the realm of dreams, begging: Remember me! . . . Denisov tightened his grip on Lora's elbow and turned toward her house, driving away the fog: they shouldn't split up, they should remain together always, united inside one pair of equation brackets, inseparable, indivisible, indissoluble, merged, like Tristan and Isolde, Khor and Kalinych, cigarettes and matches.

The cups had been stolen, so they drank tea from glasses. Snow-white Papa, cozy, like a Siberian tomcat, ate doughnuts, shutting his eyes in contentment. We, too, are like those three—the old man, the woman, the fat man—thought Denisov; we, too, have banded together high above the city; seen from the outside, what unites us? A little family, we need each other, we're weak and confused, robbed by fate: he's out of work, she's out of her mind, I'm out of a future. Perhaps we should huddle even closer, hold hands—if one of us trips, the other two will hold him up—eat doughnuts, and not strive for anything, lock ourselves away from people, live without raising our heads, not expecting fame . . . and at the appointed hour close our eyes a bit tighter, tie up our jaws, cross our hands on our chests . . . and safely dissolve into nonbeing? No, no —not for anything!

"They took all the curtains, the creeps." Lora sighed. "What do they need my curtains for anyway?"

The fog settled, or perhaps it hadn't risen to the sixteenth floor, that light summer fog. Pure blackness and the jeweled lights of distant dwellings looked into the naked windows, and on the horizon, in the Japanese-lacquer dark, the orange half-circle of the rising moon swelled, looking like a mountaintop that had pushed through, illuminated by fruit-colored morning light. Somewhere in the mountains Lora's classmate Makov, who had risen higher than everyone and remained there forever, slept an eternal sleep.

The rose-colored summit grows lighter, the cliffs are dusted with snow, Makov lies there gazing into the firmament; cold and magnificent, pure and free, he won't decay, won't grow old, won't cry, won't destroy anyone, won't become disillusioned by anything. He is immortal. Could there be a more enviable fate?

"Listen," Denisov said to Lora, impressed, "if those jerks of yours didn't know anything about this Makov, then maybe his coworkers do? . . . Couldn't a museum be organized or something? And why not rename your school in his honor? After all, he made it famous."

Lora was surprised: What museum, good Lord, Denisov, a museum, why? As a student he was nothing to brag about, he dropped out of college, then he went into the army, did this and that, and in recent years worked as a stoker because he liked to read books. He drove his family crazy, it was awful, I know from Ninka Zaitseva, because her mother-in-law works with Makov's mother. There's no way the school can be named after Makov anyway, because it's already named after A. Kolbasiavichius. And his story isn't all that straightforward either, because, you see, there were two Kolbasiavichius brothers, twins, one was killed by Lithuanian partisan rebels in '46, and the second was a rebel himself and died from eating bad mushrooms. And since their initials were the same, and even their own mother couldn't tell them apart, an extremely ambiguous situation arises. You could say that the school is named after the hero-brother, but at one time local hero-trackers came up with the theory that the hero-brother infiltrated the rebel den and was perfidiously killed by the bandits, who saw through the substitution and fed him poisonous soup, while the bandit-brother realized the error of his ways and honorably went to turn himself in, but was accidentally shot. Do you get it, Denisov? One of them is a hero for sure, but which one hasn't been established. Our director was just going crazy, she even filed a petition to have the school's name changed. But there can't even be any question of naming it after Makov, I mean, he's not some steelworker, right?

There you have it, human memory, human gratitude, thought Denisov, and he felt guilty. Who am I? No one. Who is Makov? A forgotten hero. Perhaps fate, shod in gold boots, is giving me a hint. Stop tossing and turning, Denisov—here is your goal in life, Denisov! Extricate this perished youth from nonbeing, save him from oblivion; if they laugh at you—be patient, if they persecute you—stand firm, if they humiliate you—suffer for your idea. Don't betray the forgotten, the forgotten are knocking at our dreams, begging for alms, howling in the night.

Later, as Denisov was falling asleep in the pillaged apartment high above Moscow, and Lora was falling asleep next to him, her dark hair redolent of roses, the blue moon climbed in the sky, deep shadows fell, something creaked in the depths of the apartment, rustled in the foyer, thumped beyond the door, and softly, evenly, slowly—click-clack—moved along the corridor, skipped to the kitchen, made a door squeak, turned around, and—clack-clack-clack—went back again.

"Hey, Lora, what is that?"

"Sleep, Denisov, it's nothing. Later."

"What do you mean, later? Do you hear what's going on?"

"Oh Lord," whispered Lora. "Well, it's Papa, Papa! I told you I had problems with Papa. He's a somnambulist—he walks in his sleep. I told you that they kicked him out of work, well, it started right after that. What can I do? I've been to see the best doctors! Tengiz Georgievich said: He'll run around a bit and stop. But Anna Efimovna said: What do you want, it's his age. And Ivan Kuzmich said: Just thank your lucky stars he's not out chasing devils. And through Ruzanna I found a psychic at the Ministry of Heavy Industry, but after that session it only got worse: he runs around naked. Go to sleep Denisov, we can't do anything to help him anyway."

But how could he possibly sleep, especially since the zoologist, judging by the sound, had skipped back to the kitchen, and something fell with a crash.

"Oh, I'm going to go stark-raving mad," Lora said, growing anxious. "He'll break the last glasses."

Denisov pulled on his pants and Lora ran to her father; shouts could be heard.

"Now what is he doing? Lord almighty, he's put on my boots! Papa, I've told you a thousand times. . . . Papa, for heaven's sake, wake up!"

"Warm-blooded, ha-ha!" shouted the old man, sobbing. "They call themselves warm-blooded. Mere protozoa, I say. Get your pseudopods out of here!"

"Denisov, grab him from the side! Papochka, Papochka, calm down! I'll get some valerian. . . . His hands, hold his hands!"

"Let me go! There they are! I see them!" The sleepwalker broke away, and somehow he mustered incredible strength. His mustache and beard seemed like wintry, woolly things on his naked body.

"Papa, for heaven's sake!"

"Vasily Vasilevich!"

Night flew over the world, in the distant dark the ocean seethed, distraught Australians looked around, distressed by the disappearance of their continent, the captain drenched Denisov's smoke-filled lair with bitter tears, Rykushin, famished with fame, ate cold leftovers straight out of the pot, Ruzanna slept facing east, Makov slept facing nowhere. Each was occupied with his own affairs, and who cared that in the middle of the city, many stories up, in the moon's mother-of-pearl light, real live people were in the throes of struggling, stamping, shouting, and suffering: Lora in her transparent nightshirt—a sight that even tsars would not be loath to gaze upon—the zoologist in gold boots, and Denisov, tormented by visions and doubts.

. . . The countryside around this cluster of dachas was marvelous—oaks everywhere and under the oaks, lawns, and on the lawns people playing volleyball in the reddish evening light. The ball smacked resonantly, a slow wind passed through the oaks, and the oaks slowly answered the wind. And Makov's dacha was also marvelous—old, gray, with little towers. Amid the flower beds, under the damp evening-time wild cherry tree, his four sisters, mother, stepfather, and aunt sat at a round table drinking tea with raspberries and laughing. The aunt held an infant in her arms, and he waved a plastic parrot; to the side a harmless dog lay endearingly; and some kind of bird walked unhurriedly about its business along the path, not troubling, even out of courtesy, to become alarmed and flutter off at the sight of Denisov. Denisov was a little disappointed by the idyllic scene. It would have been pointless, of course, to expect that the house and garden would be draped in mourning banners, that everyone would walk on tiptoe, that the mother, black with grief, would be lying motionless on the bed, unable to take her eyes off her son's ice axe, and that from time to time first one, then another member of the family would clutch a crumpled handkerchief and bite it to stifle the sobs—but all the same, he had expected something sad. But they had forgotten, they had all forgotten! Then again, who was he to talk, arriving with a bouquet, as if to congratulate them? . . . They turned to Denisov with perplexed, frightened smiles, looked at the bunch of carnations in his hand, crimson like a sunset before foul weather, like clotted, bloody scabs, like memento mori. The infant, the most sensitive, having not yet forgotten that frightening darkness from which he had recently been called, immediately guessed who had sent Denisov; he kicked and screamed, wanted to warn them, but didn't know the words.

No, there was nothing sad to be seen, the only sad thing was that Makov wasn't here: he wasn't playing volleyball under the slow oaks, wasn't drinking tea under the wild cherry tree, he wasn't shooing away unseasonably late mosquitoes. Denisov, having firmly resolved to suffer in the name of the deceased, overcame the awkwardness, presented the flowers, straightened his mourning tie, sat down at the table, and explained himself. He was the envoy of the forgotten. Such was his mission. He wanted to know everything about their son. Perhaps he would write his biography. A museum, but if that wasn't feasible, then he could at least arrange a corner of a museum. Display cases. His childhood things. His hobbies. Maybe he collected butterflies, beetles? Tea? Yes, yes, with sugar, thank you, two spoonfuls. He'd have to get in touch with glaciologists. It's possible that Makov's climb was in some way important for science. Immortalization of his memory. Annual Makovian readings. Let us dare to dream: Makov Peak—why not? The Makov Foundation with voluntary donations. The possibilities! . . .

The sisters sighed, the stepfather smoked and raised his gray eyebrows in boredom, the mother, aunt, and infant started crying, but it was a sun shower—all tears dried out here amid the raspberries, oaks, and wild cherry. The slow wind, flying in from distant flowering glades, whispered in his ear: Drop it. Everything's fine. Everything's peaceful. Drop it. . . . The mother squeezed her nose with a handkerchief to stop the tears. Yes, it's sad, sad. . . . But it's all over, thank God, over, forgotten, water under the bridge, it's all covered with yellow water lilies. You know how it is, life goes on. There's Zhannochka's firstborn. He's our little Vasya. Vasya, come on now, where's Grandma's nose? That's ri-iiight. Goo goo goo, ga ga ga. Vera, he's wet. This is our garden. Flower beds, do you see? Well, what else. . . . There's our hammock. Comfortable, isn't it? And this is our Irochka, she's getting married. There's a lot to do, you know. You have to get the youngsters settled, you have to take care of everything for them.

Irochka was extremely pretty—young, tanned. The mosquitoes were feasting on her bare back. Denisov couldn't take his eyes off Irochka. A breeze swayed the black berries on the wild cherry.

"Come, let's look at the garden. My tomatoes have really taken off." Makov's mother led Denisov deep into the garden and whispered: "The girls really loved Sasha. Especially Irochka. Well, what can you do. You have a heart, I can tell, you want to help. We have a request to make of you. . . . She's getting married, we're trying to get ahold of furniture for them. . . . And you know, she wants a Sylvia china cabinet. We've tried everything. After all, they're young, you know. . . . They want to live it up a bit. If Sasha were alive, he would have turned Moscow inside out. . . . In Sasha's memory . . . for Irochka . . . a Sylvia, eh? What do you say, young man?"

A Sylvia for the deceased!—cried invisible forces. Eternal memory!

"A Sylvia cabinet, Sylvia . . . Sasha would be so pleased. . . . How happy he would have been. . . . Come on, have some more tea."

And they drank tea with raspberries, and the oaks hurried nowhere, and Makov lay on high in the diamond splendor, baring his unaging teeth to the sky.

Duty is duty. All right then, let it be a cabinet. Why not? From Makov a cabinet will remain. From Aunt Rita—a glass perfume flacon. I traded the flacon. Nothing remained. Sepulchral darkness. The scorched steppe. An icy crust. The mushroom damp of a cellar. The ferrous smell of blood. One-sixth of the earth, torn out with flesh. No! I don't want to know anything. I couldn't help. I was little! I am only helping Makov, for all of them, for all, all! And when the polite, heavyset orderlies took away the sobbing captain and he grabbed onto the lintels, the mailboxes, the elevator shaft, spread his legs wide, bent his knees, and shrieked, and then they carried hundreds of little paper boats out of the apartment and gave them to the Pioneer scouts for recycling, as all the neighbors and I stood by and watched—I couldn't help then either, I am only helping Makov!

I don't want to know anything! The cabinet, only the cabinet. The cabinet, a sideboard, a wall unit with bronze inlay —a golden hair's width, no thicker—with shiny corners, delicate fretwork, and the slight gleam of diamond-shaped panes. Gentle dimples of carving—so soft and light, as though a wild hare had run past—a marvelous, marvelous piece of home.

As though a wild hare had run down the hallway. Lora's papa. Ping!—he broke something. A flacon? No, a glass. They drink tea with raspberries from glasses. Makov looks at the sky. Get hold of a cabinet in my name. All right. I'll try. I'm prepared to suffer. I'll suffer—and Makov will release me. And so will the captain. And Aunt Rita. And her comrades will lower their unbearable eyes.

Lora breathes evenly in her sleep, her hair smells of roses, the zoologist stirs in the hall, the doors are locked—where will you run away to?—let him run around—he'll wear himself out, get tired, he'll sleep better. "I knew, but I forgot, I knew, but I forgot," he mutters, and his eyes are closed and his legs lithe. Back and forth, back and forth, across the moonlit squares, past the bookshelves, from the front door to the kitchen door. Back and forth, perhaps he's put on Lora's hat or sandals, perhaps he's wound a gauze scarf round his neck or adorned his head with a colander, he likes nocturnal knick-knacks; back and forth, from door to door, with soft skips, lifting his knees high, his hands outstretched as though he were trying to catch something, but hadn't caught it yet—a festive hunt, an innocuous blindman's buff, no harm done. "I knew, but I forgot!"

In the morning the red dawn arrived, the mountain with the black bug of Makov on its peak dissolved, the weary lunatic fell sweetly asleep, degenerate city birds struck up a song, and two sky-blue tears rolled from Denisov's eyes into Denisov's ears.

In search of Sylvia, Denisov knocked on all sorts of doors, but everywhere he ran up against rejection. Are you crazy? Imports have been cut back. And Sylvia all the more so. Hah! . . . Even a general couldn't get one! Maybe a marshal, but it depends what kind, what kind of troops. No, Comrade Petryukov won't help you. Neither will Kozlov. And don't bother approaching Lyulko—there's no point. Now, Comrade Bakhtiyarov . . . Comrade Bakhtiyarov could do it, help that is, but he's a capricious, eccentric fellow, he's got a sort of florid, unpredictable personality, and the devil knows how you can pressure Bakhtiyarov. But you've definitely got to catch him out of his office, in the Woodland Fairy Tale restaurant, for instance, when the comrade is eating and relaxing. You could try going to the baths, the baths would be best of all, and it's an old trick—wait for the moment when the beauty drops her swan feathers to bathe in the spring, so to speak—then you've caught the little bird, you close in and stash the feathers somewhere, and you can ask whatever your heart desires. But Bakhtiyarov is no beauty, as you'll see for yourself, and his feathers and pants and suitcase with underwear and all kinds of tasty goodies are so well guarded, and getting into the bathhouse is so difficult—like Baba Yaga's house, it can turn its face to the forest and rear to people quick as a wink—that you shouldn't even think of getting in there without a magic password. So why don't you try to find him out of town, in the Fairy Tale? Well, what can you do, give it a try. He goes there to relax.

And the Fairy Tale came to pass.

Whew, how warm it was in there, how fancy, and how glorious it smelled. If only Lora were here, and I had a bit more money, yes, over there in that corner under the yellow lampshade, where the napkins are folded like fans and the armchairs are soft. Peace for a tormented, half-mad soul!

Waiters were passing by and Denisov asked the sweetest and friendliest of them: Comrade Bakhtiyarov isn't here by any chance, is he? And the waiter immediately took to Denisov like a brother and pointed with his little finger, directing him: The comrade's relaxing over there. In a circle of friends and lovely ladies.

Now go on over there—what will be, will be—over there —I'm not asking for myself—over there, where a dome of blue smoke billows, where giggles cavort like gusts of wind, where champagne leaps out onto the tablecloth in a frothy arc, where heavy female backs sit, where someone in a lilac-colored tie, puny, doglike, quickly prances around the Boss, incessantly adoring him. Take a step—and Denisov stepped, he crossed the line and became the envoy of the forgotten, the nameless, those who hover in dreams, who lie covered with snow, whose white bones protrude from the ruts of the steppe.

Comrade Bakhtiyarov turned out to be a round, soft, Chinese-looking person, he even seemed rather a fine fellow, and it was impossible to say how old he was, sixty or two hundred. He saw straight through people, saw everything— the liver, spleen, and heart, but he had no use for your liver or spleen—what good were they?—so he didn't look straight at you lest he pierce right through you, and he wound conversations around somewhere to the side and past you. Comrade Bakhtiyarov was consuming veal of a downright disgraceful tenderness, as well as criminally young suckling pig; and the salad—a mere three minutes separated it from the garden—was so innocent, it hadn't even had a chance to come to its senses; there it had been, minding its own business,

growing, and suddenly—whoosh!—it was picked, and before
it had time to cry out, it was being eaten.

"I love to eat young things," said Bakhtiyarov. "But you,
my little bunny rabbit, shouldn't—you have an ulcer, I can
see it in your face." He was right on target: Denisov had had
an ulcer for ages. "So I'll treat you to something that's for your
own good," said Bakhtiyarov. "Drink to my health, drink deep
to my hospitality."

And at the snap of his fingers they brought Denisov stewed
carrots and sweet Buratino soda water.

"I keep thinking, thinking," said Bakhtiyarov, as he ate.
"Day and night I keep thinking, and I can't figure out the
answer. You look like a scholarly fellow—your eyes are oh so
gloomy—come on, tell me. Why is the brewery named after
Stenka Razin? After all, my little lovebirds, it's a government
organization with plans and quotas to fill, fiscal accountability,
socialist competition, Party committees and—oh, goodness, I
can't take it—lo-ocal trade union committees. Trade union
committees. This is serious business, it's no joke. And then
they go and name it after some bandit! No, I don't get it. In
my opinion it's funny. Go on, laugh!"

The friends and ladies laughed, the lilac-colored one even
shrieked. Denisov also smiled politely and took a sip of his
warm Buratino.

"But if you look at it from the other side: Razin, Stepan
Timofeevich—he's a folk hero, an inspiration, our national
pride and joy:

> *The wench has seduced him, he's lost all his senses*
> *The cossacks they grumbled—how could he betray?*
> *So Stenka took heed and he sent for the princess*
> *And cast Persia's pearl to the swift running wave. . . .*

"That, you see, is an event with great political resonance—
and now we have some measly little factory with, you get my

meaning, a dubious profile. To my way of thinking, it's funny. Go on, laugh!"

The ladies again opened their mouths and laughed.

"Like Grandma's furs stored in the chest . . . he doesn't rot, he doesn't rust, he doesn't sweat, he gets his rest," the lilac-colored one suddenly sang, wiggling his shoulders and stamping his heels.

"See what great fun we're having here," said the contented Bakhtiyarov. "We play around and laugh like innocent children, and it's all within the bounds of the permissible, we don't go beyond what's allowed, now do we? . . . And everything's just hunky-dory, but I can see you've got a little favor to ask of me, so ask away, we'll have a listen. . . ."

"Well, actually, it's very simple, that is, it's very complicated," said Denisov, trying to concentrate. "That is, you see, I'm not really asking for myself—personally, I don't need anything. . . ."

"Oh my willow, green willow, who asks favors for himself? Nowadays nobody asks for himself. . . . Nowadays you only have to spit—and a bunch of those inspectoring fellows grab you by your little white arms—did you spit in the right place, where did you get that spit, and on just what grounds—but what do we have to do with it, we didn't do anything, we're clean as a whistle. . . . Can I call you my little chickypoo? 'You're my frost—frost, don't freeze me out,' " comrade Bakhtiyarov began to sing. "Sing, my little lovebirds!"

"Don't freeze me out!" they struck up at the table.

"Like Grandma's furs stored in a chest . . ." the lilac-colored one tried to sing against the chorus, but he was drowned out. They sang well.

"Klavdiya's soprano isn't just any old la-di-da," said Bakhtiyarov. "Our Zykina! Maria, so to speak, Callas, or maybe even better. You sing too, chickypoo."

Well, they warned me, thought Denisov, opening his mouth in time to the rhythm. They warned me, and I was prepared

—after all, it's not for myself, and you don't get something for nothing, without suffering you won't get anywhere, I just didn't realize that suffering would be so incredibly unpleasant.

"No sweat, no sweets," affirmed Comrade Bakhtiyarov, looking straight into Denisov's heart, "what did you think, my pretty boy? You need some kind of article? A ca-a-abinet, is it? Oooh, we're a naughty boy. . . . Why don't you sing for us personally, eh? Something simple, heartfelt? Give us your best consumer solo, make our spirits rejoice. We're listening. Quiet, my little lovebirds. Be respectful."

Denisov sang hurriedly, suffering under the gaze of Bakhtiyarov's guests; he sang whatever came to mind, what's sung in courtyards, on camping trips, in trains—an urban ballad about Lenka Sharova, who believed in love and was deceived, and who decided to destroy the fruit of her frivolous lapse from virtue: "She dug a hole, pushed the stones inside, and then wee Zina gave one last cry!" he sang, already realizing that he was in a desert, that there were no people about. He sang of the sentence pronounced by the heartless judges: "To the firing squad with her, to the firing squad it be!" of the sad and unjust end of the girl who'd gone astray: "I walked right up to the prison wall, and there lay Lenka in her death pall," and Bakhtiyarov nodded his soft head sympathetically. No, Bakhtiyarov himself was all right, not bad at all, really, his face even began to reveal some nice cozy nooks and crannies, and if you squinted, it was even possible to believe for a minute that here was a grandfather, an old-timer who loved his grandchildren . . . but of course only if you squinted. The others were much worse: that woman over there, for instance, an awful woman, she resembled a ski—her front was entirely encased in brocade, but her back was completely bare; or that other one, the beauty with the eyes of a cemetery caretaker; but the most horrible of them all was that fidgety giggler, that unstrung Punch with his lilac tie and toadlike mouth and woolly head; if only someone would wipe him out, exterminate

him, or burn him with Mercurochrome so that he wouldn't
dare look! . . . But then, actually, they're only horrid because
they're celebrating my humiliation, my trials and tribulations,
otherwise—they're just citizens like anyone else. Nothing special. "There lay Lenka in her death pall."

"How fine, my sweets!" exclaimed Bakhtiyarov in surprise.
"How fine our comrade sang for us. Downright pianissimo
and nothing else. No other word for it. Come on now, let's
show him our stuff. In reply. Let's give our guest a taste of
our D-flat."

The guests burst into song; the lilac fidget—all attentive-
ness—conducted with a fork, tears streamed from the beauty's
dead eyes; the diners from neighboring tables, wiping their
mouths with their napkins, joined the chorus, Klavdiya's soprano entered on a piercing, violinlike note:

> *"Mother, sweet Mother, oh, Mother dear,*
> *Why did you forsake me and leave me behind?*
> *Your son has turned into a thief I do fear,*
> *And my father—that scoundrel—you never did find."*

There, in the mountains, the snow began to fall thicker and
thicker, sweeping into drifts, burying Makov, his sprawled legs,
his face turned toward eternity. He doesn't rot, he doesn't rust,
he doesn't sweat, he gets his rest. The snowdrifts rose higher
and higher, the mountain creaked under the weight of the
snow; it groaned and cracked, and with the roar of a steam
engine the avalanche fell, and nothing remained on the peak.
A snowy mist smoked a bit and settled on the cliffs.

"Dear visitor! Aren't I your friend—to the bitter end!" cried
Bakhtiyarov, grabbing Denisov by the cheeks. "How do you
like that? I'm talking in verse. That's me. No stranger to poetry.
Eh? That's just the way I am. Drink your Buratino to my health.
Bottoms up, bottoms up! That's the ticket. You know what:

Humor an old friend. If you go to town, go all the way. Crawl under the table. For fun! Go on!"

"What the . . ." said Denisov, free of Makov. "Who do you think you are, old man? *Arrivederci* to you, I don't need your cabinet. I changed my mind." And he started to get up.

"Under the table. What's going on? What's the matter?" Bakhtiyarov tore at his coat. "We're asking you. Gentlemen!"

"Go on, go on!" shouted the ladies, friends, guests, waiters, even the cook, who appeared from out of the blue, and the entire room, rising to its feet, moving out from behind the tables, still chewing, made a scene and clapped: "Go on!"

No, for goodness' sake, no, no, no! Why? I'm a human being, and proud to be one. I won't crawl, go ahead and kill me! . . . Yes, but what about suffering? Hey, remember! Suffering! You're the one who wanted it.

He plunged into despair, as though facing death, he lost heart, he frowned—it didn't help, he wanted to take a deep breath—there was no air left to breathe. And Bakhtiyarov had already thrown back the tablecloth and seated himself sideways so that his legs wouldn't be in the way. He gestured invitingly with his hand: Go ahead, be my guest!

. . . He huddled in the half-light of the darned linen, hugging his knees like an embryo, and gazed dumbly at the women's legs, the silvered tails, and the lacquered hooves; the insidious repast had clouded his hearing and sight; the soprano set his teeth on edge. Here's what I'll do. I know. I'll erect a monument to the forgotten. Even if it's only a flat patch of land in the middle of the steppes, with no fence, no marker—let feather grass or rushes grow there, let the sun scorch the earth till the salt comes out, let gravel or broken glass litter the ground, let a jackal howl in the evenings or a boisterous crowd feast. Greetings to you, tin cans, and to you, beer caps, glory to spittle, hurrah for squashed tomatoes. A hill of garbage or a salty clearing, the whoosh of feather grass or the whistle of the wind—anything will do, it makes no difference, nothing frightens the forgotten—after all, nothing else can happen to them.

A tearstained, eyeless female face hung under the table and muttered, seeking sympathy:

"Why, tell me why's it allays rile lires, salastically yuffy for some, and others only get lurdle, glud, and droom, why?"

The heart of the wise is in the house of mourning.

The Buratino had made Denisov drowsy, and he fell asleep.

A moonbeam, breaking through a darned patch, stabbed him in the eye. The moonlit tablecloth lay on the parquet floor, a silvery garden stood beyond the window, August ignited stars in the dark. It was as if all the snow from all the mountains were cascading onto the garden, the silence, and the mute paths. Denisov creaked across the floorboards and stood by the window. He hadn't dreamt about anyone today.

The cock crowed, Bakhtiyarov and his warlocks had vanished, the shades were sleeping, the world was at peace.

And what kind of nonsense was this anyway—to be tormented by memories of nothing at all, to ask forgiveness from a dead man for something you weren't guilty of in human reckoning, to clutch handfuls of fog? There isn't any fifth dimension, and no one will keep count of your sins and victories, and there isn't any punishment or reward at the end of the road, there isn't even a road, and fame is smoke, and the soul is vapor, and if you crawled under the table, well, pardon me, my dear, but that was your choice, a matter of personal taste, and humanity will not follow after you in a grateful throng, and unseen forces won't cry out from the everlasting azure: "Good going, Denisov, attaboy! Keep up the good work! We fully approve and support you!"

He walked around the Fairy Tale, pulling on doors, all of which were locked. Well, what a pickle! Now just sit there till morning. Break a window, or what? There's probably an alarm here. It's a small village, everything's out in the open—they'll whistle, lights will blink, the police will move in; if they don't catch you in the garden, then they'll get you on the highway for sure. "The heavens are wondrous and exultant, earth slumbers in a luminous blue glow," and Denisov is going to rush about among the bushes and watchman's booths, squat behind trash cans, and rustle in the hawthorn to elude the searchlights. There's no point in it. A rampart of darkness encircles the world; incorporeal moon sugar will sift from leaf to leaf, trembling and glinting; sugar, snow, dreams, depths, everything has frozen, everything's dying, growing dull in the senseless beauty, everything's forgotten, forgiven, and anyway nothing happened, and nothing ever will.

Oh, here's the phone. Call Lora. I myself have died—help others to help themselves.

Lora sounded congested.

"Oh, Denisov, take a taxi, come over. A horrific accident happened. What do you mean, you're locked in? In what fairy tale? Have you gone out of your mind, Denisov, I'm in the middle of a nightmare, it's the problem with Papa, I took him to the country, to an old woman, you don't know her, old lady Liza, she's a healer and a wonderful woman. Ruzanna recommended her, to read Papa; how do they do that? Well, they sit you on a stool under an icon, light a candle, the wax drips into a basin, old lady Liza reads prayers, the energy field improves a lot; it's all calculated to last several sessions; so you can imagine, in the meantime I took off for the village store, they have a good selection there, men's shirts from Holland, I wanted to get you some, but they were all gone, and I got held up looking at the goods for shareholders, I don't know what shareholders, some kind of consumer co-op or something. Well, for people who bring in birch sponge mushrooms they have men's moccasins, white ones, Austrian, exactly what you need, you can get jeans for meat and felt pens for carrots, we don't need any of that, but the moccasins would be good; so I said to the salesgirls: Girls, I don't have any birch sponges, maybe you'd sell me a pair anyway? And one of them, really nice, said: Wait for the boss, maybe you can arrange something; I waited and waited, and it was already dark, but no one came, and they said: It's not likely she'll come back—her boyfriend from Severomorsk was supposed to visit her, so I went back, and old lady Liza was in a frightful panic. She said he was just sitting, sitting there and he fell asleep, and when he falls asleep, well, you know what he gets like; he fell asleep, jumped up, threw the door open and started running, and it was dark outside, and the area's completely unfamiliar, and he just ran off, I don't know what to do, Denisov, I've been to the police and they just laugh at me. Anyway, I'm home now, completely wiped out, I mean, Papa doesn't have a penny on him, he'll wake up somewhere in the forest, he'll lose his way, he'll freeze, he'll die, he doesn't know where I took him, he's lost. Denisov, what have I gone and done!"

. . . So he ran away, he broke out and ran away. He knew, he knew the road all along! The forgotten roused themselves, the shades lifted their heads, transparent apparitions pricked up their ears, listening: he's running, they've released him, go and meet him, go out on patrol, wave flags, light beacons! The sleepwalker is running along impassable paths, his eyelids closed, his arms outstretched, a quiet smile on his lips, as though he sees what the seeing cannot, as though he knows what they have forgotten, as though at night he grasps what is lost during the day. He runs over the dewy grass, through patches of moonlight and deep black shadows, over mushrooms and pale nocturnal bluebells, tiny baby frogs. He flies up hills, runs down hills, pure and bright, and under the bright moon, the heather lashes his fleet legs, night blows in his sleeping face, his white hair flutters in the wind, the forest parts, the maples blossom, light begins to appear.

Surely he'll keep running till he meets the light?

Serafim

"Go away! Go awaaay, you lousy beast!"

Someone's dog—white, matted, disgusting—not only jumped into the elevator after Serafim and whimpered, its paws pacing the dim, clunking box racing up toward the sixteenth floor, but dared to rush to the apartment, scratching insistently at the padding of the door while Serafim struggled with the keys on the landing.

"Get out of here!"

Serafim was squeamish about nudging the warm brute with his clean foot. The dog was possessed by a frightful impatience: it drummed at the door, quickly wedged its nose to the crack and snuffed the air, drummed again, insisted, would not be dissuaded.

Serafim stamped his foot and yelled—useless. He tried to trick the animal by swiftly pushing his way into the apartment, but, shuddering and wriggling like a furry snake, the filthy cur slithered in with hideous speed, rubbing against Serafim's legs in the process, and ran around the dark room, its claws clicking.

Serafim squealed, grabbed a mop, overtook the dog, struck it, struck again, kicked it out, slammed the door, and with a pounding heart collapsed against the frame. The fiend of hell quietly fluttered about on the landing, circling and rustling. It left.

His legs could still feel the revolting sensation of dog flesh slinking by. He felt nauseous.

Serafim lay against the door, calming himself. Better now? Almost.

Leave me alone. What do you all want from me? I don't want anyone. I am separate. Higher. I descended from the starry fields to this filth, and when I've completed my earthly circle, I'll go back from whence I came. Don't touch me.

Serafim took off his coat, drank a glass of cold, clean water, lit two candles, sat down in front of the mirror, and took a look at himself. Handsome. He narrowed his eyes appraisingly, threw back his head, observed from the side—excellent! That's me. Uncommonly fine! That's—me! Mind your own business, all of you. He remembered the dog. Disgusting beast. He jumped up in horror and glanced at his trousers. Just as he thought—fur. Get rid of it immediately. A hot shower. He sat down at the mirror again.

. . . What a vile world. Women, children, old people, dogs . . . Yellow, heaving swill. Flesh is nauseating. The flesh of others is revolting. Only what's mine is ravishing, pure, transparent. I am fleshless and sexless. I don't play your games. Get your muck out of here.

Serafim looked into the dark mirror. On both sides of the glass was a pure, living flame. Heavenly countenance. Candles. Heavenly countenance. But only I am permitted to admire this marvelous, inhuman sight. Turn your nasty faces away from me.

To go to work Serafim was obliged to ride the bus. He tried not to look at the swinish snouts, the camellike muzzles, the hippopotamus cheeks. People are all vile! And all of them, base, revolting, are staring at Serafim with bug eyes, grinning their grins. Yes, I am magnificent. Yes, my face shines with an unworldly light. Yes, golden curls. Snow-white wings. Angelic eyes. Part, crowd. Stand aside—Serafim goes here!

He looked in the mirror once more. Serafim's countenance swam up from the dark depths, wavering in the warm flame. A rosy glow, the reflected light of white wings behind his back. To gaze forever . . . Who are you, my beauty? Serafim sank into the divine reflection. Time to go to bed. Tomorrow would be a hard day. He blew out the flames, folded his wings together, and hung in the soft twilight.

For the Montgolfier brothers' jubilee, the district was planning a mass flight of thirty kilometers. Serafim was also participating. He had to collect various papers: a bilirubin blood test, a general urine analysis, and a certificate of residency. I'll fly higher than all of them, thought Serafim while the nurse drew his delicate blue blood through a tube. Higher than the crowd, higher than the human throng, higher than their base passions. I, a child of the ether, will spread my blinding, silky, snow-white wings like a million white hummingbirds. Oh, how magnificent my triumphant flight will be!

He strolled leisurely along the drying spring path, carrying his curly golden head high. The quacking word ZHEK—the housing office—squatted on a brown plaque. Get the residency certificate.

He pushed open the door and entered. Two old ladies were asleep in a room without curtains, furnished with rows of chairs. A middle-aged lecturer slowly read from a notebook covered with oilcloth:

"According to the absolutely aprocryphal legend, god-the-father, who doesn't exist, supposedly fertilized the so-called virgin Mary by way of the nonexistent holy spirit; the result of this fraudulent conception, according to the mendacious allegations of the clergymen, was the mythical figure of Christ, who is totally alien to us. These unfounded fabrications . . ."

The old ladies woke up.

"Come in, come in, Serafim!" cried the lecturer. "Today we're having an anti-Easter lecture on the evil of the so-called immaculate conception. Have a seat, it'll do you good to listen."

Serafim looked at him coldly, slammed the door, and left. I'm against any kind of conception. Fight, lecturer. Fight. Eradicate. I'm above human beings, above their fables about vulgar gods giving birth to idiot infants in dirty cow sheds. I am pure spirit, I am Serafim!

At the store Woodland Gifts they had pigeons. Serafim took a pair. Simmer in a covered pot for up to an hour and a half.

The pigeons bubbled in the pot. The doorbell rang. So. It's Magda, his neighbor. She wants to get married. She visits Serafim under various pretexts, the redheaded scourge! Serafim folded his arms and began looking out the window, began to heat up. Magda sat down on the edge of the chair, her legs under it; she never knows where to put her hands. She likes Serafim. Vile thing! "Khhem . . ."

She's thinking about how to start. She glances around the kitchen.

"You're boiling a chicken?"

"Yes."

"Khhem."

Silence.

"I bought some pork, too, you know, a fairly large piece, well, I mean, about three pounds, I kept looking at it, thinking, should I take it or shouldn't I, but I did; I thought I'd bake it or something, I stood in line a long time; when I got home and unwrapped it—all fat. All fat!"

Fat is nauseating muck. The whole world of flesh—is fat. Fatty, sticky children, fatty old ladies, fatty redheaded Magda.

"Ahem. I thought, maybe, I could do some washing for you, dirty sheets or whatever. You live alone."

Go away, you nauseating creature. Go away, don't soil my

clean, clear, mountain spirit with your swinish hands. Go away.

She went away.

Serafim threw out the pigeons, drank a cup of clear broth. A pure, lean bird.

There. Get the results of the blood test; one last humiliation—and upward! To the stars! Serafim knew the results beforehand: no traces of filth, nothing lowly, denigrating, or shameful would be detected. Not like these others.

Serafim got on the bus. People pressed in. Careful there, those are wings!

"You should take taxis," said a woman. But she looked at Serafim's luminous face—and smiled. Get away, you base thing!

He made his way to the middle. Someone touched one wing with a finger. Stung, he turned around. A small boy, hideous-looking—glasses, crossed eyes, no front teeth—was looking at Serafim's luxurious, swanlike feathering. His whole body winced: the snotty freak . . . with dirty hands!

Yes and here's the result of the blood test: aqua distillata [*sic!*]. What did you think it would be? . . . Swine!

The day was ending. The sweaty din, sticky dirt, stench, the human swarm—everything was loaded onto wagons and carted away. The deep blue evening, brandishing a broom, nodded to Serafim as it advanced from the east. A gentle silvery sheen set in on high. On the emptying streets each black silhouette was individually underlined. Piggish faces dared to smile at Serafim, to look into his face. Annihilate them all, thought Serafim. Incinerate every one of them. Yes, my face shines. Not for you! How dare you look!

By the time he approached his building, it was completely dark. A temptingly empty bench. I'll have a breath of fresh air. And tomorrow—the flight.

He spread his wings, looked upward. The starry wheel turns slowly, slowly. Berenice's Hair, Virgo, the Herdsman, the Hunting Dogs—clean, cold, April diamonds. That was the

place for Serafim. A sexless, shining body, he would glide in
silvery raiment through the resonant heights, let the streaming
cold of the constellations run between his fingers, dive into
ethereal currents. Dling! Dling!—the starry threads jingled like
the strings of a harp. He would drink his fill of the clean,
sparkling bubbles of the twenty-star Cup. . . . And burn up
the filthy earth. He'd pluck out the double, transfusing star
from the Hunting Dogs constellation—the Heart of Charles
. . . And he'd scorch the earth with fire.

Behind the bench, in the thick, bare bushes, something rustled, crackled, yapped—the white dog ran out, spun around,
waved its tail, jumped on Serafim's lap—joyfully, joyfully, as
if it had found a long-lost friend. It jumped about noisily,
trying to lick his face.

Serafim fell from the sky, jerked away, screamed, thrust out
his arms. The dog jumped back, sat on its hind legs, tilted its
head, and looked straight at Serafim endearingly. The sight of
the affectionate muzzle and dark dog eyes caused something
hot and dirty to rise in Serafim's chest, fill his throat. Silently,
gritting his teeth, trembling, hating, Serafim moved toward the
dog. It didn't understand and was overjoyed, wagged its tail,
grinned, and ran to meet him. Serafim kicked at the dog's eyes
with his heel, lost his footing, kicked, kicked, kicked! There
we go.

He stood for a while. The dog lay stretched out. Quiet. The
stars dripped. A woman's voice called:

"Sha-arik, Sharik, Sharik! . . . Sha-aaaarinka, Sharinka, Sharinka! . . ."

The same for you, thought Serafim. Stamp out everyone.
Trying not to make any noise with his wings, he quickly moved
toward the building.

He slept badly that night. His jawbones ached. He awoke
at dawn, and felt his alarmingly changed palate with his tongue.
Something was wrong. He yawned—and had difficulty opening his mouth. Everything had somehow become *different*.

Something's in the way. It had gotten colder. He wiped his face with his hand and looked—blood: He'd cut his palm on the end of his nose. The mirror! From the white morning murk, from the oval frame, someone was looking out at Serafim: a red, horny beak; a low forehead covered with blue-gray scales; from the mouth, the edges of a narrow slit, two large, long milk-white fangs. Serafim looked coldly into the frame. He ran the split tongue along the fangs. They're strong. He looked at the clock: Off to the dentist. The private doctor. There's time before the flight.

Tap tap tap went his claws on the asphalt. Faster—tap, tap tap tap tap . . .

"The monster Serpent Gorynych!" shouted some boys. "Look there's Serpent Gorynych!"

Serafim tucked his coat tight around him, grabbed his wide black wings, and took off at a run—the bus had already rounded the corner.

The Moon
Came Out

She was born some fifty years ago. They called her Na-tasha. The name promised large gray eyes, soft lips, a delicate silhouette, perky hair with highlights. But what came out was a fat, porous face, an eggplant nose, a dejected chest, and short, bulging bicycle calves.

In childhood she was whisked from under the gloomy arches of gray Liteiny Prospect to a dacha outside Leningrad: where exactly—had been forgotten. The name had faded, crumbled, scattered to the winds like a dry leaf; sometimes at night it thrashed against the glass, its shadow rustled—a long, long, Finnish word stretched out in the middle.

The name was lost, the days were long gone, her curly-headed little girlfriends had melted along the way—in dreams only the whisper of their feet could be heard, only the dim, distant laughter, transparent like a drawing on the air.

On lonely nights memories of gigantic trees, roads of bound-less breadth, and cupolas soaring into ceiling heights came to Natasha in dreamy gusts, like a shadow sliding by. Everything had slipped away, disappeared into thin air, vanished without a trace. Long ago in that now disintegrated world, they played the most delightful games on green lawns, and an ominous significance haunted the dark, immutable incantations that resounded like alarm bells:

> *The moon came out behind a cloud,*
> *He drew a knife and cried out loud:*
> *Now I'll stab you, Now I'll hit,*
> *I don't care, 'cause you are IT!*

And the horrid, yellow, horned moon with a human face rose up from the clouds of blue-black billowing fog, and its armor clanked dimly and its word—was law. I don't care, 'cause you are it! And they were afraid of the Moon and did not violate its oppressive, threatening will. Except when one of them cried out the colorful, catchy, lizardlike word: chooreekee! allyallyincomefree! Then for a second the horrific wheel of the world stopped running, stood rooted to the spot, the iron gates locked open, the fetters unfastened—and inside the charmed, delicate rainbow bubble of sudden freedom the little rebel himself stiffened in surprise, stopped in shock.

Heavenly valleys, tall rose-colored grasses swaying in the warm breeze; hills rising with floral breath. And in the evenings, a never-extinguished sunset beyond the black spruce peaks—orange, raspberry; in the evenings—gray, red-eyed wolves carefully distributed between the tree trunks, waiting in vain for their sinister wolfish opportunity—but no one would lie near the edge of the bed or cradle.

And in the heights above everything stretched the world of grown-ups—noisy, droning high overhead like pines in foul weather. Grown-ups: large, warm pillars, reliable, eternal columns that held out glasses of milk and offered trays of latticed blueberry pie, that ran out with prickly wool sweaters in their outstretched hands and got down on their knees to fasten small dusty sandals.

And then something broke, something went wrong. The kaleidoscope—and everything in it—shattered: a handful of dull glass shards, bits of cardboard, and strips of fiery, crimson-backed mirror. The world began to dwindle and wither, the grass receded, the ceiling lowered, borders started to show through, the delightful games were forgotten. The evening fog, the wolves and the forest, it turned out, were painted on canvas carelessly tacked on wood stretchers that leaned against the cold wall. Grown-ups broke all the rules and died: Father was crossed out by the red line of war, Mother shriveled and extinguished; their faces dissolved in a tremulous netting of rain. The only one to dig in, hold on, the only one to stay—was Grandmother. And like a barrier, like Baba Yaga's pike fence, impenetrable, pitch-black adolescence rose up in front of Natasha: twisted dead-ends, shameful thoughts, revolting conjectures.

The sky was silent, the earth died. Slushy rains fell for centuries. Natasha dragged the swelling caldron of her body, lumbering along on her pawish feet—there are five of them, seven of them, they're in the way; in the mirror, heavy, clumsy eyes looked out at her from a thick, rubbery face. People walked around up to the waist in filth, they concealed stench and open sores under their clothes, and all of them thought only of one thing. And with a shudder, suspecting her own unclean, female, animal nature, Natasha felt attacked night and day by a foul wind blowing and blowing from below at her gut, at her unprotected depths.

She began to dream of silent ravines, closed underground dens, staircases with collapsing steps. Every night, ripping her nails, Natasha tore off the cold, padded doors, and behind one of those doors her dead father, his huge mouth yawning, blew a monstrous black bubble from ash-colored lips—a hellish balloon.

And Natasha lay for hours, covering herself with a blanket from head to toe so that neither humans nor the stars could discern the marshy rubbish heap writhing like putrid mushrooms in her soul, so they wouldn't recognize the unmentionable.

At this time Konovalov began to drop in.

He came in from the cold, took out a handkerchief and carefully dried his nose as it defrosted in the warmth; he gazed intently with his blue eyes, wiped his hands, made friends with Grandmother's cheesecake: Natasha attracted him. Konovalov helped Grandmother with money, gave advice about Natasha's future, moved the furniture, screwed in pale light bulbs high up on the ceiling and, flustered, even offered a princely gift: he rented them a cheap dacha for the summer. And Natasha waited for the squeak of the door from the communal hall, the shudder of the dusty ball fringe on the door curtains, waited for the moment when, bearing a questioning blue fire in his eyes, Konovalov would enter.

But Konovalov was clean and Natasha was dirty, and she battened down all the hatches, caulked all the cracks, stood like a mute black tower. Konovalov's blue flares fizzled out against her cold surface.

Like a frenzied falcon, Konovalov looked this way and that, circled, clicked his beak, and then, unwillingly, shot up into the air and hid himself far beyond the deep blue forest. No one ever loved her again.

. . . But that summer, that summer in the country, the magical farewell feather that Konovalov let fall.

In a tight sundress, with a waffle towel slung over her neck, Natasha went out on the June porch. An early sun—timid, cold, pure—trembled on high, entangled in the pine. The air was colored in unsteady morning tones—not quite color, but the intimation of color: a sigh of pink, a hint at transparency. The earth was black, firm, the grass wet, thick, and under every bush lay a hard block of lilac shade. It was damp, lush, shadowy, the garden was neglected. And the sun climbed upward and pierced the pine summits with pale rainbow knitting needles. There, at the very top, dark-blue birds flitted about, and the tiny, green, sharp-tipped umbrellas shone with an unbearable, sun-filled happiness. There the morning was being made, a holiday was being celebrated, there was joy, joy, joy —a young June bride.

Beneath one's feet was a green, prickly country, dove-gray blueberry undergrowth, the green-pea shapes of unripened wild strawberries, whitish pink fields of cockles, and beyond the bright forest—the smooth quiet of a lake burning under the sun.

And Natasha carried in her soul a limpid golden glass of champagne happiness.

By autumn she was despondent, her heart pounded, she heard voices, had dreams. From rows of late gypsy poppies, spun from gentle soporific substances, the wind blew potions, visions of bedchambers, connecting suites, cool boudoirs, light blue lacy bridges over misty waterways, muddled paths that led to a nocturnal country: a pliant, soft, brown, elusive country; to a sleepy forest with neat yellow paths, literate bears that walked on their hind legs, friendly old women who willingly lived alone in thickets and waved plump hands from gingerbread windows; and you walk farther and farther on, you've already made it past the round table buried in the ground, and the old gray hammock stretched between resinous spruces, you've passed the abandoned, child-size watering can; and you see yourself, sitting on your haunches, with a yellow silk ribbon in your hair; and on the bench, ornamented by bark beetles, your dead parents are sitting and waiting. Now you remember their faces. Mama wears white tennis shoes and a white beret; Papa sports a mustache. He's drawing a word of some sort on the sand with a black umbrella. A strange word, you can't quite make it out. You're on the verge of getting it . . . but no. They're looking straight at Natasha, they're silent, smiling:

What's the problem? Well? Didn't you understand? Just a minute, wait, any second now . . . there . . . but the thick cloth curtains of dream quiver, the faces blur, the forest grows thin as gauze, and like a fish jerked out of the water, panting and weighty, Natasha is once again here. Upon awakening the un-ambiguous temples of her today throb. The obscure water closes up, the lid slams shut, on the white ceiling the un-deciphered abracadabra—the futile missive from her dead father—melts swiftly.

Grandmother took Natasha to the doctor, Natasha swal-lowed white tablets, and she no longer dreamt of anything except sighing, black waves of air.

After graduating from the institute, Natasha taught geography to schoolchildren. The word "geography" caused vast expanses to unfold in her mind: a hawk glided above the poppy fields, the muffled, nighttime sea roared, poisonous lily-white flowers swayed high overhead, and at the very bottom of the heavy, round earth, where the blue string bag of the meridians tightens into a stiff knot, a frost-covered skier, following the trail of whining dogs, slowly wandered upside down among the del-icate ice glades of Queen Maud Land. But she didn't know how to talk about this, and for that matter, no one asked her to; in fact, there was no science on earth devoted to study-ing the fragrance of a garden at night, the moan of sea foam, the dark splendor of the ocean's pearls, and the dull thud of a lonely heart. What if the children were to guess—how shameful—that Natasha, their melancholy, large-nosed teacher, imagined "bauxite deposits" as forest caves from which fat, reddish, short-haired dogs in round boxing gloves tumbled one after another, and "Tung Sten" as a raven-haired Chinese prince in a robe of iridescent cast? So, afraid of being found out, Natasha spoke in a dull, confusing manner, gazed imploringly at the awkward, chapped-knuckled eighth graders, whom she feared, hinted at the answers herself, and drew pretty blue A's on their papers with a sense of relief.

Time was passing, her heart beat, and no one arrived to love Natasha. But there were omens, premonitions, and visions, those ambiguous signs that fate proffers every so often—hadn't the Yellow Moon, emerging with a knife from the blue billows of misty clouds, promised her something ominous, enormous, and petrifying? But now the Yellow Moon was silent and only played with the carved black shadows on Grandmother's grave.

A long communal corridor ran through Natasha's dwelling; overhead in the half-dark swam washbasin tambourines, dusty Aeolian bicycle harps, and over the exit, rising like a plague cemetery up in arms, the black skulls of electric meters huddled together; as night fell the white stripes of their teeth, each row marked by a single bloody tooth, began madly spinning to the right. In the evening, soccer games whistled and blazed blue behind other people's doors, other people's husbands argued loudly; grandmothers sitting on high beds scratched their legs. A cheerful plumber reached for his rosy young neighbor in the kitchen; the neighbor woman flapped her elbows and the cheerful plumber exclaimed delightedly: "Goooood and spunky!"

In the evenings Natasha played poker with yellow, tobacco-permeated Konkordia Benediktovna, who gave her advice on how to dress; Konkordia Benediktovna herself wore a dark, glinting brooch at her breast, she fetched large faceted beads from little boxes, turned cups over and tapped her fingernail against the porcelain bottoms with their pale blue pedigree stamps—antiques, ancient antiques. Natasha gazed at the worn little cards and wanted to look like the Russian Queen of Diamonds—soft, blue-eyed, dressed in a white gathered head scarf and a sable vest. The old widower Gagin would stop in, looking like a graying crane in a red muffler; every year he

drew a crazed Santa Claus and a violently lunatic Snow White
for the windows of the vegetable store: mammoth, red-faced,
ready to take on anything, they raced furiously through a curly
blizzard on princely sleighs with silver spangles.

In the morning there was the humiliating visit to the toilet
with its oozing pistachio walls, carefully torn rectangles of
Socialist Industry or *The Week*, and a swaying dog-leash chain
ending in an old-fashioned porcelain pear, on which some wise
Englishman, to help things along, had written the black word
"Pull" in English and had even drawn a tiny pointing hand in
a black cuff: which direction to pull. But just for fun, the
cheerful plumber always deliberately disobeyed the Englishman's directions, and while Natasha fumed indignantly in the
slime-covered isolation booth, old lady Morshanskaya, ailing
and disheveled in her nightgown, was already pounding on the
door, shouting in her whiskered voice:

"Have some consideration for old people! . . . Natalia, is
that you? . . . Your insides will fall out! . . ."

The bathroom window opened onto the back stair, and old
lady Morshanskaya, fearing an attack by Young Pioneer scouts
out collecting materials for recycling, barricaded it with a
wooden washtub—the very same cracked one, the last hand-
me-down from the Magic Golden Fish. The bathroom was
used exclusively for washing clothes—they went to the baths
to wash themselves. Natasha went as well: she looked at the
strange, undressed women, pink, like wet ham, and found fault
with them all. Once, in the steam room, on the slippery, slop-
ing floor, the fat, naked high-school headmistress passed by
with a wet knot of hair on her forehead and a tub tucked
under her arm like a class register, the same headmistress who, that very morning, had sternly declared: "We,
pedagogues, collectively recognize." And long afterward,
whenever the headmistress—her face purple, her medal
clinking—yelled at adolescents who giggled during the cere-

monial lineup, all Natasha could see was the horrid, red, distended creature that shuffled hurriedly past along the wet, terra-cotta tile.

On the summer boulevards sat old women who had known a better life: gilded cups, the frosty flora of lace hems, the tiny antlike facets of foreign fragrance vials, and perhaps—indeed, most likely—secret lovers; they sat with one leg crossed over the other, their gaze lifted to where the heavenly evening theater silently lavished burning crimsons, golden treasures; and the loving western light crowned the blue hair of these former women with tea roses.

But nearby, heavily spreading their swollen legs, with drooping hands and drooping heads wrapped in dotted kerchiefs, flames all snuffed out, like dead swans sat those who had lived for years in brown communal kitchens, in dim corridors, those who had slept on iron frame beds next to deep-set windows, where beyond the speckled blue casserole, beyond the heavy smell of fermentation, beyond the tearstained glass, another person's wall darkens and swells with autumn anguish.

And Natasha began to dream: If old age must come to me as well, then let me turn into a clean, pink, white-haired old lady, a beloved schoolteacher, kind and funny, like a hot cross bun. But she wasn't made to be a hot cross bun and so was obliged to become a stooped, muddy-gray old lady with jowls.

She only made it to Moscow once, by chance. In a taxi, scared stiff, she zoomed along the nighttime streets squeaky with frost; she gazed up at the enormous buildings—rearing black chests of drawers, the gloomy castles of vanished titans, gigantic honeycombs crowned with bloody embers standing guard. And in the morning she looked out of the hotel window onto a hushed thaw, the soft, gray day, the jumble of little two-story yellow buildings and annexes pierced by morning lights—muslin is

drawn back from a small window, a kettle whistles, a grandmother in felt boots entertains her grandson with white rolls
—sweet, soft, Russian Moscow!

She immediately wanted to live there, wanted to exhale frosty
steam in the small lanes, clear little paths in the snowdrifts,
wear loose, ample blouses untucked, drink tea with hard round
pretzels purchased in a little, ruddy, golden shop.

Elated by the strong morning air, by Moscow's slapdash
shabbiness, by the smoldering geranium lampposts in low windowsills, Natasha awoke, threw her arms open wide, laughed,
and fell in love—swiftly and uninhibitedly, on meeting the
bearded, sandy-haired Pyotr Petrovich from the city of Izium,
who had come to Moscow to go shopping. Happy, she laughed,
leaning her chest on the table of the dumpling shop, and
watched with shining eyes as Pyotr Petrovich heartily tossed
the steaming white blobs into his large mouth; she trotted
around to stores with the cheerful Iziumer like a dog, waved
from long lines, helped him lug blue shoeboxes, elbowed her
way through to the steep Eliseevsky counter windows, and in
the crowd accidentally pressed her cheek to the wide, fragrant
back of that beloved sheepskin coat.

And Pyotr Petrovich, unaware, laughed joyfully, turned
around toward Natasha as he swayed in the roaring surf at the
counters of Children's World, and in a booming voice called
through the storm of heads: "Miss! Over here, Miss! Give me
a tabletop ring toss." And from afar he raised his victorious
hands and linked them over his head, nodding to Natasha: I'm
alive, alive, I bought it, await me on the shore. . . .

And at the station, near the train to Izium, he shook Natasha's hand joyfully: Thank you, you're a wonderful woman,
come visit Izium, you'll get on splendidly with my wife, you'll
meet my children. . . .

Pyotr Petrovich sank, Natasha howled like a wolf after the
departing green train, and her howl—a wartime, train station
howl—flew over the ringing rails, over the redbrick barracks,

over the cruel, bitter-cold earth. And behind Natasha, holding her firmly by the shoulder, stood old age, like a stern, patient doctor who has prepared his usual instruments.

She began to like gray goosedown scarves, to be pickier about her shoes: were they well-cut, did they pinch? She went to visit old lady Morshanskaya, and inspected her boxes of homeopathic remedies: sulfur iodine, salvia, hamamelis. For the old woman's birthday she gave her an enema bag: light blue, cheerful, with a relief drawing: little bouquets of lily of the valley against a sunrise. Konkordia Benediktovna returned from visiting her sister in Paris and brought Natasha a red plastic spoon. The widower Gagin would drop in with a crossword puzzle: Now then, Natasha, this is your territory—a river in Kazakhstan, five letters, ending with "sh"?

At New Year's, Gagin drank champagne and offered Natasha his heart and hand; Natasha laughed, Gagin laughed too; he was a jovial old man, and every year his drunken Santa Clauses and pedigree milk-cow Snow Whites turned out cheerier and cheerier.

Natasha moved the buffet and remembered Konovalov; at first he flared like a blue spark in the dark, then he flew in more and more often, hovered in the air, blotted his nose, and timidly disappeared if someone knocked at the door. While canning tomatoes, throwing the whole weight of her body onto the stiff lids of the jars, Natasha imagined how Konovalov, gratefully surprised, would fish out a soft, cool, dripping ball with two fingers, and ask for seconds.

Asleep in Serafimovsky Cemetery, Grandmother approved of Konovalov, but she'd gone and taken his address with her. Natasha flipped through the phone book: Konovalovs multiplied like cards in a deck, they scattered about the city like ants, their little black numbers blinked—one lived here, on Liteiny. It was easy to say: find Konovalov . . . A copper bell with a round inscription: "please turn." Brrring, brring, brrriiinngg! Silence. Slip-slap—footsteps. The bar clanks; squealing, a two-foot-long iron-smelling hook flies off; a chain scrapes. A suspicious old lady sticks a yellow, hairy nose out from the darkness, the smell of kasha wafts through the door: "Who do you want?"—"Konovalov."—"He's not home." Bang!—the door slams shut. Maybe he lives in a new building, on Rzhevka, or Grazhdanka, or on Silvery Boulevard, all riddled with rusty wire? . . . "Who's there?" "I'm looking for Konovalov, please. . . ." A surprised wife—dark, thin—wipes her hands on her apron, perplexed: Come in, please, but . . . Behind her—an unfamiliar, alien apartment, *their* apartment, the unread story of a life that has passed without me. . . . Konovalov comes out, chewing: "Who are you? . . ." No, but maybe he actually lives out of town? In some two-story wooden house. . . . A rooster wanders about the yard, tiger lilies bloom near the porch, the ground is trampled, packed down by feet. . . . A front door—like a dacha outhouse, and farther on, up a steep stair—a dark entryway, a hanging horse collar, wooden washtubs. . . . "It's Konovalov you want? Upstairs, upstairs, knock on the door. . . ." And he's lying in his boots on the bed, a cigarette in his hand, flowers in the windows, a grandfather clock: ticktock, ticktock; the pinecone weight crawls down. . . . And what will I say to him? "Oh, Konovalov! If once you loved a green, unripe sapling, then won't you now take autumn's withering, rotting fallen fruit? . . ."

In the cemetery where old lady Morshanskaya was buried there was also a Konovalov, but that one was four years old, and in the last century for that matter; and besides, the little tombstone angel, pressing a green finger to his mossy lips, invited silence.

Natasha knitted Gagin a pair of socks: The old man's room was damp. She mustn't forget to caulk the windows for the winter. Some wonderful star pupils presented her with a colorful album for her birthday: *Cats of Europe*. The elevator began to break down more frequently. You can rarely buy good tea nowadays. Did you hear, there's a cold front coming in tomorrow? Listen to that wind howl. And Natasha went to the window and listened, and nothing, nothing could be heard but the din of passing life.

Night

In the mornings Alexei Petrovich's mama yawns loud and long: hurrah, onward, a new morning gushes in through the window; the cactuses shine, the curtains quiver; the gates of the nighttime realm have slammed shut; dragons, mushrooms, and frightening dwarfs have plunged below the earth once again, life triumphs, the heralds blow their horns: a new day! a new day! Da-da-da da da-daa!

Mamochka combs her thinning hair oh so quickly with her hands, throws her bluish legs over the high bed frame—let them hang for a moment and think: all day they'll have to drag around the 135 kilos that Mamochka has accumulated in the course of eighty years.

Alexei Petrovich opened his eyes: Sleep slips serenely from his body; everything is forgotten, the last crow flies off into the gloom; the nocturnal guests, gathering their ghostly, ambiguous props, have interrupted the play until next time. A breeze sweetly fans Alexei Petrovich's bald spot, the newly grown bristle on his cheeks pricks his palm. Isn't it time to get up? Mamochka will give the order. Mamochka is so big, loud, and spacious, and Alexei Petrovich is so little. Mamochka knows everything, can do everything, gets in everywhere. Mamochka is all powerful. Whatever she says, goes. And he—is a late child, a little bundle, nature's blunder, a soap sliver, a weed intended for burning that accidentally wormed its way in among its healthy brethren when the Sower generously scattered the full-blooded seeds of life about the earth.

Can I get up already, or is it early? Don't squawk. Mamochka is carrying out her morning ritual: She honks into a handkerchief, pulls her stockings, sticking and prickling, onto the columns of her legs, fastens them under her swollen knees with little rings of white rubber. She hoists a linen frame with fifteen buttons onto her monstrous breast; buttoning it in the back is probably hard. The gray chignon is reattached at Mamochka's zenith; shaken from a clean nighttime glass, her freshened teeth flutter. Mamochka's facade will be concealed under a white, pleated dickey, and, hiding the seams on the back, the insides out, napes, back stairs, and emergency exits—a sturdy dark blue jacket will cover the whole majestic building. The palace has been erected.

Everything you do is good, Mamochka. Everything's right.

Everyone is already awake in the apartment, everyone's stirring, all the Men and Women have started talking. They slam doors, burble water, jingle on the other side of the wall. The morning ship has left the slip, it cuts through the blue water, the sails fill with wind, the well-dressed travelers, laughing, exchange remarks with one another on the deck. What shores lie ahead? Mamochka is at the wheel, Mamochka is on the captain's bridge, from the crow's nest Mamochka looks onto the shining ripples.

"Alexei, get up! Shave, brush your teeth, wash your ears. Take a clean towel. Put the cap back on the toothpaste. Don't forget to flush. And don't touch anything in there, you hear me?"

All right, all right, Mamochka. How right everything you say is. How much sense everything immediately makes, how open the horizons become, how reliable a voyage with an experienced pilot. The old colored maps are unrolled, the route is drawn in with a red dotted line, all the dangers are marked with bright, clear pictures: there's the dread lion, and on this shore—a rhinoceros; here a whale spouts a toylike fountain, and over there—is the most dangerous creature, the big-eyed, big-tailed Sea Girl, slippery, malicious, alluring.

Alexei Petrovich will wash up, put himself together; Mamochka will come and check whether he messed anything, or else the neighbors will yell again; and then it's food time. What did Mamochka make today? To get to the bathroom you have to go through the kitchen. Old ladies grumble at the hot stove, they're stewing poison in pots, they add the roots of terrible plants, follow Alexei Petrovich with bad looks. Mamochka! don't let them hurt me!

Dripped a little on the floor. Oh no.

There's already a crowd in the hallway: the Men and Women are leaving, noisily checking for their keys, coin purses.

The corner door with opaque glass is wide open; on the threshold stands that brazen Sea Girl, smirking. She winks at Alexei Petrovich; she's all tilted; she puffs Tobacco, her Leg is stuck out, her nets laid—don't you want to be caught, eh? But Mamochka's to the rescue, she's already racing like a locomotive, her red wheels pound, she whistles, out of the way!

"Shameless hussy! Get out of here, I say! Not enough for you . . . have to have a sick man as well! . . ."

"Ga-ga-ga!" The Sea Girl isn't afraid.

Dart—and into the room. Saved. Yu-u-ck. Women—are terrifying. It isn't clear what they're here for, but they're very unsettling. They walk by—smelling like they do . . . and they have—Legs. There are lots of them on the street, and in every house, in this one, and that one, and that one, behind every door, they've hidden, they're doing something, bending, rum-

maging around, giggling into their fists; they know something
and they won't tell Alexei Petrovich. He'll sit down at the table
and think about Women. Once Mamochka took him with her
out of town, to the beach; there were lots of them there. There
was one . . . a wavy sort of fairy . . . like a little dog . . . Alexei
Petrovich liked her. He went up close and looked at her.

"Well, what are you staring at?" shouted the fairy. "Get out
of here, you retard!"

Mamochka came in with a bubbling pot. He looked in. There
were the pink weenies of sausages. He was glad. Mamochka
sets the table, moves, wipes up. The knife pops out of his
fingers, strikes the oilcloth somewhere to the side.

"In your hands, take the sausage in your hands."

Ah, Mamochka, guiding star! Heart of gold! You'll fix everything. Wise, you'll unravel all the tangles, you'll destroy all the
back alleys, all the labyrinths of this incomprehensible, un-
navigable world with your powerful hand, you'll sweep away
all the walls—here's an even, leveled plaza. Boldly take one
more step. Farther on—wind-fallen trees.

Alexei Petrovich has his own world—in his head, the real
one. Everything's allowed there. But this one, outside—is bad,
wrong. And it's very hard to remember what's good and what's
bad. They've set up and agreed upon written Rules that are
awfully complicated. They've learned them, their memory is
good. But it's hard for him to live by someone else's Rules.

Mamochka poured coffee. Coffee has a Smell. You drink
it—and the smell goes over to you. Why aren't you allowed
to make your lips into a tube, cross your eyes to look at your
mouth, and smell yourself? Let Mamochka turn her back.

"Alexei, behave yourself!"

After breakfast they cleaned the table, set out the glue,
cardboard, scissors, tied a napkin around Alexei Petrovich:
he's going to glue boxes. When he's done a hundred of
them—they'll take them to the pharmacy. They'll get some
money. Alexei Petrovich loves these boxes, he doesn't like to

part with them. He wants to hide them on the sly, save at least some for himself, but Mamochka watches carefully and takes them away.

And then other people carry them out of the pharmacy, eat little white balls from them, and they tear up the boxes and throw them away. They throw them right in the trash bin, even worse, in their apartments, in the kitchen, in the trash he saw a ripped-up, dirtied box with a cigarette butt inside. A fearful black rage then filled Alexei Petrovich, his eyes flashed, he foamed at the mouth, forgot words, fiery spots flashed in front of his eyes, he could have strangled, torn them to pieces. Who did this? Who dared do this? Come on out, why don't you! He rolled up his sleeves: Where is he? Mamochka ran over, calmed him down, led the enraged Alexei Petrovich off, took away the knife, tore the hammer from his convulsed fingers. The Men and Women were afraid and sat quietly, hidden in their rooms.

The sun has moved to another window. Alexei Petrovich has finished his work. Mamochka fell asleep in the chair, she's snoring, her cheeks gurgle, she whistles: pssshhew-ew-ew . . . Alexei Petrovich oh so quietly takes two boxes, ca-arefully, on tip-tip-tippy-toes—goes to his bed, ca-aarefully, carefully puts them under his pillow. At night he'll take them out and sniff them. How the glue smells! Soft, sour, muffled, like the letter *F*.

Mamochka woke up, it's time to take a walk. Down the stairs, only not in the elevator—you can't close Alexei Petrovich up in the elevator: he'll begin to flail and squeal like a rabbit; why don't you understand?—they're pulling, pulling on my legs, dragging them down.

Mamochka floats ahead, nods at acquaintances. Today we'll deliver the boxes: unpleasant. Alexei Petrovich deliberately drags his feet: he doesn't want to go to the pharmacy.

"Alexei, don't stick out your tongue!"

The dawn has fallen behind the tall buildings. The gold

windowpanes burn right under the roof. Special people live
there, not the same kind as us: they fly like white doves, flitting
from balcony to balcony. A smooth, feathery breast, human
face—if a bird like that roosts on your railings, tilts its head
and starts to coo and bill—you'll look into its eyes, forget
human speech, and start clucking in bird language, you'll jump
along the iron poles with fuzzy little legs.

Under the horizon, under the bowl of the earth, giant wheels
have started turning, monstrous conveyer belts are winding,
toothed gears are pulling the sun down and the moon up. The
day is tired, it has folded its white wings, flies westward, big,
in loose clothes, it waves a sleeve, releases stars, blesses the
people walking on the chilling earth: good-bye, good-bye, I'll
come again tomorrow.

They're selling ice cream on the corner. He'd really like
some ice cream. Men and Women—but especially Women—
stick money into the square window and get a frosty, crunchy
goblet. They laugh; they throw the round, sticky papers on
the ground or stick them on the wall, they open their mouths
wide, lick the sweet, needlelike cold with red tongues.

"Mamochka, ice cream!"

"You're not allowed. You have a sore throat."

If he mustn't, he mustn't. But he really, really wants some.
It's awful how much he wants some. If he had one of those
monies, like other Men and Women have, one of the silvery,
shiny ones; or a little yellow piece of paper that smells like
bread—they also take those at the square windows. Ooh, ooh,
ooh, how he wants ice cream, they're all allowed, they all get
ice cream.

"Alexei, don't twist your head around!"

Mamochka knows best. I'm going to listen to Mamochka.
Only she knows the safe path through the thickets of the world.
But if Mamochka turned away . . . Pushkin Square.

"Mamochka, Pushkin—is he a writer?"

"A writer."

"I'm going to be a writer too."

"Of course you will. If you want to—you will."

And why not? He wants to, so he will be. He'll get some paper, a pencil, and he'll be a writer. There, that's decided. He'll be a writer. That's fine.

In the evenings Mamochka sits in a spacious armchair, pushes her glasses down on her nose, and reads thickly:

> *"A pall the storm casts on the sky,*
> *And whirls the twisting snow,*
> *First like a beast she'll howl and cry,*
> *Then like a child sob soft and low."*

Alexei Petrovich really loves this. He laughs heartily, baring his yellow teeth; happy, he stamps his foot.

> *"First like a beast she'll howl and cry,*
> *Then like a child sob soft and low."*

The words get to the end—and turn around, get to the end again—and turn around again.

> *"Apall thus tormcas tson thus ky,*
> *An dwhirls thet wistings no!*
> *First likab eastsheel howland cry,*
> *Then likach ild sobs off tandlow!"*

Very good. This is how she'll howl: oo-oooooo!

Shhh, sshhh, Alexei, calm down!

The sky is all sprinkled with stars. Alexei Petrovich knows them: little shining beads, hanging all by themselves in the black emptiness. When Alexei Petrovich lies in bed and wants to go to sleep, his legs start growing on their own, down, down, and his head grows up, up, to the black dome, up, and sways like the top of a tree in a storm, while the stars scrape his skull like sand. And the second Alexei Petrovich, inside, keeps shrinking and shrinking, compressing, he disappears in a poppy seed, in a sharp needle tip, in a microbe, in nothingness, and if he's not stopped, he'll vanish there completely. But the outside, giant Alexei Petrovich sways like a pine log mast, grows, scratches his bald spot against the night dome, doesn't allow the little one to disappear into a dot. And these two Alexei Petroviches are one and the same. And this makes sense, this is right.

At home Mamochka undresses, demolishes her daytime corpus, puts on a red robe, becomes simpler, warmer, more comprehensible. Alexei Petrovich wants Mamochka to pick him up. What nonsense! Mamochka goes out into the kitchen. It seems like she's been gone an awful long time. Alexei Petrovich checked whether the boxes were still there, sniffed the oilcloth, took a chance, and went out into the hall. The corner door, where the guests of the Sea Girl giggle at night, was cracked open. A white bed was visible. Where's Mamochka? Maybe she's in there? Alexei Petrovich peeped in the crack cautiously. No one. Maybe Mamochka hid in the closet? Should he go in? The room is empty. On the Sea Girl's table—an open tin can, bread, a nibbled pickle. And—a little piece of yellow paper and silver circles. Money! Take the money, run downstairs along the dark staircase, into the labyrinth of streets, look for the square window, and they'll give him a sweet cold cup.

Alexei Petrovich grabs, jingles, knocks things over, runs, slams the door, breathes loud and fast, trips. The street. It's dark. Which way? That way? Or this way? What's in his fist? Money! Someone else's money! The money shows through his hairy fist. Stick his hand in his pocket. No, it'll show through anyway. Someone else's money! He took someone else's money! Passersby turn around, whisper to one another: "He took someone else's money!" People press to the windows, shoving each other: Let me look. Where is he? There he is!

He has money! Aha! You took it, did you? Alexei Petrovich runs in the dark. Clink clink clink clink—the coins in his pocket. The whole city has spilled out onto the street. The shutters are thrown open. Hands point from every window, eyes shine, long red tongues stick out: "He took the money!" Let out the dogs. The fire engines blare, the hoses uncoil: Where is he? Over there! After him! Crazed, Alexei Petrovich rushes about. Throw it away, tear it from his hands, away, away, there it is, there it is! With his foot! Stamp on it with his foot! Traaaammmpple it! That's it. . . . There. . . . It's not breathing. It's quiet. It's died out. He wiped his face. There. Now where? Night. There's a smell. Where's Mamochka? Night. In the entryways wolves stand in black columns: they're waiting. I'll walk backward. I'll trick them. Good. It's stifling. I'll unbutton. I'll unbutton everything. Good. Now? Women with Legs walked by. They turned around. Snorted. So that's the way it is? Whaaaat? Me? I'm a wolf! I walk backward!!! Aha, scared are you? I'll catch up with you, I'll pounce, we'll see just what these Legs of yours are! He rushed at them. A cry. A-a-a! A blow. Don't hit! A blow. Men smell of Tobacco, they hit you in the stomach, the teeth! Don't! Forget it, leave him alone—don't you see? . . . Let's go.

Alexei Petrovich leans against a drainpipe, spits something black, whines. Little one, so little, alone, you got lost on the street, you came into this world by mistake. Get out of here, it's not for you! Alexei Petrovich cries with a loud howl, raising his disfigured face to the stars.

Mamochka, Mamochka, where are you? Mamochka, the road is black, the voices are silent, the paths lead into a deep swamp. Mamochka, your child is crying, dying, your only one, beloved, long-awaited, long-suffered. . . .

Mamochka is running, Mamochka is gasping, she stretches out her hands, shouts, grabs, presses him to her breast, feels him all over, kisses him. Mamochka is sobbing—she's found him, found him!

Mamochka leads Alexei Petrovich by the reins into a warm den, into a soft nest, under a white wing.

The swollen face is washed. Alexei Petrovich snuffles at the table, a napkin tied round him.

"Do you want a soft-boiled egg? Soft-boiled, a runny one?"

Alexei Petrovich nods his head: Yes, I want one. The grandfather clock ticks. It's peaceful. Delicious hot milk, soft, like the letter N. Something clears inside his head. That's right, he wanted to be . . .

"Mamochka, give me paper and a pencil! Quick! I'm going to be a writer!"

"Lord almighty! My poor baby! Why on earth . . . Well, now, don't cry, calm down, I'll give you some; just wait, you have to blow your nose."

White paper, a sharp pencil. Quickly, quickly, while he hasn't forgotten! He knows everything, he has understood the world, understood the Rules, grasped the laws of connection of millions of snatches and of odd bits and pieces! Lightning strikes Alexei Petrovich's brain! He frets, he grumbles, grabs a piece of paper, pushes the glasses aside with his elbow, and, surprised at his own joyful renewal, hurriedly writes the newly acquired truth in big letters: "Night. Night. Night. Night. Night. Night. Night. Night. Night. Night . . ."

Heavenly
Flame

This Korobeinikov, he would come over to the dacha from the neighboring sanatorium. They operated on him there for an ulcer. That's what doctors always say: for an ulcer. After all, you don't just go cutting someone open without rhyme or reason, although I know a lot of people think it'd be interesting to get opened up, so they can take a look and see what's in there just in case. But you can't go and do that for no reason. So they give a reason to cut—an ulcer, let's say—and then it's up to God; our citizen goes and dies for some entirely different reason, and the doctors had nothing to do with it.

So anyway, Korobeinikov would come visit the dacha from his sanatorium. It's a nice walk, not hard, a couple of kilometers among hills, through a little birch forest. It's August; the birds aren't singing anymore, but it's pure bliss all the same. The weather's dry, the leaves are turning yellow and dropping off, here and there a mushroom sticks up. Korobeinikov would pick the mushroom and bring it to the house.

You can't make anything with one mushroom, but it was

still a gift. An offering to the house. Olga Mikhailovna would
stand on the porch, watching him come from behind the high-
spiked birch-trunk fence, and say, "Here comes Korobeinikov,
he's got a mushroom." And her words made everyone feel
good, kind of peaceful, like in childhood: the sun shines serenely; the seasons slip by serenely; serenely, with no shouting
or panic, autumn draws near. A nice man is coming, carrying
a bit of nature. How sweet.

Who knows how or why he got into the habit of going over
to their place, why he became attached to them. But they were
glad to have him. Having company in the country—it's not
like having company in the city. There's a pleasant lack of
obligation. In the city a guest won't just drop in, he'll phone
first to say, I'd like to come by and visit you. The hostess will
glance quickly at the floor: is there a lot of dust?—she'll do a
mental check: is the bed still unmade?—she'll give a nervous
thought to the refrigerator shelves—all in all, it makes for
tension. Stress. But in the country none of that matters: what
to sit on, what to drink, or from what cups. And it's no disaster
if you leave a guest alone for five minutes—in the city that's
a cardinal sin, but not in the country. It's a different type of
hospitality. The guest lounges in a wicker armchair, has a
smoke or just sits quietly, gazing out the window at the view,
at the sky, and there's a sunset playing through all its colors
—it'll give off a red or lilac stripe, then a golden crust will
flare on a cloud, or everything will be tinged with a frosty green
or lemon—a star will sparkle. . . . Better than television.

Then the hostess returns carrying a teapot under a padded-
cotton cozy, she slices a loaf of pound cake, turns on the light.
Moths fly in from the garden, flutter about. Small talk, this
and that, everyone laughs, argues, sits around, sighs. Korobeinikov would be better off not smoking, what with his ulcer,
but he smokes, launches into his discussions of mysterious
phenomena. He believes in aliens, in little green men; he's
concerned about giant spiders, and triangles in the Nazca des-

ert. In the newspaper *Labor* he read that a flying saucer came
and hovered over the city of Sverdlovsk, that the sky near
Leningrad shone with a strange light and no one knew why.
This disturbs him. It disturbs Olga Mikhailovna too: she's
always wanted to meet little green men; she has plans for them.
Korobeinikov says that in South America the little green men
took this woman Dolores up with them in their saucer, gave
her a ride, showed her a bird's-eye view of the earth, then set
her down—in the city of Boston. Dolores, a simple peasant
woman, was completely bewildered—she didn't know the language, didn't know where to go. She's got sixteen children at
home howling to eat, and here she is, gadding about the city
of Boston like a chicken, while her husband, José, also a simple
peasant, doesn't have a clue what's going on either, and is so
furious he's sharpening his switchblade and threatening to take
care of his faithless wife—just let her cross the threshold of
their house! Olga Mikhailovna both believes and doesn't believe, but she's extremely annoyed: *she* would have figured
things out just fine over there in the city of Boston, what with
her common sense and clear thinking; *she* would have known
what was what right away—these little green men are forever
picking up the wrong people. Everyone laughs and gives Olga
Mikhailovna instructions about what to bring them from Boston if the same thing ever happens to her. Olga Mikhailovna's
husband says just let her try; he'll sharpen his switchblade,
too, he won't stand for any of these little men. Someone says
aliens only take people to Boston if they're from South America; anyone from the Moscow suburbs, it stands to reason,
they'd take somewhere like Tyumen or the Matochkin Strait,
and what would Olga Mikhailovna do in that case? Olga Mikhailovna's husband says this is all nonsense—as if *Labor* was
any authority!—and that there's no such thing as aliens, it's
all meteors with megahertz. What hertz? Well, he couldn't say
for sure, he's no astronomer, but they've all got megahertz.
Oh, there goes Olga Mikhailovna's husband again with his

cheap materialism—he's always reducing the dreams of pro-
gressive mankind to some little turd. One witty fellow immediately starts punning. "Whatever hertz, a person blurtz."
Who hertz where, comrades? Korobeinikov's ulcer hertz, but
he feels good here at this dacha; everything is so relaxed that
he somehow forgets about his pain. One hour of time spent
with pleasant people, a single hour an evening, is worth all the
medicines they cram down him at the sanatorium.

Korobeinikov savors one last cigarette: he taps it against the
table; he kneads the hollow cardboard tip, lights a match; the
pale flame illuminates his yellowish face, the fat lenses of his
glasses, a bulging forehead with locks of thick black hair. Korobeinikov has extraordinary hair: the man is nearly sixty years
old, and look what a mane he's got! Everyone else already has
bald spots of various shapes, except for the young people, of
course. Olga Mikhailovna's husband, glancing at Korobeinikov, runs his hand over his own balding head with chagrin—
oh well, to each his own. At least I don't have an ulcer.

But now it's dark outside the window—in August it gets
dark early—and time for Korobeinikov to go. He's expected
for supper at the sanatorium: his piece of baked cheese pie
with its beggarly puddle of sour cream has already grown cold,
and the tea urn, too, and the lights have been turned out. He'll
sit in the half-empty cafeteria, deep in thought, brushing
crumbs off the tablecloth, staring at his shaggy reflection in
the black windowpanes, listening closely to the mustard-hot
pain somewhere inside him—to the pain that awakens with
the darkness and drones, drones like a distant transformer.

Dolores—that is, Olga Mikhailovna—walks Korobeinikov
out to the porch, and everyone else stands up as well, nodding
and shaking his hand: It's not too cold for you? Maybe you
should take a jacket? No? Are you sure now? He will carefully
step down from the porch, his glasses glinting, he'll turn on a
pocket flashlight, the bright circle will play at his feet, catching
a bit of the green grass, the fence spikes, the trampled path,

the startled, white tree trunks. Korobeinikov directs the beam
to the skies, but the weak light scatters and the skies remain
just as dark as ever; only the top branches and the crows' nests
are lit for a moment. Playful, he turns the flashlight back toward
the porch, and then nothing can be seen in the night but a
white star where Korobeinikov had been standing.

At some point Olga Mikhailovna finds out that Dmitry Ilich
has also rented a little dacha in their village—Dmitry Ilich,
whom she knew slightly in the city; she'd run into him at
friends' houses, and they even kind of took to one another.
Olga Mikhailovna thinks it's only natural that people like her;
she's considered pretty, and from Dmitry Ilich's viewpoint
she's still quite young. Dmitry Ilich is an interesting man, too:
he's a sculptor, and he knows tons of stories and amazing
incidents, like for instance how once they unveiled a monument
and it was headless! Well, and stuff like that. Dmitry Ilich
limps, he walks with a stick, and it suits him. He says things
like "No, I'm not Byron, I'm something else," but somehow
it ends up that he *is* sort of Byron, after all—he's lame, he
writes a little poetry, and he was in Greece for a day and a
half on a cruise. He's seen Europe, and this automatically
commands respect. He says, "Italy—huh, nothing special. But
Greece, now—Greece is something," and though everyone
understands that Italy is probably not exactly nothing special,
he's been there and they haven't, so it's hard to argue. Well,
he says a lot of other things—he's had plenty of adventures
in his time. He was at the front for a speck, and in the
camps—he "went camping" in Siberia for two years, as he
puts it, not for any particular reason, naturally—but he doesn't
hold a grudge, he believes in destiny and has a sense of humor.
So when Olga Mikhailovna runs into him in the village, she
says, "Drop by and see us some evening," and he thanks her
and says, "I will be sure to limp by." He's really a gorgeous

man—he plays the bohemian, of course, but so what?—he has hair down to his shoulders, streaked with gray, a slightly pockmarked face, yellow hawk eyes, and he wears a smock. He says to Olga Mikhailovna, "I must sculpt you."

So he actually does come to see them one evening, and they slice a pound cake and put the kettle on. Dmitry Ilich tells them about his cruise, and about how one old guy in their group blew all his foreign currency the first day out, and when they were already on their way home through Turkey he suddenly remembered that he hadn't bought anything for his wife, so then he raced down to the Turkish market and traded his hearing aid—which he passed off as a radio—for a necklace. And he brought his old lady this necklace. Everyone's laughing, including Olga Mikhailovna's husband, and Olga Mikhailovna looks out the window and says, "Here comes Korobeinikov, he's got a mushroom. Oh, he's such a dear, and he tells the most amusing stories—about this woman named Dolores and all!"

Dmitry Ilich says, "Korobeinikov! Which Korobeinikov? Could it really be the same Korobeinikov?" And he doesn't explain what he means. Olga Mikhailovna is intrigued, of course, and looks to and fro, and in comes Korobeinikov with his mushroom and his stories, sweet and affable as ever—he likes it here, and it's a nice day, and the air is good, and the woods are lovely, and the people are nice, and he'd be happy to stay forever.

The guests are introduced to each other, everybody has tea, the evening chitchat begins. Korobeinikov, it must be said, is in top form, and Olga Mikhailovna is simply thrilled, but Dmitry Ilich is watching sort of intently, and there's some thought glimmering in his yellow eyes. Olga Mikhailovna is dying of curiosity—what did he mean?—her eyes shine, and everyone finds her charming. As always, for that matter.

"Hmm. Well, what do you know?" says Dmitry Ilich, after the ulcer patient, playing with his flashlight, has disappeared into the grove. "Who would have thought?"

"Well, what? What is it?"

"No, who would have thought?" And he drums his fingers on the table. Then he lays out everything he knows about this Korobeinikov. They were in school together, as it happens. In different classes. Korobeinikov, of course, has forgotten Dmitry Ilich—well, it's been forty years now, that's only natural. But Dmitry Ilich hasn't forgotten, no sir, because at one time this Korobeinikov pulled a really dirty trick on him! You see, in his youth Dmitry Ilich used to write poetry, a sin he still commits even now. They were bad poems, he knows that—nothing that would've made a name for him, just little exercises in the fair art of letters, you know, for the soul. That's not the point. But, as it happened, when Dmitry Ilich had his little legal mishap and went camping for two years, the manuscripts of these immature poems of his ended up in this Korobeinikov's hands. And the fellow published them under his own name. So, that's the story. Fate, of course, sorted everything out: Dmitry Ilich was actually glad that these poems had appeared under someone else's name; nowadays he'd be ashamed to show such rubbish to a dog; he doesn't need that kind of fame. And it didn't bring Korobeinikov any happiness: he got neither praise nor abuse for his reward; nothing came of it. Korobeinikov never did make it as an artist, either: he changed professions, and now he does some kind of technical work, it seems. That's the way the cookie crumbles.

"How do you like that," says Olga Mikhailovna.

"How do you like that," says her husband. "What a bastard!"

"Now then, I wouldn't call him a bastard," said Dmitry Ilich, softening. "At that time people saw things differently. Who could have known that I would come back? And this way my humble verse didn't perish—at least it saw the light of day. Maybe he was even prompted by noble motives."

"But he could have apologized after your return," says Olga Mikhailovna. "That's what I would have done, at any rate."

"Those were different times, my child," Dmitry Ilich explains indulgently. Olga Mikhailovna likes it when he calls her a child. At forty, it's pleasant. "Different times. And how would he have known that I came back? I didn't report to him. We weren't even really acquainted. God will forgive him, and I already have. Right here and now I've forgiven him."

So once again evening falls, and from the woods comes that vile Korobeinikov, carrying his foul toadstool. Everyone already knows about his treachery, about the mark of Cain on him. Olga Mikhailovna stands on the porch. "You have to forgive him," said Dmitry Ilich, but she doesn't want to forgive him. "Judge not, that ye be not judged," said Dmitry Ilich. All right, so she'll be judged, but at least she'll have the satisfaction of making judgments herself. She loves truth, what can you do, that's how she is. Of course, she's not about to persecute Korobeinikov—he has an ulcer, after all—but inside, in the pure house of her soul, she has the right to keep things in their proper place. And the place for trash is the kitchen, not the parlor.

There he sits, in the wicker chair, weaving a lot of nonsense about miracles. There he goes, slurping tea and chomping on cake. There he goes, singing like a nightingale about how some kind of mysterious voids were supposedly found deep inside the pyramid of Cheops, and what could this signify? You're the pyramid of Cheops yourself, thinks Olga Mikhailovna. "Megahertz . . ." mutters Olga Mikhailovna's husband. And everyone else thinks hostile thoughts. And Korobeinikov can't help but feel this.

Korobeinikov is confused; Korobeinikov mumbles on—about how one fine evening, see, the skies over Petrozavodsk convulsed and a heavenly flame descended, a column of horrendous force, and everything turned bright as day, while crimson stripes ranged the sky and the whole shebang flashed and quaked, and what could this possibly signify? But knowing what they now know about Korobeinikov, the hosts and their guests no longer ooh and ah, no longer laugh, no longer cry out in disbelief. Olga Mikhailovna forces a smile, even though it's about as easy for her to smile as it would be to lift weights, and she curses herself for her fake smile, her female cowardice: if only she could somehow give Korobeinikov to understand that that's it—that's it!—he needn't come around here again, that's enough, we don't want him anymore. We know about your low-down dirty trick. And your ulcer is no excuse! Your ulcer is a heavenly flame sent down on you as a punishment, that's what! We wish you no ill—go and get yourself cured, take your little vitamin pills, go drink buttermilk in your sanatorium—but don't come around here! And don't bring us any mushrooms.

Korobeinikov, of course, can feel that the temperature at the dacha has dropped for some reason. He's nervous; he smokes one cigarette after another; behind the thick lenses of his glasses his eyes watch, frightened and uneasy; he thinks the problem must be his stories—maybe he's repeating himself, maybe they aren't interested in this stuff. He hastens to inform them about the Filipino healers—it doesn't help; he remembers a marvelous story about the Berdichev bonesetter who puts hopeless paralytics back on their feet—useless; the ice stays ice; they stare at him, their eyes hard as nuts. Finally he gets up to leave, and they all nod, but it's not quite the same; they offer him the jacket again, but they don't even pretend to rise, don't walk him out to the porch, don't see him off— it's as though their joints had turned to stone. True, Olga Mikhailovna can't help but do her duty as hostess: she opens the front door, waits for him to descend from the porch, turn on his flashlight, and disappear deep into the birch grove. The beam floats steadily, thoughtfully, through the severe, white tree trunks; it doesn't soar or circle, doesn't dance in the darkness.

Korobeinikov's ashtray is full of butts—geez, look how much he smoked! Everyone stares after the ashtray meaningfully as Olga Mikhailovna's husband goes to dump it—that mound of empty, stinking cardboard tips—as if it measured the guilt of an unclean man.

Korobeinikov walks through the unsheltering grove. The birch trunks are chilly, and the ground feels cold through his shoes; ahead smolder the lights of the sanatorium, a vale of woe: the beds there are white and the bed tables are white, the walls shine with white oil paint, white lamps hang from the ceilings, and on the staircase landing, where Korobeinikov goes to smoke, a fire hose is curled up in a white cabinet with glass doors. The hose is brown, flat, long—infinitely long, longer than life—and at night, when Korobeinikov falls asleep, headless orderlies will sail into the ward without touching the floor and order Korobeinikov to swallow the hose—that's what you have to do before an operation—and, choking, he will swallow, swallow those long, endless yards of dull, rough ribbon.

The next day, Korobeinikov sits at his boring meal, listlessly pokes at his fish balls with a fork, stares out the wide sanatorium windows to where August burns with gold, green, and deep blue—he'll go for his usual walk and then he'll drop by that house after all: he was only imagining things, he must have been in a bad mood himself, it's just the illness, it's the pain, the rumble, the spoonful of fire he must have swallowed somehow by mistake, those people have nothing to do with it. He walks through the grove, touches the cold bushes, leans his spectacles earthward, looking for a mushroom, but there aren't any; lots of people hunt for them here.

He sits on the veranda, trying to joke and be entertaining, but Olga Mikhailovna only narrows her eyes, and Olga Mikhailovna's husband, who whenever he hears a good joke repeats it again and again, asks, "So how's your megahertz—still hurts?" although the question is really unnecessary. And the conversation flags, halts, dries up, as if everything on earth had already been said.

It must be boring for them to listen to the same thing over and over again—why hadn't he considered that? Now, when that yellow-eyed sculptor puts on a show, they're all pleased as Punch, they all laugh. Still, an old friend is better than two new ones, Korobeinikov thinks vaguely to himself; no matter, he'll just have to outtalk him. He'll prepare something for tomorrow. About life after death, for instance. What a person sees when he faints or is in a coma, when he's clinically dead. Oh, there's a lot of gripping stuff! The witnesses are completely reliable. He actually talked to one of these people. This guy told him that on the other side, everything is sky blue and transparent, but there's no air, and you don't need to breathe, you don't even miss it. And, you know, the feeling is like when you're young, or you just got out of the army, or you just had a son—a really good feeling. And then someone appears— you can't exactly see anyone, but he's *there* all the same—and this someone talks to you, but without any voice. "It's not time yet," he says. In a kind of respectful way. And then, whoosh!—you're suddenly back on the operating table again, everybody's running around you, frantic, but you're lying there and you're thinking, What do any of you know! . . . Yes, that's a good story. Only it has to be told with élan, with spirit. Have to rouse the audience, right? . . . No, I won't go there anymore, thinks Korobeinikov, heading back, tripping over a root. It's humiliating, for heaven's sake! If only it weren't for the white-ness of the hospital, the dull shine of the linoleum, the sterile, deathly cigarette bucket! If only the fire hose didn't come sneaking up in the evenings, didn't stick to you with suction cups, didn't sting you to the very core.

Completely yellow, Korobeinikov walks along the evening path. Dmitry Ilich embraces Olga Mikhailovna in the birch forest.

"Why does he keep dragging himself over here?" says Olga

Mikhailovna indignantly, her eyes following the gaunt figure.

"Oh, don't pay him any mind, little one," says Dmitry Ilich, kissing her.

"How do you stand him, Dima, you're simply a saint!"

"Don't be silly, my child, what's there to get excited about! He's got it bad enough as is, let him live out his life in peace! For him the time has come to wither; for you, to blossom. You see, even my walking stick is blooming at the sight of you." Olga Mikhailovna's head spins; if no one could see her she'd jump up and down and do cartwheels—wow, what a romance! Dmitry Ilich combs back his hair with his fingers, flashes his hawk eyes and feasts them on Olga Mikhailovna.

It grows dark. Korobeinikov, completely black, shuffles from the village to the sanatorium; a little ball of light bounces about on the roots. Dmitry Ilich has no secrets from Olga Mikhailovna: "By the way, my child, I was only joking," he says, knocking leaves from a bush with a stick. "It was a practical joke—punish me. That story about the poems—it never happened, and I've never seen that Korobeinikov of yours before in my life."

"What do you mean, Dima?" says Olga Mikhailovna, scared.

"The devil led me astray. Or maybe I was jealous of him. I thought, Who is this Korobeinikov character? But I pulled it off, didn't I?"

"Ohhhh, Dimochka, you're so bad," pouts Olga Mikhailovna. "What are we going to do with you? Come on, let's go have our tea. My husband is probably sharpening his switchblade by now."

Over tea they giggle like conspirators. "What's with you two?" says Olga Mikhailovna's husband, surprised. So they have to tell about how Dmitry Ilich played a joke on Korobeinikov. Dmitry Ilich is very amusing about doing penance—he clasps his hands together and begs to be forgiven. He even wants to get down on his knees in front of everyone, only his lame leg gets in his way. "Don't be ridiculous!" everyone shouts. No, he insists, he'll get down on his knees! At least on one knee. He's repented, repented! On one knee, and the other leg cocked like a pistol: how do you prefer the other leg—in front or behind? Everyone laughs: this Dmitry Ilich is so awfully artistic! And though Korobeinikov may be vindicated now, he's a bore anyway. And somehow they've got used to thinking badly of him. Oh, to hell with him! "Heavenly flame!" "Megahertz!" "It hertz until it stoptz!" "Did you hear that?" shouts Olga Mikhailovna's husband. "It hertz until it stoptz!" Anyway, he always talked such a lot of nonsense, and told such lies—did you notice? And tomorrow he'll drag himself over here again. He ought to at least be ashamed—he can see how people feel about him; he could just stay put in that sanatorium of his! Spit in his face and he thinks it's a spring rain!

The next day Olga Mikhailovna feels very uncomfortable. First of all, around her husband, who doesn't suspect a thing—oh well, that doesn't matter—and secondly around Korobeinikov. It would be better if he didn't come. It's uncomfortable to look someone straight in the eye when we've treated him like crap for no reason and we can't admit it. But, on the other hand, he's been cleared. And now we don't have to live with that awful feeling of having invited a bastard into the house. Dima behaved badly, of course. But he's repented—and all on his own, too, no one twisted his arm. It takes guts to do that, whatever you say. That's courage.

But Korobeinikov does come, of course. And he tries really hard. Why does he try so hard? It's all over with! And Olga Mikhailovna puts up with him, soiled as he is, and she's solicitous, emphatically solicitous, as she pours him tea and feeds him pound cake. "Everything they give you in the sanatorium is probably mush—isn't it? At least here you can eat like a real person." Korobeinikov is startled, he looks bewilderedly through his thick glasses. He doesn't understand—what was all that about, last week? What's going on now? There's some kind of tension in the air. And does anyone like this tension? No one does. It's hard to be with him, Korobeinikov. He's already turned completely yellow. And it would be nice if he'd realize that, since the conflict is resolved and everything's cleared up now, it would just be better if he didn't come here anymore. Because it's hard to be with him. And when he looks closely into their faces, trying to understand, that's hard too. And there's no point staring. As it turns out, it's nothing to do with him. He's been acquitted and now he can just leave.

Olga Mikhailovna looks at Korobeinikov with hatred. These nightly visits drive her crazy. And they drive everyone else in the house crazy, too. What—don't we have the right to live like human beings? Among our own friends? Honestly, it would be better if he died. Yes, well, that's what'll probably happen soon. That's no ulcer he's got, oh no. It's not an ulcer; see how lemony-looking he is, and he's aged right before our very eyes. And another sign that the end is near is that insensitivity and tactlessness, that thickheaded stubbornness—when the sick person doesn't care about proprieties anymore and just clings to life, to people, to whatever there is. Yes, as an honest person, she freely admits it to herself: she wishes he would die. There you have it. Everyone would rest easier.

The nights are cold: she goes out on the porch, offers Korobeinikov a jacket, knowing that he won't take it; she waits while he lights the flashlight, steps down from the porch; she listens greedily to his feeble feet shuffling through the fallen leaves. She hopes that she's right about the symptoms. Soon, very soon. It would be nice if it were before the end of the summer. She stands for a long time and watches the flashlight's pale fire count the hospital-white birch trunks, watches the corridor of light close in, the darkness thicken, the heavenly flame sweep blindly by, searching out its victim.

Most Beloved

At night spring blows through Leningrad. River wind, garden wind, and stone wind collide, whirl together in a powerful rush, and race through the empty troughs of the streets, shatter the glass of attic windows with a peal and lift the damp, limp sleeves of laundry drying between rafters; the winds fling themselves flat on the ground, soar up again and take off, speeding the scents of granite and budding leaves out to the night sea where, on a distant ship under a fleet sea star, a sleepless traveler crossing the night will raise his head, inhale the arriving air, and think: land.

But by early summer the city begins to wear on the soul. In the pale evening you stand at the window above the emptying street and watch the arc lamps come on quietly—one moment they're dead and silent, and then suddenly, like a sick, technological star, a rosy manganese point lights up, and it swells, spills, grows, and brightens until it shines full strength with a dead, lunar whiteness. Meanwhile, outside of town, the grasses have already quietly risen from the earth, and without a thought for us the trees rustle and the gardens change flowers. Somewhere out there are dusty white roads with tiny violets growing along their shoulders, the swish of summer stillness at the summit of century-old birches.

Somewhere out there our dacha is aging, collapsing on one side. The weight of February snows has crushed the roof, winter storms have toppled the double-horned chimney. The window frames are cracking and weakened diamonds of colored glass fall onto the ground, onto the brittle litter of two years' flowers, onto the dry muddle of spent stems; they fall with a faint chime no one will hear. There's no one to weed out the stinging nettle and goosefoot, sweep the pine needles from the rickety porch, no one to open the creaky, unpainted shutters.

There used to be Zhenechka for all this. Even now it seems she might be limping along the garden path, in her hand the first bouquet of dill, raised like a torch. Perhaps she actually is somewhere around here right now, only we can't see her. But the cemetery is definitely not the right place for her—for anyone else in the world, yes, but not for her. After all, she meant to live forever, until the seas dry up. It never even crossed her mind that she could stop living, and, truth be told, we too were certain of her immortality—as we were of our own, for that matter.

Long, long ago, on the far side of dreams, childhood reigned on earth, the winds slept quietly beyond the distant, dark blue woods, and Zhenechka was alive. . . . And now, from the herbarium of bygone days which grows with every year—green and motley days, dull and brightly colored ones—memory fondly extracts one and the same pressed leaf: the first morning at the dacha.

On the first morning at the dacha, the damp glassed-in veranda still swims in green, underwater shadow. The front door is open wide, cold creeps in from the garden; the pails are in place, empty and resonant, ready for a run to the lake, to the smooth, blinding lake, where the reflected world fell upside down in the early hours of the morning. The old pail gurgles, a distant echo gurgles. You ladle the deep, cold silence, the stilled, smooth surface, and sit for a while on a fallen tree.

Cars will soon start honking outside the gates of the dachas, summer folk will pour out of the automobiles, and, sighing and moaning, a taxi-truck will turn around in the narrow, wooded dead end of the road, scraping on the low branches of maples, breaking off the fragile flowering elder. It will give a gasp of blue smoke and fall quiet. In the returning silence the only sound will be the thunder of the truck's wood side-panels dropping, and on its high platform strangers' belongings, crowned with an upturned Viennese chair, will be shamelessly revealed to the eye.

And one automobile will drive straight through the gates, and from the wide-flung door will emerge a firm, elderly hand gripping a walking stick, then a leg in a high-buttoned orthopedic shoe, then a small straw hat with a black ribbon, and finally smiling Zhenechka herself, who will straightaway cry out in a high voice: "Look at the lilacs!" and then, "My suitcases!" But the bored driver will already be standing with the canvas bags in both hands.

Zhenechka will hurry into the house, exclaiming loudly over the aromas of the garden; she'll push open the casements impatiently, and with both hands—strong like a sailor's—pull branches of lilac into the rooms, their cold, purple curls rustling with noisy importance. Then she'll hurry to the sideboard to see whether the winter mice have broken her favorite cup, and the cabinet will grudgingly open its swollen doors, behind which Zhenechka's treasure whiled away the January nights alone in the stale, empty depths, alone with a graying, forgotten cookie.

She will walk through the rooms, as yet unwarmed by the

sun; she'll unpack, hand out presents crackling with paper, shake fruit fudge and sweet cakes from packets, cram the corners of the rooms with bouquets of wild flowers, hang our smiling photographs above her bed; then she'll clear the desk, and stack it with textbooks, dictionaries, and dictation books. Not a single idle day will she allow us; she'll sit us each down for at least an hour of lessons geared to our respective ages. "We are legion—you can't teach us all!" We'll wriggle and hop about in front of Zhenechka. "Yes, I can," she'll answer calmly, looking for the inkwell. "Take pity on yourself," someone will whine. "Like Pushkin says, we're disgusting, lazy— no curiosity. . . ." "All of you are going to grow up to be educated people." "We won't grow up! We're slaves to our stomachs! We're denizens of the dark kingdom! Take the books and burn them all!" "Never mind, we'll manage," says Zhenechka, and she'll seize us roughly and kiss us each harshly with a convulsive love we accept indulgently: All right, let her love us. Already she's dragging the first victim to her lesson, saying, as always, "I taught your mama, you know. Your grandmother and I were childhood friends. . . ." And on her chest, in the folds of her dress, her hearing aid begins to chirr like a nightingale—the hearing aid that for some reason never works quite right. Well, then, we're back to lessons again, exercises and dictations; once again, sitting in the creaky wicker armchair, propping her bad leg against the walking stick, Zhenechka, in her measured voice, will begin patiently turning us into educated people, and with the heedlessness of childhood, we will again start to bait her. We'll crawl into the room where the current captive languishes at the copybook; we'll crouch behind Zhenechka's armchair—her hunched linen back, her clean soap smell, the willow creak—and take advantage of her deafness to prompt the giggling victim with wrong or indecent or ridiculous answers, or pass notes with calls to rebel against the slave driver, until Zhenechka notices something's up and, all in a dither, banishes the spies.

And beyond the windows, beyond the tinted panes: a fresh, flowered stillness, warm shadows beneath the pines, and the midday lake filled with blue, glinting through the boughs, all covered with patches of sun, with fleet wedges of rippled brightness. . . . But here we are, locked indoors, the table covered in green blotting paper, the thumbtacks rusted over the winter, the ink stains bleeding an official-looking lilac rainbow. And everything Zhenechka says—is boring, correct, old. If only she'd go into the garden or go drink coffee! "Zhenechka, how much longer?" "Underline the subject with one line, the predicate with two. . . ." "Zhenechka, the summer will be over!" The willow armchair gives a heavy sigh, the blue eyes gaze with calm reproach, the patient voice says: "There's a time to sow and a time to reap. . . . Sluggards never make scholars. . . . Live and . . ."

Ohh, isn't there something she's dying to do?

The evening fades, the dust on the road grows cold, dogs bark far away. We lie in our beds on cool pillows, listening to the sighs and purrs of the day winding down, the whispers of doors, muffled laughter. From the attic—lighter than shadow, quieter than dust—dreams descend, surging in a transparent wave and confusing what has been with what never was.

Knocking, squeaking, and rustling, groping through the twilight of the house, Zhenechka makes her way to our beds, settles in and takes up an unending story about bygone years—about the children she taught and loved, about the wind that scattered them throughout the wide world: some disappeared, some grew up and forgot, some returned to dust. Dreams swirl like a warm shadow; from the invisible cloud of soap and mint only her voice emerges, sympathetic and soft, then cooing and enraptured, unhurried, like a blissful June day. Transparent visions float in dozing waters: a boy surfaces, a faraway dark-eyed, light-haired, antique boy, who long, long ago lay just like this in a dizzyingly distant white bed and listened to the murmur, the gurgle, the rise and fall of Zhenechka's voice—a boat rocking on waves of drowsiness. His eyes drooped and shut, his fingers relaxed, his speechless lips parted—for the dark-eyed boy was mute. That's why Zhenechka was asked to come: to pity, love, and care for him; to croon lullabies and babble fairy tales about dark forests, about the cat and the wolf, about the seven orphaned goats; and, as the boy fell asleep, his muteness mingled with the night's, and his bed set sail under the low vault of dreams.

Zhenechka had been in our house from time immemorial, and through the darkness of infancy I can make out her blue gaze bent over me on the day when the good fairies customarily gather with gifts and greetings for the newborn. I don't know what gift she intended for me: amid the bounty of gifts called life, Zhenechka's own gift, humble and small, could easily have been lost, or maybe she had nothing to offer but herself, nothing but the steady glow of love and tranquillity that emanated from her smooth, clear soul.

Once she gave one of us, one of her girls, a pretty box: luxurious, satin, full of light blue envelopes for love letters. Embarrassed, she threw back the top, so that its taut blue silk reins quivered; on the inner side, hidden from idle eyes, she had written in her clear schoolteacher's hand: "If you were to ask for advice, I would say only one thing: Don't wish to be the prettiest, wish to be the most beloved." And we did wish this. But nothing came of it, of course, no more than it did for Zhenechka herself.

Her mouth was not made for kissing. No. It was simply a dry, prim, pedagogical mouth, which with age acquired that particular array of surrounding wrinkles that unmistakably indicates honesty, goodness, and simplicity—all those tiresome, well-meant, inarguable truths that its owner hastens to share with you: The north is cold, the south is hot; May mornings are better than November fogs; sun, lilies of the valley, and golden curls are good; tornadoes, toads, and bald patches are bad. And roses—roses are the best thing on earth.

Zhenechka always stuck to her routine, of course. She exercised in the morning. In all seasons, she kept the window cracked open at night, and made a point of waking early— not because she liked gray, dank dawns, but because she could be useful in the mornings. The luxury of idleness was unknown to her, coquetry beyond her ken, playfulness alien, intrigue incomprehensible, that's the reason Hymen ran from her, not because he was the least bit scared off by her hearing aid or her orthopedic shoe. No, those trifles appeared later—after the war, after the bomb that exploded close to her, when Zhenechka was already over fifty. That wasn't the reason, of course. After all, even legless people can get married and have a family; it's the soul that counts. And her soul was—well, they don't come any simpler.

If our souls are usually constructed like a kind of dark labyrinth—so that any feeling running in at one end comes out the other all rumpled and disheveled, squinting in the bright light and most likely wanting to run back inside—then Zhenechka's soul was built rather like a smooth pipe, with none of those back streets, dead ends, secret places, or, God forbid, trick mirrors.

And the face matched the soul: simple blue eyes, a simple Russian nose. It would even have been quite a nice-looking face if it hadn't taken forever to get from the nose to the upper lip. Short, fluffy hair, a style called "smoke." Braids when she was young, of course.

She wore simple muslin dresses, undergarments that were clean and cheerless; in winter she put on a shabby quilted cotton coat that she called her "fur," and covered her head with a tall boyar's hat; summer or winter she never removed her amber beads, worn not for beauty's sake but for her health, because she believed some sort of electricity emanated from them.

She taught Russian her whole life, and—if you think about it—how could it have been otherwise?

Giving presents was her favorite activity. Winters in our Leningrad apartment, at the core of my childhood, there would be a ring at the door, and—smiling, squinting, treading heavily on her orthopedic shoe, leaning on her staff—little boyar Zhenechka would enter in her cloth "fur," a real fur hat over her puffed hair, a fresh ruddiness on her middle-aged cheeks, in her hands a pastry box and other tiny, mysterious bundles.

We would all run out into the foyer; smiling silently, Zhenechka would hand over her things—the staff to the right, the tall hat to the left—and unbutton her heavy coat. Freed from its padding, the hearing aid on her chest filled with our cries and greetings, the smack of our kisses, shouts about how young she'd gotten and how well she looked. Having combed the fluffy smoke at the mirror and straightened the heavy amber beads, Zhenechka got down to passing out her gifts: for the grown-ups, useful, serious books that got leafed through, set aside, and never picked up again; for us, tiny flasks of perfume, little notebooks, or surprising trifles miraculously preserved from prerevolutionary times—statuettes, embroidered brooches, ancient cups with broken handles—treasures to take any little girl's breath away. Amazing how all these easily lost, perishable little things filtered down through the years. Time's meat grinder readily destroys big, solid, cumbersome objects —cabinets, pianos, people—while all manner of fragile odds and ends that appeared on God's earth to gibes and raised eyebrows—all those little porcelain dogs, miniature cups, minuscule vases, rings, drawings, snapshots, boxes, notes, knick-knacks, thingamajigs, and whatchamacallits—pass through unscathed. Zhenechka's tiny apartment somewhere on the edge of the city near the sea was crammed with all this marvelous junk, while her sisters—the three here and the fourth, who'd gone to live in Helsingfors, beyond that sea, beyond its sad, gray waters—had vanished like smoke. We were all she had left in the world.

Having handed everything out and received the happy squeals and kisses due her, Zhenechka picked up her pastries and marched off to the parlor to drink coffee.

The pastries, of course, were from Nord—the best. On her bad legs, Zhenechka had stood in a long line for them in that magical basement, that gathering place for all believers in sugary terrestrial bliss, where impatient ladies intent on instant happiness elbow their way over to the side gripping a pastry in tremulous fingers and—pressed by the crowd to the mirrored column, to their own agitated reflections—snort like eager fairy-tale stallions, their nostrils exhaling a double, swirling puff of sweet powder that slowly settles on their silver-fox collars.

Zhenechka would open the box wherein reposed the grand, monarchical pastries Napoleon and Alexander; beside them, like Dmitry the Pretender, the despised shortbread ring, that constant of railroad snack bars, had wormed its way in. No one would eat it, but to Zhenechka it, too, seemed wonderful—the ruddy embodiment of a sated, crumbly dream dreamt during the not-yet-forgotten hungry nights of the wartime blockade.

Until the pastries are gone, being with Zhenechka holds my interest, and then, alas, it's boring. She talks in detail about her health, the contents of a book she read, the flowers that grow so luxuriantly in summer at a friend's house near the Peri station (from the station walk straight ahead, turn left, then one more turn, and it's the second house) but don't grow at all in winter because of the fact that in the winter the ground is covered with snow, which falls from the sky, and thus unfortunately nothing can grow, but as soon as spring comes and the days get longer and the nights shorter and the sun starts warming things and leaves appear on the trees, then, of course, the flowers will bloom again. . . .

I slip quietly out of the room and off to the kitchen; that's where real life is! Marfa, the housekeeper, is drinking tea with the lady who operates the elevator. Marfa is a tall, bald, cunning old peasant woman who was washed up at our door by the war; she knows absolutely everything better than everybody.

". . . So he says keep an eye on my suitcase, lady, will you? I'll be back, he says, in the wink of an eye. So she takes it from him. Right away he's up and gone. Well, he's gone for an hour, and he's gone for two, and now she has to go home. She's bone-tired of waiting. She figures she'll hand it over to the police, but she thinks, well, I'll just take a look-see. So she peeks inside." Marfa raises her eyebrows up high, pokes the sugar lumps with the tongs.

"Well?" says the elevator lady, alarmed.

"Well to you too. A fine how-de-do! She thought maybe there's valuables in there, or something. Opens it up—Heavenly Mother of God! . . . A head, with mustaches!"

"Chopped off?!"

"Right to here. Just a head, deary, with mustaches. Some guy, not too old. And the head tells her: Shut the suitcase, he says, and don't stick your nose where it don't belong!"

"Oh my! The head says that?"

"Yes. Well, she's off and running for all she's worth. And the head yells after her: 'Shut the suitcase, you stupid fool, or you'll be in big trouble!' And he starts cussin' her something fierce."

"No!"

"These was a pack of thieves, deary. That's what they was. They'd take him along in that suitcase, give him to someone in line to hold on to, and from inside there he hears everything—who's got bonds hidden where, or lengths of cloth."

"So that's what they do!"

Horrified, I ask:

"The head, who was it?"

"Who, who, what's it to you? You go play. . . . That what's-her-name of yours—she still here? The one with the beads?"

Marfa doesn't like Zhenechka: she doesn't like her shabby coat, her beads, her nose. . . .

"What a nose—a regular hose! If I had me a horn like that, I'd toot it on holidays! Such a laaa-dy! The same old gab all the time—yackety yackety yak . . ."

Marfa laughs, the elevator lady also laughs, politely, into her hand, and I laugh along with them, betraying poor unsuspecting Zhenechka, may she forgive me! But it's true, she does go on—yackety, yackety . . .

"And I heard another," Marfa starts.

But there's already a deep blue beyond the windows, and there are voices in the foyer—Zhenechka is getting ready to go home. Exhausted, everyone rushes to kiss her, a bit ashamed that they were so blatantly bored and Zhenechka, a pure soul, didn't notice anything amiss.

And someone walks her to the tram while the rest watch out the window: under softly falling snow, leaning on her staff, in her tall hat, Zhenechka slowly shuffles away, back to her lonely dwelling.

And the tram will rush past wastelands, snowdrifts, fences, past low brick factories that send a roaring appeal into the steely winter murk, past buildings decimated by the war. And somewhere at the edge of town, where the cold fields begin, a wizened amputee tumbles into the dim, clanking car, stretches out his accordion, and sings, "Oh, woe is me, a poor old cripple, I'm only half a man, they think; if you don't help, my cares will triple, for I still need to eat and drink," and warm, shame-ridden coppers fly into his filthy hat.

The snowflakes are thicker, the white shroud denser, the

streetlamp sways, seeing off the small, lame figure, the snow-storm sweeps away the faint, barely visible footsteps.

But she was actually young once! Just think—the sky above was not a whit paler than it is now, and the very same velvety black butterflies fluttered above the splendid rose beds, and the whistle of the grass under Zhenechka's cloth shoes was just as silky when she walked down the drive, canvas suitcase in hand, to her first pupil, the mute, dark-eyed boy.

His parents were good-looking and rich, of course; they had an estate, and the estate had a greenhouse with peach trees, and young Evgeniya Ivanovna, who had just finished school with honors, was photographed among the peach blossoms—homely, smiling pleasantly, with two long, fluffy braids remarkable for the fact that they grew thicker and fluffier at the bottom. The picture faded to an iodine yellow, but Zhenechka's smile and the peach blossoms still showed, while her mute charge had bleached away entirely—all we could see was a bright patch nestled up against Zhenechka.

When she came to that long-ago family, the boy could speak only his name: Buba. The rest of the world was engulfed in his silence, although he heard everything and loved everyone, and must have come to love Zhenechka especially, for he often sat close by her, gazed at her with his dark eyes, and stroked her face with his little palms.

It was enough to move a person to tears, and the rich parents wept, blowing their noses into lacy handkerchiefs, while the bearded family doctor, whom they paid exorbitant sums to examine Buba, gave his indulgent approval to the new governess, though he didn't find her pretty. But Zhenechka wasn't touched and she didn't weep. All business, she immediately established a daily routine and never deviated from it in all the years that she lived with her charge. After a while, to the amazement of the parents and the envy of the bearded doctor, the boy began to talk—quietly and slowly, glancing at serious, attentive Zhenechka, forgetting by morning the words that he had learned the night before, mixing up his letters and losing his way in the maelstrom of sentences, but, still and all, he did begin to talk, and could even draw some scribbles. The letter *izhitsa* came out best—the least used, most unnecessary letter in the Russian alphabet.

On Zhenechka's instructions the rich parents bought dozens of lotto games, and mornings she would wake to a knock at the door; the boy was already waiting for her, holding under his arm a rattling box full of little cardboard squares covered with elusive, difficult, slippery black words: ball, bird, hoopstick.

Once she took a vacation and paid a visit to her Petersburg sisters—she was not destined to see the fourth, the most beloved one, in far-off Helsingfors. Called back to the peach estate by an urgent telegram, she found the rich parents sobbing, the bearded doctor tranquilly triumphant, and the boy silent. The flimsy film of words had washed from his memory during Zhenechka's absence; the enormous rumbling world, fearsome and noisy, had reared up in menace and crashed down on him in all its nameless inarticulateness, and only when Zhenechka hurriedly unpacked her canvas bag and retrieved the bright ball she'd bought him did the boy cry out in recognition, gasping: "Moon, moon!"

They wouldn't let Zhenechka go off again; now her Petersburg sisters had to come to her. But her favorite sister somehow couldn't manage to get away from Helsingfors for a visit. And she never did.

There was some fear that Zhenechka would marry and abandon the peach family—a needless fear: her youth fluttered by and departed without attracting anyone's attention. There must have been men Zhenechka liked, who appeared and disappeared in her life, just as, if you turn a kaleidoscope for a long time, a rare, yellow shard of glass will occasionally tumble free and bloom like a broken star. But not one of them asked more of Zhenechka than true, steady friendship; there was no one whose eyes misted over at the thought of Zhenechka, and no one who made a secret of his acquaintance with her—such a pure, respectable, ennobling acquaintance. Zhenechka is an extraordinarily good person, someone would say, and everyone else would ardently take up the cry: Oh, yes, wonderful! Simply unique! So honest. And decent. Uncommonly conscientious. A crystal-pure soul!

There was one short, stunted, meager love in Zhenechka's life; there was someone who troubled Zhenechka's clear soul— perhaps for a week, perhaps for her whole life; we never asked. But whenever she told the story of how she lived and whom she taught before the war, one episode trembled plaintively through the years; there was one episode she always faltered over, and her high, calm voice would suddenly break for a moment, always on the very same phrase: "Good tea, Evgeniya Ivanovna. It's hot." That's what someone said to her at three o'clock on one prewar February afternoon, in a warm wooden building. At the time, Zhenechka was teaching Russian in a quiet sewing school, vegetating amid the apple trees and kitchen gardens somewhere on the outskirts of the city. Tearing themselves away from the subtleties of constructing "Undergarments, Women's Winter" and bolero jackets, uncounted generations of young seamstresses plunged into the refreshing, well-ordered streams of Russian grammar, only to forget forever the blur of Zhenechka's face after leaving their alma mater. They scattered around the world, loving, giving birth, stitching, pressing; they sang, saw husbands off to war, cried, grew old, and died. But, resolutely taught by Zhenechka, even on their conjugal beds they remembered the correct spelling of negative prefixes, and on their deathbeds, in a mortal swoon, they could, if necessary, have parsed a sentence.

Zhenechka traveled to the seamstresses through the black dawn by ice-cold tram; she ran, cold and ruddy, into the thoroughly heated wooden office and immediately looked about for the one she cherished: a rather gloomy, stoop-shouldered history teacher. He would walk toward her without noticing her and pass her by, and she dared not gaze after him. Her face burned, her hands trembled a little as she opened the workbooks, but he—he walked about the same building as she and thought his own thoughts. Such was the love that was her lot.

No one knew, and no one will ever know, what words she silently sent him while he stood by the window of the teachers' lounge and looked out at the snowy yard, where sparrows swayed like dark berries on branches. She probably yearned to say something honest, serious, and unremarkable, to make a modest request: Notice me, love me—but who says that sort of thing out loud? No one knew where he had been before, this man, nor where he went, but he must have come from somewhere. Dark-faced, taciturn—he'd been gassed in the first war, people said. He coughed dully in the wooden corridors, clutching his sunken chest in its soldier's shirt, and he smoked, smoked in the cold vestibule, where clumps of cotton batting stuck out of the insulated doors, where a feeble pink sun shattered against frosty purple stems on the frozen sill. He warmed his hands at the tile stove, smoked another cigarette, and left to lecture the seamstresses on history; the sound of his cough and his quiet, rather strained voice came from behind the tightly closed doors. Such was the man who pierced Zhenechka's heart, but neither of them said anything important to the other. And then who was Zhenechka to him? Just a good coworker. There was nothing between them except the mugs of tea that she poured for him in the teachers' lounge after lessons—trembling, her knees weak from her own foolhardiness. Madness, madness . . . It was no ordinary cup; it was a loving cup, adroitly disguised as a comradely one: Zhenechka poured tea for all the teachers, but she didn't give everyone so much sugar. A dark blue, chipped mug with a black border—that was all. And he drank it gratefully and nodded: "Good tea, Evgeniya Ivanovna. It's hot." And Zhenechka's love—a homely, barefoot orphan—danced for joy.

That was it, and there was nothing more at all, and soon he disappeared, and there was no one to ask.

Far outside the city, beyond the wasteland of the outskirts, beyond the weedy alder copses, off the big roads, amid the pine forests and glades of fireweed, abandoned, surrounded by overgrown lilac, the dacha quietly ages. The lock is rusting, the porch rots, thistle has strangled the flower beds, and prickly raspberry edges away from the fence and across the garden, timidly at first, then ever more boldly, twining into the nettle to form a burning hedge.

At night the wind rises and flies over the blustery, deserted lake; collecting a misty dust and the hum of uninhabited expanses, it tears an iron sheet from the roof, rumbles it about, and flings it into the garden. The wind-bent grass whistles, wild berries and the seeds of wild plants scatter on the humid night earth, sowing a gloomy harvest of dragon's teeth. And we thought Zhenechka was immortal.

We didn't listen to the end of her stories, and now no one will ever know what happened to the mute boy; we threw out unread the books she gave us; we promised to come visit her in her Leningrad apartment but we didn't mean it; and the older we grew the more excuses we found to avoid her cold, lonely home. And when we finally did come, how she rushed to and fro with joy, how she clutched us—already grown a head taller than she—with small, dry hands, how she flung herself from the table to the stove, where an apple pie was already well under way, how hurriedly she straightened a festive tablecloth on the round table, anchoring it firmly with a vase of autumn roses! And how hastily she smoothed out the high bed's worn silk coverlet, pale, like the fluid, frayed petal of an enormous rose abandoned by August and possessed by a dusty, indoor spirit, a coverlet so light it couldn't be thrown over the bed with one broad flap; rumpling in a slow glide, slack and indifferent, it descended unevenly, riding handfuls of stale household air as it fell and shuddering long after it landed, stirred by the thin streams of a warm draft, by the rumble of trucks outside. And, having eaten her pie, we would depart feeling awkward and relieved, and we would relish the autumn air, and laugh at everything, looking all around us eagerly for the arrival of love, which we expected any minute now—long, true love, everlasting and unique—while the love that leaned against the windowpane above and watched us go was too simple and mundane for us. But Zhenechka, thank God, didn't realize that. And she fervently awaited the new summer, awaited her rendezvous with the old dacha, with the new flowers, and with us, her beloved ones.

And summer came.

The era of cooks passed. Fed up, Marfa left, taking away in her trunk the little capital she'd accumulated from milk bottle deposits; the silver fox furs rotted in the storerooms, the factory fences fell apart, and Leningrad gardens turned crimson with wild roses. The school years were coming to an end, the examinations loomed ahead, and energetic Zhenechka prepared for a decisive summer of work. But all this voluntary service —drumming Russian grammar into the heads of ungrateful, sarcastic lazybones day after day; clearing the jungles of dense, stubborn, wily ignorance; planting the cleared terrain with shapely grammatical trees, their spreading branches sibilant with the fuzzy suffixes of Russian participles; trimming away

dry knots; grafting flowering branches into place and gathering
the fallen fruit—all this toil was apparently not enough for
her. The uneasiness of the eternal cultivator drove her into the
garden, once as untended and wild as the heads of her pupils.
We would urge her to stretch out in the chaise lounge in the
sun: What could be better for an old person—just cover your
head with burdock leaves and doze till dinnertime. But instead
it was we who collapsed in the chaise lounge, languid from
sun and adolescence, while Zhenechka tied a kerchief on her
head and marched into the overgrowth with shears and a rake.
Who had the time to notice that in place of molehills and
mountains of stinging nettle, swaying flowers rose in a gentle
froth. In her hands flowers seem to soar: ornate pink hydran-
geas like bombs ready to burst into red, or else blue ones like
a mousse of whisked sky tinged with smoky thunderheads;
thick peonies of dark, swooning velvet; and some frizzy, nameless trifle that was splashed all about like a quivering white
rain. Only her beloved roses did poorly, no matter how hard
she tried. We knew that Zhenechka dreamed of a genuine red
rose, pure and deep like the sound of a cello; but either the
meager northern warmth held them back, or the earth in our
garden rejected the timid roots—the roses grew small, waifish,
consumptive.

Zhenechka would come onto the veranda greatly distressed,
and casting an alarmed look at us, she'd say, "Worms are eating
the roses." "Give 'em the old one-two," we answered, bored.
"Make an example of them." "Cut off their quarterly bonus."
    But she was afraid of them—of flower worms, and rain
worms, and especially of mushroom worms; it was difficult to
slip a basket of mushrooms past her watchful eye. Arrest,
inspection, and destruction threatened our booty, so we had
to hand the basket straight through the low kitchen window
while someone stood watch. Hastily dashing icy well water

over the slippery, jumping, liplike brown boletuses stuck with leaves, or the pale, wide russulas that crumbled like shortbread and squeaked in our hands, we would throw them into the noisily boiling pot, using a straining spoon to hold back the mushrooms crawling over the rim and to skim off the turbid foam full of dead, floating worms. At the clunk of Zhenechka's orthopedic shoe we would work faster, bustling and giggling, and by the time she ceremoniously entered the kitchen, pushing open the door with a royal gesture, the burbling broth already shone with a dark, transparent purity.

"No worms?" she would ask, grave and anxious. "No, no, Zhenechka, perfectly wonderful mushrooms each and every one!" And she would calm down, never dreaming that we could possibly fib, while behind her back, wild with adolescent laughter, someone would wipe the straining spoon clean of the dried gray foam teeming with white corpses.

And everyone else would look away in embarrassment, as if we'd deceived a child.

. . . August approaches, evening descends; the dark forest stands with its back to us, facing the sunset, and watches the liquid crimson islands burn out in orange seas high overhead. The first star is out. The night damp gathers. Women sitting on porches pull the hems of their skirts over their knees, speak more softly, raise their dark faces to the heavenly stillness. A black tomcat steps noiselessly out of the black grass, places a black mouse on the stoop. Soon the last heavenly island will be extinguished, darkness will move in from the east, the lake will speak in heavy, muffled waves; the wild lake wind will billow, straighten out, and moan, tearing off into dark, unpeopled expanses to bend bushes, fell ripe seeds, drive nameless, prickly orbs through cooling clover valleys and through untrodden copses; with a drone, it will ascend to the agitated sky in order to blow away the first wisps of feeble, ephemeral stars as they slip into the abyss. Soon it will be time to get up, sigh, shake off specters, walk across the old boards; cups will clink, gas burners will flare like blue asters, the evening tea will trill. Refrigerators will clank open, and the women, back from the stars, will stare mindlessly into their rumbling, dimly lit interiors, slowly recognizing the contours of terrestrial cutlets or dense, frozen cottage cheese.

Zhenechka, quietly aging, goes through the house, opens the kitchen drawers, whisks some sort of rag about, and steps out onto the silenced porch, holding her breath so as not to frighten the stillness. She puts her hands on my shoulders— dry old hands, chilled to the marrow—and I suddenly feel how small and light she is, how easily the night wind could carry her away to the dark, clamoring distances.

A lengthy, tranquil moment sets in, one of those moments when superstition says an angel is passing over, and Zhenechka begins, "Now, I remember . . . ," but we've all come to, started talking, and stood up; the porch clatters under our feet, and Zhenechka rushes to tell us the rest, but it's too late, the angel has come and gone in a gust of wind that covers her words. I see her lips moving, her naive, loving gaze reach out; the wind grabs Zhenechka, the years spill from the sky like stars and fall onto the greedy earth where they grow like thistle, goosefoot, and couch grass; the grasses rise higher, close in; the old house chokes and dies, footsteps are erased, paths are lost, and oblivion blossoms everywhere.

An old person is like an apple tree in November: Everything in him is falling asleep. In anticipation of night the sap stops flowing, the insensitive roots grow chill and turn to ice, while slowly, slowly the split branch of the dusty Milky Way spins overhead. With its head leaning back, its dry stumps stretched to the frost-furred stars, the obedient, perishable creature waits, submerged in somnolence, expecting neither resurrection nor spring, waits for the dull, speechless swell of time to roll over it, carrying everything along.

Time passed, and we became adults. Busy with our urgent affairs and our friends, our books, and our children, we brushed Zhenechka's life aside; it was harder and harder for her to leave her house, and she would phone to relate things that interested no one.

For a minute or two, I listen to her slow voice, then lay the receiver softly on the telephone table and run off: in the kitchen pots are boiling, hot oil is shooting from the skillet; in the dining room there's lively conversation, laughter, and news, and they're calling me to share it all. The doorbell rings, a frozen, rosy crowd enters in raucous fur coats, there's the clatter of skis, the thud of feet, the floors shake, the windowpanes shake, and beyond the windowpanes the frosty trees shake, bathed in a dusky winter gold.

Zhenechka's voice lies cozily on the tablecloth, unhurriedly telling the telephone book, ashtray, and apple core about its joys and worries. Complaining and marveling, admiring and wondering, her soul flows from the telephone receiver holes in an even stream, spills over the tablecloth, evaporates like smoke, dances like dust in the last rays of the sun.

"Why is the receiver off the hook?" someone asks. I grab the phone with barely wiped wet fingers, and shout: "Yes, Zhenechka! Of course, Zhenechka!" and rush away again. Her hearing aid sings and chirps; she doesn't notice a thing.

"Well, what's she saying?" asks a passing member of the household.

"Let me listen. . . . Something about some Sofia Sergeevna who went to the sanatorium last summer and the roses they had there. . . . She says the roses were red and their leaves were green . . . in the sky was the sun . . . but at night the moon . . . and the sea was full of water . . . people swam, and got out of the water . . . and dressed in dry clothes and the wet clothes dried out . . . oh, and she asks how we are. Fine,

Zhenechka! I said, we're fine, Zhenechka! Just fi-ine! Yes! I'll
tell them! I'll tell them!''

We were all she had left in the world.

But there came a day in the middle of winter when—shaken
to the depths of her soul, armed with a cracked walking staff,
the remains of her boyar hat pulled low—Zhenechka appeared
on the threshold with a long blue envelope in her hands.

Words buzzed and fluttered in the envelope, telling her that
she was not alone in this world; that quite close by—just a
stone's throw away, beyond the cold gulf, beyond the arc of
green ice and the swishing pines, in the snow-covered city of
Helsinki (formerly Helsingfors), in an A-frame house, around
a cheerful fireplace—there lived the offspring of Zhenechka's
long-lost favorite sister; that these offspring were waiting,
couldn't wait for dear Aunt Eugénie to enter under the peaked
roof, into their hospitable half-Finnish embraces, and to lay
cellophane-wrapped flowers on the grave of her dear sister,
who rests in a neat Finnish cemetery.

We saw Zhenechka off at the station. She was flustered and
embarrassed, like Cinderella stepping into the pumpkin car-
riage drawn by mice; she clutched her canvas suitcase with her
toothbrush and a change of underclothes inside it. We had
seen these undergarments at the dacha, on the lakeshore at
dawn, when Zhenechka did the hygienic exercises suitable for
her age. The shifts consisted of rectangular, sackcloth panels,
meticulously joined with a solid, eternal seam; these severe,
soldierly items knew neither darts, nor flounces, nor any other
tailor's mischief—they were just sturdy panels, like the white
pages of a story about an honest, hardworking life, usefully
lived.

A month later we went to meet her at the same station, ran
the entire length of the train and couldn't find her. From one
car emerged an impressive old lady with eyebrows black like
a fallen angel's and thickly blushed cheeks, dressed in fluffy
furs and a dignified hat. The porter carried her scented suit-

cases. Someone recognized Zhenechka by her orthopedic shoe.

"Well?" we asked.

"They've got everything over there," she said. And, over-come, she nearly fainted.

We took her home and made her tea.

After that, Zhenechka went to Finland every spring. And then each summer—shining and crazed, happy and youthful, she grew unheard-of flowers from Finnish seeds in the fragrant, revitalized garden of our dacha. Zhenechka's lacy underwear, celestial and lemon-colored, hung on a line above the flowers, and in her room incredible objects were heaped on her shelf: perfumes, lipsticks, nail polish. And the roses—red roses which had behaved capriciously for many years—suddenly flourished under Zhenechka's hands, shooting out new buds in swift succession. The Finnish fertilizer must have helped.

Zhenechka would catch us at the front door or in the garden, and excitedly thrust photographs at us for the umpteenth time: Zhenechka on a Finnish sofa in the living room, Zhenechka with her great-nephew—her new, adored pupil—clinging poignantly to her hand (what's his name again, Zhenechka? Koko or Pupu?), Zhenechka in the dining room at dinner: lettuce leaves and a couple of green weeds.

"They're very thrifty. And they follow a strict diet."

We looked at Zhenechka's belatedly blackened eyebrows and yawned, listening as she sang her hymns to the untold riches of the fish stores.

"But Zhenechka, do they have sprats in tomato sauce?"

"No, now I don't think I saw any sprats."

"Well, there you are. How about Wave fish paste?"

"I don't think so."

"Well, then! They're way behind us! Just look, our shelves are filled with them!"

And earnest Zhenechka did her best to argue and persuade.

"And where did you go while you were there?"

"Oh, I stayed at home. I took care of my great-nephew."

"And them?"

"They went to the Azores. They'd already bought the tickets," she said in justification.

So while the relatives lolled about on ocean beaches, the infatuated Zhenechka watered, weeded, and coddled her new sapling with the stubbornness of an insane gardener; she drew the barbarian alphabet on blue paper, so that the boy could meet his suntanned parents with a Russian poem or unpronounceable greeting. On her return to Leningrad, she took to writing postcards, choosing the prettiest: bouquets, golden Petersburg bridges, and the statue of the Bronze Horseman (her relatives mistook Peter the Great on his horse for the anarchist Kropotkin). And new love, which never comes too late, thundered and raged and cascaded over her from head to toe.

And we believed that Zhenechka was immortal, that youth can return, that a candle once lit will never go out, and that virtue, whatever we might think of it, will eventually be rewarded.

We'll choose a day, lock the doors behind us, descend the cold staircase, go out into the stuffy morning city, and leave for the dacha. Out there, pink grass sways and rustles in the warm wind, pine needles cover the old porch; with a slight shush there passes through the emptied, abandoned house the shadow of a shadow of she who once lived, simple as a leaf, clear as light, still as morning water: she who once naively desired to be most beloved.

We'll step off the train onto the bare cement platform, walk under the aspen hum of the wires and on—through marsh and thicket, across hills and copses—to where the empty house sleeps beyond the glades of overgrown fireweed, where lilac has gone wild, where a crow taps his beak along the porch, where mice say to one another: "Let's live here for a while."

We wade through the grass, parting the dense overgrowth with our hands like swimmers; we find the long-forgotten keys and look around, stretching arms numb from the weight of the bags. It's a damp, lushly blooming northern June. The old, crooked dacha sinks into the grass like a half-drowned boat. Lilac darkens the rooms, pines have crushed the veranda's fragile breast. The brittle fifes of bedstraw have opened their white umbrellas; disturbed, a mysterious young bird cries loudly; and tiny veronica blossoms litter every sunny clump of dry earth with dark blue.

There are no roads or paths in the ocean of grass yet, the flowers are not yet crushed, only a slight corridor can be discerned where we walked from the gates to the porch. It's a shame to break the dense, stiff clusters of lilac—a blue, snowy shadow lies on them as on a new-fallen, sparkling crust of ice. It's a shame to trample the quiet, thick grass forests.

We drink tea on the veranda. Let's spend the night. Why don't we ever come here? We could live here! But it's a long way to lug supplies. We should weed out the nettle. Plant some flowers. Repair the porch. Prop it up somehow. The words fall into the stillness, the impatient lilac has burst through the open windows and sways as it listens to our empty promises, our impossible projects, our rosy dreams fading in an instant: it's not true, no one will come, there is no one to come, she's gone, she's a shadow, and the night wind will blow away her dilapidated dwelling.

Once again Zhenechka packed her bags to go visit her Finnish relatives: for the baby an ABC book, for the nephews something stronger. She was only waiting for the letter, and it arrived. The relatives came straight to the point—they couldn't invite dear Eugénie to visit them anymore. She would understand, of course; after all, she had reached such a venerable age that what had happened to their neighbors' Aunt Nika could happen to her any minute. And enclosed was a photograph of this aunt in her coffin, all dressed up and motionless, surrounded by Russian Orthodox lace and Finnish bouquets. Look how badly Aunt Nika behaved; if dear Eugénie were to do the same thing during her visit there might be complications, trouble, misunderstandings . . . and who would pay for it all? Had dear Eugénie considered this? And she needn't write anymore, why strain her eyes—and she might get a cramp in her hand!

Zhenechka stood and stared at the photograph of an unknown old lady in a neat coffin, a graphic reproach to Zhenechka's lack of foresight. And the nightingale that had sung songs on her chest for many years grew deaf and shut its eyes tight. And fate, like a black wind flying into an open window, turned, stuck out its tongue, and shouted, "Just try and be most beloved!" and with a deafening cackle snuffed the candle out.

. . . A light Karelian night. There's neither darkness nor crimson dawn: an endless white dusk. All the colors have drained away; the grainy half-moon seems a cloudy brushstroke in the luminous heights; gray garden shadows and crevasses of clotted twilight crawl along the earth; between the tree trunks in the distance, the flat lake glimmers in lackluster coves. A mosquito whines, eyes close. There's a rustling in the gray grass, the creak of cracked shutters. Overnight yet another colored pane will fall from the veranda, overnight the grasses will rise still higher, the path we walked in the morning will be swallowed up and our footsteps will vanish; fresh mold will bloom on the front porch, a spider will spin the keyhole shut, and the house will fall asleep for another hundred years—from the underground passages where the Mouse King roams, to the high attic vaults from which the fleshless steeds of our dreams take flight.

The Poet and
the Muse

Nina was a marvelous woman, an ordinary woman, a doctor, and it goes without saying that she had her right to personal happiness like everyone else. Of this she was well aware. Nearing the age of thirty-five after a lengthy period of joyless trial and error—not even worth talking about—she knew precisely what she needed: a wild, true love, with tears, bouquets, midnight phone vigils, nocturnal taxi chases, fateful obstacles, betrayals, and forgiveness. She needed a—you know—an animal passion, dark windy nights with streetlamps aglow. She needed to perform a heroine's classical feat as if it were a mere trifle: to wear out seven pairs of iron boots, break seven iron staffs in two, devour seven loaves of iron bread, and receive in supreme reward not some golden rose or snow-white pedestal but a burned-out match or a crumpled ball of a bus ticket—a crumb from the banquet table where the ra-diant king, her heart's desire, had feasted. Well, of course, quite a few women need pretty much the same thing, so in this sense Nina was, as has already been said, a perfectly ordinary woman, a marvelous woman, a doctor.

She had been married: it was as if she'd done an interminable, boring stretch on a transcontinental train and emerged—tired, dispirited, and yawning uncontrollably—into the starless night of a strange city, where the only kindred soul was her suitcase.

Then she lived the life of a recluse for a while: she took up washing and polishing the floors in her spotless little Moscow apartment, developed an interest in patterns and sewing, and once again grew bored. An affair with the dermatologist Arkady Borisovich, who had two families not counting Nina, smoldered sluggishly along. After work she would drop by his office to see him. There was nothing the least bit romantic about it; the cleaning lady would be emptying out the trash cans and slopping a wet mop across the linoleum while Arkady Borisovich washed his hands over and over, scrubbing them with a brush, suspiciously inspecting his pink nails and examining himself in the mirror with disgust. He would stand there, pink, well fed and stiff, egg-shaped, and take no notice of Nina, though she was already in her coat on her way out the door. Then he would stick out his triangular tongue and twist it this way and that—he was afraid of infection. A fine Prince Charming! What sort of passion could she find with Arkady Borisovich? None, of course.

Yet she'd certainly earned the right to happiness, she was entitled to a place in the line where it was being handed out: her face was white and pretty and her eyebrows broad, her smooth black hair grew low from her temples and was gathered at the back in a bun. And her eyes were black, so that out in public men took her for a Moldavian Gypsy, and once, in the metro, in the passageway to the Kirovskaya station, a fellow had even pestered her, claiming that he was a sculptor and she must come along with him immediately, supposedly to sit for the head of a houri—right away, his clay was drying out. Of course she didn't go with him; she had a natural mistrust of people in the creative professions, since she had already been through the sorry experience of going for a cup of coffee with an alleged film director and barely escaping in one piece—the fellow had a large apartment with Chinese vases and a slanted garret ceiling in an old building.

But time was marching on, and at the thought that out of the approximately 125 million men in the USSR fate in all its generosity had managed to dribble out only Arkady Borisovich for her, Nina sometimes got upset. She could have found someone else, but the other men who came her way weren't right either. After all, her soul was growing richer as the years passed, she experienced and understood her own being with ever greater subtlety, and on autumn evenings she felt more and more self-pity: there was no one to whom she could give herself—she, so slim and black-browed.

Occasionally Nina would visit some married girlfriend and, having stopped off to buy chocolates at the nearest candy shop for someone else's big-eared child, would drink tea and talk for a long time, eyeing herself all the while in the dark glass of the kitchen door, where her reflection was even more enigmatic, and more alluring in comparison with her friend's spreading silhouette. Justice demanded that someone sing her praises. Having finally heard her friend out—what had been bought, what had been burnt, what ailments the big-eared child had survived—and having examined someone else's standard-issue husband (a receding hairline, sweatpants stretched at the knees—no, she didn't need one like that), she left feeling dismayed. She carried her elegant self out the door, onto the landing, and down the staircase into the refreshing night: these weren't the right sort of people, she should never have come, in vain had she given of herself and left her perfumed trace in the drab kitchen, she had pointlessly treated someone else's child to exquisite bittersweet chocolate—the child just gobbled it down with no appreciation; oh, well, let the little beast break out in an allergic rash from head to toe.

She yawned.

And then came the epidemic of Japanese flu. All the doctors were pulled out of the district clinics for house calls, and Arkady Borisovich went, too, putting on a gauze face mask and rubber gloves to keep the virus from getting a hold on him, but he couldn't protect himself and came down with it, and his patients were assigned to Nina. And there, as it turned out, was where fate lay in wait for her—in the person of Grisha, stretched out completely unconscious on a bench in a custodian's lodge, under knit blankets, his beard sticking up. That was where it all happened. The near-corpse quickly abducted Nina's weary heart: the mournful shadows on his porcelain brow, the darkness around his sunken eyes, and the tender beard, wispy as a springtime forest—all this made for a magical scene. Invisible violins played a wedding waltz, and the trap sprang shut. Well, everybody knows how it usually happens.

A sickeningly beautiful woman with tragically undisciplined hair was wringing her hands over the dying man. (Later on, to be sure, it turned out that she was no one special, just Agniya, a school friend of Grisha's, an unsuccessful actress who sang a little to a guitar, nothing to worry about, that wasn't where the threat lay.) Yes, yes, she said, she was the one who'd called the doctor—you must save him! She had just, you know, dropped in by chance, after all he doesn't lock his door, and he'd never call for help himself, not Grisha—custodian, poet, genius, saint! Nina unglued her gaze from the demonically handsome custodian and proceeded to look the place over: a large room, beer bottles under the table, dusty molding on the ceiling, the bluish light of snowdrifts from the windows, an abandoned fireplace stuffed with rags and rubbish.

"He's a poet, a poet—he works as a custodian so he can have the apartment," mumbled Agniya.

Nina kicked Agniya out, lifted her bag from her shoulder,

and hung it on a nail, carefully took her heart from Grishunya's hands and nailed it to the bedstead. Grishunya muttered deliriously, in rhyme. Arkady Borisovich melted away like sugar in hot tea. The thorny path lay ahead.

On recovering the use of his eyes and ears, Grishunya learned that the joyous Nina meant to stay with him to the bitter end. At first he was a bit taken aback, and suggested deferring this unexpected happiness, or—if that wasn't possible—hastening his meeting with that end; later, though, softhearted fellow that he was, he became more complaisant, and asked only that he not be parted from his friends. Nina compromised for the time being, while he regained his strength. This, of course, was a mistake; he was soon back on his feet, and he resumed his senseless socializing with the entire, endless horde. There were a few young people of indeterminate profession; an old man with a guitar; teenage poets; actors who turned out to be chauffeurs and chauffeurs who turned out to be actors; a demobilized ballerina who was always crying, "Hey, I'll call our gang over, too"; ladies in diamonds; unlicensed jewelers; unattached girls with spiritual aspirations in their eyes; philosophers with unfinished dissertations; a deacon from Novorossisk who always brought a suitcase full of salted fish; and a Tungus from eastern Siberia, who'd got stuck in Moscow—he was afraid the capital's cuisine would spoil his digestion and so would ingest only some kind of fat, which he ate out of a jar with his fingers.

All of them—some one evening, some the next—crammed into the custodian's lodge; the little three-story outbuilding creaked, the upstairs neighbors came in, people strummed guitars, sang, read poems of their own and others, but mainly listened to those of their host. They all considered Grishunya a genius; a collection of his verse had been on the verge of publication for years, but a certain pernicious Makushkin, on whom everything depended, was blocking it—Makushkin, who had sworn that only over his dead body . . . They cursed

Makushkin, extolled Grishunya, the women asked him to read more, more. Flushed, self-conscious, Grisha read on—thick, significant poems that recalled expensive, custom-made cakes covered with ornamental inscriptions and triumphant meringue towers, poems slathered with sticky linguistic icing, poems containing abrupt, nutlike crunches of clustered sounds and excruciating, indigestible caramel confections of rhyme. "Eh-eh-eh," said the Tungus, shaking his head; apparently he didn't understand a word of Russian. "What's wrong? Doesn't he like it?" murmured the other guests. "No, no—I'm told that's the way they express praise," said Agniya, fluffing her hair nervously, afraid that the Tungus would jinx her. The guests couldn't take their eyes off Agniya, and invited her to continue the evening with them elsewhere.

Naturally, this abundance of people was unpleasant for Nina. But most unpleasant of all was that every time she dropped by, whether during the day or in the evening after her shift, there was this wretched creature sitting in the custodian's lodge—no fatter than a fork, wearing a black skirt down to her heels and a plastic comb in her lackluster hair, drinking tea and openly admiring Grisha's soft beard: a person named Lizaveta. Of course, there couldn't possibly be any affair going on between Grishunya and this doleful aphid. You had only to watch her extricate a red, bony hand from her sleeve and reach timidly for an ancient, rock-hard piece of gingerbread—as if she expected any moment to be slapped and the gingerbread snatched away. She had rather less cheek than a human being needs, and rather more jowl; her nose was gristly; in fact, there was something of the fish about her—a dark, colorless deepwater fish that slinks through the impenetrable gloom on the ocean floor, never rising to the sun-streaked shallows where azure and crimson creatures sport and play.

No, no love affair, there couldn't be. Nonetheless, Grishunya, the beatific little soul, would gaze with pleasure at that human hull; he read poems to her, wailing and dipping on the rhymes, and afterward, deeply moved by his own verse, he would blink hard and turn his eyes up toward the ceiling as if to stanch his tears, and Lizaveta would shake her head to show the shock to her entire organism, blow her nose and imitate a child's sporadic whimpers, as if she, too, had just been sobbing copiously.

No, this was all extremely unpleasant for Nina. Lizaveta had to be gotten rid of. Grishunya liked this brazen worship, but then, he wasn't picky; he liked everything on earth. He liked swishing a shovel about in the loose snow in the morning, living in a room with a fireplace full of trash, being on the ground floor with the door open so anyone could drop in; he liked the crowd and the aimless comings and goings, the puddle of melted snow in the vestibule, all those girls and boys, actors and old men; he liked the ownerless Agniya, supposedly the kindest creature in the world, and the Tungus, who came for who knows what reason; he liked all the eccentrics, licensed and unlicensed, the geniuses and the outcasts; he liked raw-boned Lizaveta, and—to round things out—he liked Nina as well.

Among the little outbuilding's visitors, Lizaveta was considered an artist, and indeed she did exhibit in second-rate shows. Grishunya found inspiration in her dark daubings, and composed a corresponding cycle of poems. In order to concoct her pictures, Lizaveta had to work herself into an unbridled frenzy, like some African shaman: a flame would light up in her dim eyes, and with shouts, wheezes, and a sort of grubby fury she would attack the canvas, kneading blue, black, and yellow paint with her fists, and scratching the wet, oily mush with her fingernails. The style was called "nailism"—it was a terrible sight to behold. True, the resulting images looked rather like underwater plants and stars and castles hanging in the sky—something that seemed to crawl and fly simultaneously.

"Does she have to get so excited?" Nina whispered to Grishunya once as they observed a session of nailism.

"Well, I guess it just doesn't happen otherwise," dear Grishunya whispered back, exhaling sweet toffee breath. "It's inspiration, the spirit, what can you do, it goes its own way." And his eyes shone with affection and respect for the possessed scrabbler.

Lizaveta's bony hands bloomed with sores from caustic paints, and similar sores soon covered Nina's jealous heart, still nailed to Grisha's bedstead. She did not want to share Grisha; the handsome custodian's blue eyes and wispy beard should belong to her and her alone. Oh, if only she could become the fully empowered mistress of the house once and for all, instead of just a casual, precarious girlfriend; if only she could put Grisha in a trunk, pack him in mothballs, cover him with a canvas cloth, bang the lid shut and sit on it, tugging at the locks to check: Are they secure?

Oh, if only . . . Yes, then he could have whatever he wanted—even Lizaveta. Let Lizaveta live and scratch out her paintings, let her grind them out with her teeth if she wanted, let her stand on her head and stay that way, trembling like a nervous pillar beside her barbaric canvases at her annual exhibitions, her dull hair decked out with an orange ribbon, red-handed, red-faced, sweaty, and ready to cry from hurt or happiness, while over in the corner various citizens sit at a rickety table cupping their palms to shield against inquisitive eyes as they write their unknown comments in the gallery's luxurious red album: "Revolting," perhaps; or "Fabulous"; or "What *does* the arts administration think it's doing?" or else something maudlin and mannered, signed by a group of provincial librarians, about how sacred and eternal art had supposedly pierced them to the core.

Oh, to wrest Grisha from that noxious milieu! To scrape away the extraneous women who'd stuck to him like barnacles to the bottom of a boat; to pull him from the stormy sea, turn him upside down, tar and caulk him and set him in dry dock in some calm, quiet place.

But he—a carefree spirit ready to embrace any street mongrel, shelter any unsanitary vagrant—went on squandering himself on the crowd, giving himself out by the handful. This simple soul took a shopping bag, loaded it with yogurt and sour cream, and went to visit Lizaveta, who had fallen ill. And of course Nina had to go with him—and, my God, what a hovel! what a place! yellow, frightful, filthy, a dark little closet, not a single window! There lay Lizaveta, barely discernible on an iron cot under an army blanket, blissfully filling her black mouth with white sour cream. Bent over school notebooks at a table was Lizaveta's fat, frightened daughter, who bore no resemblance to her mother but looked as though Lizaveta had once upon a time bred with a St. Bernard.

"Well, how are you doing here?" asked Grishunya.

Lizaveta stirred beside the dingy wall: "All right."

"Do you need anything?" Grishunya insisted.

The iron cot creaked. "Nastya will take care of everything."

"Well then, study hard." The poet shuffled about and stroked fat Nastya on the head; he backed into the hallway, but the enfeebled Lizaveta was already dozing, a stagnant lake of unswallowed yogurt apparently frozen in her half-open mouth.

"She and I should really, er, hook up or something," Grishunya said to Nina, gesturing vaguely and looking the other way. "You see what problems she has getting an apartment. She's from way up north, from Totma, she can only rent this storeroom, but what talent, no? And her daughter's very drawn to art, too. She sculpts, she's good—and who can she study with in Totma?"

"You and I are getting married. I'm all yours," Nina reminded him sternly.

"Yes, of course, I forgot," Grishunya apologized. He was a gentle man; it was just that his head was full of a lot of nonsense.

Destroying Lizaveta turned out to be as hard as cutting a tough apple worm in half. When they came to fine her for violating the residence permit in her passport, she was already holed up in a different place, and Nina sent the troops over there. Lizaveta hid out in basements and Nina flooded basements; she spent the night in sheds and Nina tore them down; finally, Lizaveta evaporated to a mere shadow.

Seven pairs of iron boots had Nina worn out tramping across passport desks and through police stations, seven iron staffs had she broken on Lizaveta's back, seven kilos of iron gingerbread had she devoured in the hated custodian's lodge: it was time for the wedding.

The motley crowd had already thinned out, a pleasant quiet reigned in the little house in the evenings, and now it was with due respect that the occasional daredevil knocked at the door, carefully wiping his feet under Nina's watchful gaze and immediately regretting that he had ever come by. Soon Grishunya would no longer be slaving with a shovel and burying his talent in the snowdrifts; he would be moving to Nina's where a sturdy, spacious glass-topped desk awaited him, with two willow switches in a vase on the left, and, on the right, from one of those frames that lean on a tail, Nina's photo smiled at him. And her smile promised that everything would be fine, that he'd be well fed and warm and clean, that Nina herself would go to see Comrade Makushkin and finally resolve the long-drawn-out question of the poetry collection: she would ask Comrade Makushkin to look over the material carefully, to give his advice, fix a few things, and cut up the thick, sticky layer cake of Grisha's verse into edible slices.

Nina allowed Grishunya a final good-bye to his friends, and

the innumerable horde poured in for the farewell supper—girls and freaks, old men and jewelers. Three balletic youths with women's eyes arrived prancing on turned-out toes, a lame man limped in on crutches, someone brought a blind boy, and Lizaveta's now nearly fleshless shadow flitted about. The crowd kept coming; it buzzed and blew around like trash from a vacuum cleaner hooked up backward; bearded types scurried past; the walls of the little house bulged under the human pressure; and there were shouts, sobs, and hysterics. Dishes were broken. The balletic youths made off with the hysterical Agniya, catching her hair in the door; Lizaveta's shadow gnawed her hands to shreds and thrashed on the floor, demanding to be walked all over (the request was honored); the deacon led the Tungus into a corner and questioned him in sign language on the faith of his people, and the Tungus answered, also by signs, that their faith was the best of all faiths.

Grisha beat his porcelain brow against the wall and cried out that fine, all right, he was prepared to die, but after his death—you'll see—he'd come back to his friends and never be parted from them again. The deacon didn't approve of such proclamations. Neither did Nina.

By morning all the scum had vanished, and, packing Grishunya into a taxi, Nina carried him off to her crystal palace.

Ah, who could possibly paint a portrait of one's beloved when, rubbing his sleep-filled blue eyes and freeing a young, hairy leg from beneath the blankets, he yawns with all his might. Entranced, you gaze at him: Everything about him is yours, yours! The gap between his teeth, and the bald spot, and that marvelous wart!

You feel you're a queen, and people make way for you on the street, and your colleagues nod respectfully, and Arkady Borisovich politely offers you his hand, wrapped in sterilized paper.

How fine it was to doctor trusting patients, to bring home bags full of goodies, to check in the evenings, like a solicitous sister, to see what Grishunya had written during the day.

Only he was a frail thing: he cried a lot and didn't want to eat, and he didn't want to write neatly on clean paper but, out of habit, kept on picking up scraps and cigarette packs, and doodling or else just drawing flourishes and curlicues. And he wrote about a yellow, yellow road, on and on about a yellow road, and high above the road hung a white star. Nina shook her head: "Think about it, sweetheart. You can't show poems like that to Comrade Makushkin, and you should be thinking about your book. We live in the real world." But he didn't listen, and kept on writing about the road and the star, and Nina shouted, "Did you understand me, sweetheart? Don't you dare write things like that!" And he was frightened and jerked his head about, and Nina, softening, said, "Now, now, now," and put him to bed. She fed him mint-and-lime-blossom tea, infusions of adonis and motherwort, but the ungrateful man whimpered and made up poems that offended Nina, about how motherwort had sprouted in his heart, his garden had gone to seed, the forests had burned to the ground, and some sort of crow was plucking, so to speak, the last star from the now silent horizon, and how he, Grishunya, seemed to be inside some hut, pushing and pushing at the frozen door, but there was no way out, there was only the pounding of red heels in the distance. . . . "Whose heels are those?" demanded Nina, waving the piece of paper. "I'm just interested—whose heels are they?"

"You don't understand anything." Grishunya snatched the paper.

"No, I understand everything perfectly well," answered Nina bitterly. "I just want to know whose heels they are and where it is they're pounding."

"Aaa-agh!!! They're pounding in my head!!!" screamed Grishunya, covering his head with the blanket, and Nina went into the bathroom, tore up the poems, and scattered them into the watery netherworld, the little domestic Niagara.

Men are men; you have to keep an eye on them.

Once a week she checked his desk and threw out the poems that were indecent for a married man to compose. And once in a while she would rouse him at night for interrogation: Was he writing for Comrade Makushkin, or was he shirking? And he would cover his head with his hands, lacking the strength to withstand the bright light of her merciless truth.

They managed this way for two years, but Grishunya, though surrounded by every care and concern, did not appreciate her love, and stopped making an effort. He roamed the apartment and muttered—muttered that he would soon die, and the earth would be heaped over him in clayey, cemeterial layers, and the slender gold of birch coins would drift over his grave mound like alms, and the wooden cross or pyramid marker (whichever they didn't begrudge him) would rot beneath the autumn rains, and everyone would forget him, and no one would visit, only the idle passerby would struggle for a moment to read the four-digit dates. He strayed from poetry into ponderous free verse as damp as pine kindling, or into rhythmic lugubrious prose, and instead of a pure flame a sort of white, suffocating smoke poured from his malignant lines, so that Nina coughed and hacked, waved her hands about, and, choking, screamed, "For heaven's sake, stop writing!"

Then some kindhearted people told her that Grishunya wanted to return to his little house, that he had gone to see the custodian hired in his place—a fat woman—and bargained to see how much she would ask for handing him back his former life, and the woman had actually entered into negotiations. Nina had connections in the Municipal Health Department, and she dropped hints that there was a wonderful three-story building in the center of town, it could be taken over by an institution, hadn't they been looking for something? Municipal Health thanked her, it did suit them, and very soon

the little building was no longer a custodian's lodge: the fireplace was torn out, and one of the medical institutes settled
its faculty there.

Grisha fell silent, and for about two weeks he was quiet and
obedient. Then he actually cheered up, took to singing in the
bath and laughing—but he completely stopped eating, and he
kept going up to the mirror and pinching himself. "What are
you so cheerful about?" Nina interrogated him. He opened
his identity card and showed her the blue margins freshly
stamped with fat lilac letters reading "Not Subject to Burial."
"What does that mean?" asked Nina, frightened. Grishunya
laughed again and told her that he had sold his skeleton for
sixty rubles to the Academy of Sciences, that "his ashes he
would outlast, and the worms elude," that he would never lie
in the damp ground, as he had feared, but would stand among
lots of people in a clean, warm room, laced together and in-
ventoried, and students—a fun crowd—would slap him on
the shoulder, flick his forehead, and treat him to cigarettes;
he'd figured it all out perfectly. And he wouldn't say another
word in answer to Nina's shouts; he simply proposed that they
go to bed. But she should keep in mind that from now on she
was embracing government property and thus was materially
responsible before the law for the sum of sixty rubles and
twenty-five kopecks.

And from that moment on, as Nina said later, their love seemed
to go awry, because how could she burn with full-fledged
passion for public property, or kiss academic inventory? Nothing about him belonged to her anymore.

And just think what she must have gone through—she, a
marvelous, ordinary woman, a doctor, who had indisputably
earned her piece of the pie like everyone else, a woman who
had fought for her personal happiness, as we were all taught
to do, and had won her right in battle.

Despite all the grief he'd caused her, she was still left with pure, radiant feelings, she said. And if love didn't turn out quite the way she had dreamed, well, Nina was hardly to blame. Life was to blame. And after his death she suffered a good deal, and her girlfriends sympathized with her, and at work they were kind and gave her ten unpaid days off. And when all the red tape was done with, Nina made the rounds of her friends and told them that Grisha now stood in the little house as a teaching aid, tagged with an inventory number they'd given him, and she'd already gone to have a look. And everything was actually just as he had wanted: the students joke with him, they tug on his wrist to make him dance about, and they put a white cap on his head. The place is well heated, at night he's locked up in the closet, but otherwise he's always around people.

And Nina also said that at first she was very upset about everything, but then it was all right, she calmed down after a woman she knew—also a lovely woman, whose husband had also died—told her that she, for one, was even rather pleased. The thing was that this woman had a two-room apartment and she'd always wanted to decorate one room Russian style, just a table in the middle, nothing else, and benches, benches all around the sides, very simple ones, rough wood. And the walls would be covered with all kinds of peasant shoes, icons, sickles, spinning wheels—that kind of thing. And so now that one of her rooms was free, this woman had apparently gone and done it, and it's her dining room, and she always gets a lot of compliments from visitors.

Limpopo

Judy's little grave was dug up last year and a highway was laid down in its place. I didn't go out to see it: it's already done, I was told, cars whoosh and zoom by, children sit in the cars eating sandwiches and dogs smile zipping along in the embrace of their mistresses—they come and go in a flash. What would I do there?

In cases like this a condolence letter is usually sent to the near and dear: Step lively, so to speak, and get your dear departed ashes out of here, because we've got a shock crew on the job, the fires of the five-year plan are burning and stuff like that. But Judy had no near, no relatives—at least not in our hemisphere—and of dear there was only Lyonechka, and where can you find Lyonechka these days? There is that group of energetic enthusiasts who've been looking for him, of course, but more on that later.

Last year was the fifteenth anniversary of Judy's death, and not knowing anything about the highway, I lit a candle as I always do on that day, set an empty glass out on the table, covered it with a piece of bread, sat down across from it, and drank a toast to her memory with rowanberry cordial. The candle burned, and the mirror watched from the wall, and a snowstorm raged out the window, but nothing danced in the flame or passed across the dark glass or summoned me from the snowflakes. Maybe that wasn't the right way to remember poor Judy, maybe I should have wrapped myself up in a sheet, lit incense sticks and beat on a drum until daylight, or shaved my head, spread lion's fat on my eyebrows, and squatted facing a corner for nine days—who knows how it's done over there in Africa?

I don't even remember exactly what her name was: you had to sort of howl in a special way, clack your teeth, and yawn —and you'd said it. You couldn't write it down on paper in our letters, but, Judy told us, it was really a very sweet, lyrical name, which according to the dictionary meant "a small plant of the liliaceous order with edible tubers"; in the spring they all go off into the hills to dig this stuff up with sharp sticks, and then they bake it in cinders and dance all night until the cold dawn, dance until the huge, crimson sun rises to dance in turn on their faces, black as oil, on the poisonous blue flowers stuck in their wiry hair, and on their dogs' teeth necklaces.

Whether that's what they really do over there or not is hard to say now, especially since Lyonechka—in a burst of inspiration further encouraged by Judy's ear-to-ear smile—wrote tons of poems on the subject (they're still lying around here somewhere); fact and fancy got so mixed up that now, after all these years, you can't figure out whether shining black people did in fact dance in the hills, joyfully greeting the rising sun, whether a blue river, steaming in the dawn, ever flowed at the foot of those hills, whether the equator curved like a morning rainbow melting in the sky, whether Judy actually did have sixty-four cousins, or whether it was true that her maternal grandfather thought he was a crocodile and would hide among the dry rushes to grab the legs of children and ducks swimming by.

Everything's possible! Why not? Everything's exotic over there, but here, nothing but nothing at all ever happens anywhere, anytime, anyhow.

Dances are all well and fine, but Judy apparently managed to grab a scrap of some kind of education somewhere, for she came to us to do a residency (in veterinary school, for heaven's sake!). We unwound scarves, scarves, and more scarves; wraps, plaid shawls, shawls made of goat yarn with knots and splinters, shawls that were gauzy and orange, with gold threads, shawls of blue linen and striped linen; we unwound; we looked: what was there left of her to reside? There was nothing to reside, much less fight with livestock and swine: horns, tails, hooves, tripe, and abomasum, dung and udders, moo-oooo and baaa-baaaa, horrors! To combat this rough host—only a little pillar of living darkness, a slice of shadow shivering from the cold, with dark brown dog eyes—that was all there was. But Lyonechka was instantly captivated, bewitched, spellbound; moreover, the reasons for this sudden gush of passion were, as were all of Lyonechka's reasons, purely ideological, a mental tornado, or to put it simply you could say that rationalism was always one of his dominant characteristics.

Well, first of all, he was a poet, and motes of distant countries carried a lot of weight on his poetic scales; second, as a creative individual he was constantly protesting something—exactly what didn't really matter, the subject of the protest emerged in the process of indignation—and Judy arose like protest incarnate, like a challenge to everything in the world, a scrap of darkness, a coal amidst the snowstorm, tangerine shawls in the fierce Moscow January, almost Candlemas—to quote Lyonechka. As I saw it—nothing special. Third, she was not just black, but black like a stoker, Lyonechka enthused, and stokers were Lyonechka's favorite heroes—along with custodians, night watchmen, woodsmen, doormen, and more or less anyone who froze in a sheepskin jacket under the cruel stars, or wandered in felt boots squeaking with snow to guard a construction site at night with the bared fangs of its vertical piles, or kept a drowsy watch on the hard chair of an official building, or stood next to pipes wrapped in rags, checking the pressure gauge in the dim light of a boiler. I'm afraid that his notion of a stoker was either unnecessarily romantic or outdated— stokers, as far as I know, are not at all that black. I knew one once—but we'll forgive the poet.

Lyonechka admired all these professions as the last bastions of the genuine intelligentsia. Because outside, the times were such—in Lyonechka's words—that the spiritual elite, no longer able to watch its weak but honest candle crackle and smoke in the foul air of the epoch, had retreated, had turned away, and, accompanied by the hooting of the mob, gone into the basements, the watchmen's lodges, shacks, cracks, and crevices, in order, having hidden itself, to preserve the last candle, the last tear, the last letter of its dispersed alphabet. Almost no one returned from the cracks: some were lost to drink while others went mad, either on paper or in reality, like Seryozha B., who got a job guarding the attic of a cooperative apartment building and one spring saw heavenly bouquets and silver bushes with sparkling lights in the dark sky beckoning to his ensavaged soul with a portent of the Second Coming, which he went to meet, stepping from the window of the fourteenth floor right into the fresh air, thereby casting a pall on the pure delight of the working classes out to enjoy the holiday fireworks.

Many people flew off into stern, high-minded flights of fancy about pure, princely air, about maidens in green peasant frocks, about dandelions growing next to wooden fences, about radiant waters and faithful steeds, embroidered ribbons and emboldened riders; they sorrowed and saddened, cursed the course of the times and grew significant, golden beards; they hewed birch blocks to carve spoons, bought themselves samovars, grandfather clocks with cuckoos, woven doormats, crosses, and felt boots; they condemned tea and ink, walked with a ponderous gait, would say "A lady, and you stink" to women who smoked, and with a third eye, which opens forth on the forehead after lengthy fasts and mental stoppages, they began to see sorcery and black magic everywhere.

And there were those who ripped open their shirts to free their suffocating throats, tore off their clothes, fouled by poison and pus, and renounced henceforth and forevermore, crying out: Anathema to Augeas and his works, to his wives and his heirs, his steeds and his chariots, his golden stores, and his servants, his idols and his sepulchers! . . . And, having screamed their fill, they wiped away their saliva, tightened the belts and strings on their bundles and duffel bags, took their children in their arms and old people on their shoulders, and, without looking back or crossing themselves, dissolved into the sunset. A step forward—over the hunchbacked bridge—through the waters of the Lethe—a wood trampoline—darkened air—a whistling in the ears—the sobbing of the globe, quieter and quieter, and then: the world is different, blossoming thistle, spring blackthorn, wormwood cordial, capers shall scatter and the grasshopper shall be a burden, and . . . Ah, the new stars are so innocent, and the thronging lights below are so golden, as if a burning being had passed by and left traces, his step wide and uneven—golden, segmented worms and shining tentacles wriggle and burrow, and then the cake of an alien city spins, bloody-blue, doused with rum and set ablaze, stinging the eyes and fingers, hissing in the black water, while the sea with its smoking river tongues inches forward into space—a cooling, darkened, sluggish space already covered with a thin film. Farewell, you who were too slow, farewell, you who remain, forever, forever farewell.

And others survived, preserved themselves, guarded against changes, laid low behind the strips of unglued wallpaper, behind the loosened doorframes, under the tattered felt, and now they emerged, honest and old-fashioned, redolent of ancient virtues and devalued sins. They emerged and couldn't understand, they recognized neither the air, nor the streets, nor a single soul—"this is not the same city, nor is the night the same!" They came out, carrying under their arms valuables safeguarded in their lethargic sleep: decayed novelties, frayed audacities, moldy discoveries, expired insights, amen; squinting, strange, rare, and useless, they came out the way an antiquarian, albino cockroach might emerge from a pile of old newspapers, and the hosts, amazed by nature's play, can't bring themselves to raise their slippers and crush the creature, who seems as noble as a Siberian fox.

But that's now. Then—it was January, a black frost, two-sided, double-lobar love, and the two of them, standing opposite each other in the foyer of my old apartment, gazing at each other in amazement—oh, to hell with them, I should have pulled them apart right away and nipped imminent misfortune and the whole disgraceful mess in the bud.

I guess it's no good talking about it now.

We forgot her real name and simply called her Judy; as for the country she came from, well, I couldn't find it in the new atlas, and I turned the old one in for recycling—in a hurry, without thinking, since I urgently needed to buy the recycled edition of *Backcountry River* by P. Raskovyrov: everyone remembers that those two volumes traded well for Baudelaire, and Baudelaire was needed by a masseur I knew, who knew the fixer who finally helped me to get the apartment, though he ended up creating a lot of bad blood along the way. However, that's beside the point. But I couldn't find the country. Apparently, after the usual battles, partitions, witchcraft, and cannibalism, Judy's compatriots tore apart the hills, the smoky river, and the fresh morning valley, sawed the crocodiles in three, dispersed the people, and scorched the straw huts. It happens. There was a war going on there, that's the thing, that's why Judy ended up stuck here with us: no money, no home, and no one answered any letters.

But in the beginning she was just a muffled, freezing young woman who didn't understand much of anything, who wanted to nurse animals and who believed Lyonechka's every word.

I knew him well, however. I knew Lyonechka from grammar school, and therefore I could neither trust nor respect him, but as for others—well, I never stopped anyone else from respecting him. All in all he was a great guy, a childhood friend—you don't respect those kind of people, you just love them—and at one time he and I hurried together through the same iron-gray morning gloom, past the same snowdrifts, fences, and swaying streetlamps to the same redbrick school whose facade was girded with medallions sporting the alabaster profiles of frostbitten literary classics. And we shared the melancholy of green walls and floors smeared with red floor-polish, of echoing staircases and warm coatroom stench, and of stern-eyed Saltykov-Shchedrin on the landing of the third floor—a scary, murky presence who wrote obscurely about a carp which you had to condemn in the biannual exam that bore the purple stamp of the city board of education. This Saltykov was always either "castigating ulcers" or "revealing birthmarks," and behind his rabid, arrested gaze there arose the bloodied apron of the sadist, the torturer's tense tongs, and the slimy dock, at which it was better not to look.

Those painted floors, and the muddy carp, and the ulcers, and the hiss of the strap that Lyonechka's father used to thrash him—all that had passed; the horizon, as they say, was lost in haze, and what does any of it really matter? Lyonechka was now an inspired liar and a poet—which is much the same thing—a small, bowlegged young man, with a head of mutton-blond hair and the round, not fully closed mouth of a skinned rabbit. Friends are like that. They aren't pretty.

He fought for truth, of course, wherever he imagined it to be. If the coffee in the cafeteria was watery, Lyonechka would run into the Food Inspectorate offices and, saying he was a public inspector, demand an accounting and a response; if the train couchettes were made up with damp linens, Lyonechka would blow up and, banging the walls, crashing through the cars, break in to see the conductor, announcing himself as an inspector of the Ministry of Transportation and threatening to smash this thieves' jalopy of theirs to smithereens, including the engineer's cabin and the radio room, and especially the dining car: he'd mash the mashed potatoes and spatter all their borscht with the impact of powerful fists, and he'd bury each and every one of them under an avalanche of hard-boiled eggs.

At the time I'm talking about they'd already kicked Lyonechka off the editorial staff of the evening newspaper, where, under the banner of truth and sincerity, he had tried without authorization to add a literary luster to the obituaries:

In horrible torment

TER-PSIKHORIANTS,
ASHOT ASHOTOVICH

passed on. Head engineer of a sugar-refining factory, member of the CPSU since 1953.
We can't speak for the whole collective, but most of the packing department workers, two of the accountants and the assistant director of the local committee, L. L. Koshevaya, will remember him with a quiet, not unkind word for at least a little while.

or

The long-awaited death of

POPOV
Simon Ivanovich

former director of a soft toy factory, came
during the night of February 2–3, neither
surprising nor upsetting anyone in particular. He'd lived long enough. Ninety
years old, that's no joke! Whoever wants
to show up at the funeral, well, it'll probably be on Wednesday the sixth, if they
deliver the coffins, but then anything can
happen here.

or

Noticed to be missing only a week later

POLUEKTOVA
Klarissa Petrovna,

an individual with no particular occupa-
tion, born in 1930, a confirmed drunk.
Found by her neighbors on the balcony,
she gave no signs of life, and she certainly
won't give any now. It'll happen to all of
us one of these days, what can we say?
Too bad.

or, finally,

Baby PETER played with matches,
Now he's up in heaven fair,

Where bananas grow in batches,
Baby PETER, hear our prayer!

Lyonechka was outraged by the narrow-mindedness and
callousness of his newspaper colleagues, who didn't accept his
style. He felt that their position was based on poverty of in-
tellect, acceptance of the cliché, lack of inspiration, and per-
secution of the creative intelligentsia—quite justly, in my view;
he deplored their indifference to the Russian word, so powerful
and poisonous and yet loving and lithe; he saw their disincli-
nation to expand the limits of genre, and most important—
he perceived their dishonesty, their dishonesty and their scorn
for the simple, terrifying event that awaits us all, for the trap-
pings of a simple man's death.

Lyonechka drank tea in my communal apartment kitchen,
drawing my neighbor Spiridonov into arguments and shouting
matches. Spiridonov had also suffered in the struggle with
indifference: the perforated five-kopeck paper piece he invented had cost him an early heart attack, divorce from his
wife, expulsion from the Party, and the loss of his illusions.
Once a fanatic and now a lifeless, gray-haired man, Spiridonov
would show up with tea in a railway tea-glass holder presented
to him by his coworkers for his jubilee, set out hard vanilla
cookies, and the two of them would grumble and shout at
each other. "Dim-witted Hegels . . . he says to me: Did you
substantiate the documentation? . . . The imagination of a
worm . . . I said, how much metal alone are we throwing under
a dog's tail, these are the Altai Mountains we're talking about
. . . fly-brains with sclerotic arteries. . . . All the bus fleets—
right? the whole subway—right?" They embraced and cried
about all that was pure, fresh, and untarnished, about trust in
ideas, love of one's fellowman, about a simple smile—they
cried about a lot of things in those days. Woe is me, oh, ach,
alas and alack—as Barkhudarov and Kryuchkov, compilers of
a glossary of our native tongue's sighs, wrote sadly once upon

a time. "They've done in Pushkin!" Spiridonov shouted ardently: "Ekh, if only Pushkin were here!" "Pushkin will come! We'll make another Pushkin," Lyonechka promised.

He laid out his plan to Spiridonov. I'm supposed to be an intellectual, right? said Lyonechka. An intellectual . . . you know, you've seen the posters . . . the one shown in the back, behind the worker and the peasant woman, wearing glasses just begging to be smashed by, say, a length of pipe or a chunk of cement—the one with a kind of watery, uncertain smile ready to turn into a humiliated smile any second: as if he's saying, I know, I know my place! The intellectual on the posters knows his place: it's in the back, in the doorways, at the threshold—and one undrawn foot is already groping backward for the step down, the way back, the path to retreat; that's the place where they chuck out leftovers, hand-me-downs, scraps, rags, dregs, dribbles, butts, slops, slivers, splinters, mismatches, misreadings, mis-seeings, mis-thoughts. What, you dare to stand up! I'll teach you! Aha, so you don't like it . . . You don't li-i-i-ke it? Take that, take that, take that! Sic 'im! son of a b——. Now he's trying to bite, is he? . . . Look, he's baring his teeth . . . he doesn't li-i-i-ke it. So get the hell outta here! Bastard. Kick 'im, kick 'im out, hey, guys, let's go, let's give it to him! Aha, he ran off. Run, run . . . You won't get far, ha! And he wanted to talk his way out of it, the louse.

It's no accident, oh no, it's no accident that intellectuals are placed in the back on official paintings—posters, that is—it's not by chance they're depicted as second-rate, last and least, just like the posters calling for friendship of peoples, by the way, treat black people as second-rate—behind the whites, set back a little. As if to say, friendship is all well and good, but, well, comrades, they're still black . . . you know what I mean.

It therefore followed that the intellectual (Lyonechka) and the black (Judy) should be joined in the bonds of matrimony, and this union of the insulted and injured, the wounded and outcast, this minus, multiplied by a minus, would yield a plus—a curly-headed, plump-bellied, swarthy little plus: if our luck holds we'll get a Pushkin right off; if not, we'll go at it again and again, or wait for our grandsons, great-grandsons— and going to the grave my blessing will I give!—decreed Lyonechka. "Go for it," sighed Spiridonov, and left, taking away his jubilee tea-glass holder, on which three silver satellites orbited a pea-sized earth with one lone country on its bulging side.

Lyonechka went for it.

It was the most nebulous possible time for this, it must be said, since it was precisely then that Judy, or whatever her name really was, turned out to have no citizenship status. That is, she simply had no status of any kind—in place of her African homeland a theater of military operations had opened up. One country wouldn't recognize her, another wanted to expel her, a third invited her to be interned for an indefinite period, and our country exceptionally regretted, shrugged its shoulders, scratched its head, blew the dandruff off its comb, smiled politely, and looked distractedly out the window, but could definitively propose nothing comforting at that given nebulous point. Just be glad it's no worse.

Aunt Zina, Lyonechka's aunt, not yet suspecting what a dirty trick her nephew was planning to play on her and her well-being, said to Judy, "Chin up, daughter. Life is hard on everyone." But her husband, Uncle Zhenya, whose diplomatic career was taking off—and who was expecting appointment to the corner of the African continent opposite Judy's at any moment, as it so happened—did not approve of contact with the foreign citizen, even though she was homeless. As the hour of the final paperwork on his appointment drew nearer, he became more strict and vigilant, so as not to take a false step in any direction. Thus, he forbade Aunt Zina to subscribe to *Novyi Mir*, remembering that its poisonous aura had not yet evaporated; he crossed all suspiciously surnamed acquaintances out of his address book, and hesitating, even crossed out a certain Nur-

mukhammedov (which he bitterly regretted later, when, straining his eyes, he held the page up to the light in an attempt to
restore the telephone number, since the guy turned out to be
nothing but a car repair swindler); and in the last, crisis-fraught
week, he even smashed all the jars of imported food in the
house and threw them into the incinerator, including the Bul-
garian apple jam, and was already eyeing products from the
other republics, but Aunt Zina protected the beet horseradish
with her body.

And then, if you please, just as he had brought himself to
an unheard of, unbelievable, inhuman ideological purity, just
when he virtually glowed, like a good, ripe persimmon—all
the pits shine through and there's not a bruise to be found
whichever way you turn it—no, no, no, I am not now nor have
I ever been under investigation, I never participated, possessed,
belonged, intended, pronounced or met, never even considered, never heard of in my life, never entertained the least
thought, never had the foggiest notion; but he rested not day
or night, saying: holy, holy, holy Lord God Almighty, Which
was, and is and is to come—at this very moment a boy, a snot-
nosed boy, his nephew, scientifically speaking, a near relative,
sullies, do you understand, his reputation, compared to which
the hermits of Mount Athos are simply delinquents, vandals
writing indecent words in elevators, mongrels, sorcerers, for-
nicators, murderers, and idolaters!

So Uncle Zhenya had a screaming fit and flailed about on
the floor. Because of Lyonechka's matrimonial intentions his
career hung on a thread, and in his mind he had already
traveled, served his time, and returned, bringing oodles of stuff
with him: wall masks, and rugs, and a fuzzy lampshade, not
to mention large-scale items. He could already picture how
future guests—the ones that might arise five or six years from
now—would change from their boots into slippers and peruse
the living room in apparent impartiality, their souls in fact
racked with envy; how he would then relieve the tension of

the evening with jokes: he'd take a Hong Kong rubber spider out of a packet and throw it against the wall—sticking and tearing itself away, and sticking again, the loathsome thing would crawl down, provoking happy cries and frightening the ladies; he envisioned how they would drink tea from a blue tin with a kind of dancing girl in bloomers—a diamond in her nose, and in her eyes, you know, a certain something, a sort of false innocence; Indian tea would they drink, while the small fry would make do with Georgian tea. In short, Uncle Zhenya planned to live luxuriously, to live forever. But God ruled differently. Jumping ahead, I'll say that after a few glorious months of his African career—which did happen after all— when he visited the national animal preserve where he teased a baboon with a stick, he got distracted and was torn into teensy pieces by one of those African animals passing by. Before his end, however, almost as if he'd had a premonition, as if he were uneasy, he did manage to send Lyonechka a present —the above-mentioned sticky spider; but the parcel took so long to arrive that when it came the spider had expired and it wouldn't crawl, it simply splatted; it took so long that even the newspapers promising that Uncle Zhenya's memory would remain forever in our hearts had been handed over for recycling, to return, in the eternal circulation and transformation of matter, as eighty-kopeck wallpaper, the line for which was long and dismal, as if in mockery of our aspirations.

But all this was later. At that moment Uncle Zhenya was still alive and happy. His wife was just what was called for— the daughter of a military man—and the tile in the john was lettuce green, Czechoslovakian, and on the wall hung a bala-laika, a sign of loyalty. So his screaming was completely natural and justified.

He screamed at Lyonechka's father—the right of a younger, but successful brother—for giving who the hell knows what kind of upbringing to his children: Lyonechka, who had failed miserably in the corridors of the press—the pup could have grown into a strong, international sports journalist if he'd only listened to his uncle; Svetlana, Lyonechka's sister, an undisciplined girl prone to hanging around cafés and riding in cars with God knows whom; Vasilyok, the youngest, a fifth-grade pupil, also got his share, though he was definitely not guilty of anything and had even just taken second place in the municipal skating olympics. He screamed at his wife, Aunt Zina, accusing her of permissiveness, absentmindedness, self-indulgence, and of the fact that the husband of her second cousin once considered working for the Planning Department, and for that matter the grandfather of one of the former employees of this Planning Department lived next to a peasant who had owned two cows in 1909, and this could be regarded as wittingly dangerous proximity to kulak circles; he screamed at the cat, who with the approach of March looked ever more frequently out the window; he screamed at the custodian, at the radish seller in the courtyard entrance, at the elevator lady, at the cooperative parking lot guard, at the head of the housing office, and even at the hamster living in a cage in the kitchen—and as a matter of fact, the hamster, having listened to Uncle Zhenya, up and died.

Anyway, Uncle Zhenya's screams were horrible, as horrible, no doubt, as the scream of a falling man slipping into the abyss, who tries to hold on by clumps of grass: the pliant dry soil raises dust and crumbles, and the roots swell, leaving their earthy nest; close, close to the eyes a startled spider or ant has already run out of his little house. He'll remain, but you'll fly off, blossoming for a short while like a bird, like a towel, like a still-warm, living bundle swaddled in its own cry; the feet are already scratching the empty air, and the world is ready, spinning and turning, to offer you its fluffy, green, rough bowl.

And I felt sorry for him, as one always feels sorry for those who've been beaten to a bloody pulp, as one pities the eyeless people you see in dreams.

Meanwhile, Lyonechka, having ordered Vasilyok to take up

the jigsaw and make the shelves on which he planned to place
the future Pushkin's works, applied himself in earnest to Judy's
education, to her initiation into his poetic faith. He couldn't
bring her home, nor to his uncle's, needless to say, and my
communal kitchen, enlivened by the invalid Spiridonov, resounded with Lyonechka's crazed texts, protests, and toasts.

"Well, what do you want? Tell me! I'll take care of everything," said Lyonechka, strewing the standard lovers' promises,
drinking his fill of tea and crunching the invalid's cookies.

Judy was embarrassed. She wanted to become a veterinarian
as soon as possible. . . . She wanted to be useful and nurse
little animals. . . . Cows, horses . . . "Sweetheart, those aren't
little animals, those are large, horned livestock!" "Horses don't
have horns. . . ." "That's fallacious thinking. That's a fallacy!"
seethed Lyonechka. "Horses used to have horns, but they fell
off in the process of evolution when the horse came down from
the trees in obedience to social demands and went to work for
man in the fields, where horns only got in the way. Do you
have cows and horses in Africa? And do they hibernate in the
winter?" the poet amused himself. And he explained to Judy
that the cow, having taken care of her business and seen to
the calf, goes off into the forest, digs a hole, and, settling in
cozily, curling up like a bun, sleeps until the spring, swept by
snow, with a gentle smile, her lovely eyes closed, eyes whose
praises have been sung in epics ours and not ours, and she
dreams of swift streams, lo, and green meadows scattered with
daisies; meanwhile, forming a chain, hunters are already out
on the winter hunt with flashlights and red flags; and they poke
the snowdrifts with rakes and lift the sleeping cow with oven
forks—that's why we only have frozen meat here. These aren't
any of your plain old zebu.

When the snows melt, Judy dear, we'll go to the country,
to the thick forests and wide fields—the fir trees are dark,
their stumps are huge—and you'll see our northern fauna:
curly-headed silky nightingales with blue eyes, white-fleeced

sheep with silver hooves who sing wonderful refrains above
the fleet waters; and what cats we have, dressed in caftans of
ribbed velvet with copper buttons, and what goats—if only
you knew—politically literate, tidy, with uncompromising civic
attitudes, in steel-framed glasses. And our spiders, our flies—
jolly creatures in red boots with gingerbread cookies under
their arms—tell her, Spiridonov! Chin up, Spiridonov, let's
drink to the spider.

I can't say that I liked this evening Sabbath very much, this
daily commotion and tea drinking on my tiny territory—I had
my own plans for life, and a few dreams: to marry, to move
Mama to my place from the suburb of Friazino or exchange
my communal rooms for a one-room apartment. Frankly, although barely defined, these plans were somehow getting all
confused and falling apart; it wasn't that there weren't any
husbands or opportunities to exchange apartments—everything was there, but it was all somewhat shopworn, squalid,
fifth-rate, with cavities and defects, abscesses and flaws.

It was impossible, for instance, to take my suitor Valery
seriously: strong and tall, and ardently admiring himself for
these qualities, with the face of a policeman or an executive,
Valery ate a lot of meat, kept weights, springs, a bicycle, skis,
and other unnecessary sports thingamajigs at home; his dream
was to buy a blue jacket with metallic buttons, but none could
be found for love or money. Without the jacket Valery felt
himself to be out of life's mainstream. Once we took a walk
in the autumn along the windy embankment of the Yauza: it
was a cold, orange evening, the last leaves were flying about,
a clear star shone in the sky and there was a feeling of winter's
closeness in the air, a feeling of melancholy, of the meaningless,
ineluctably nearing New Year; the wind rose and tossed freezing urban dust at us. Valery stopped and burst into tears. I
stood there, waiting through it, looking at the sky and the star
in the emptiness. I understood that words meant nothing, that
no comfort was needed, I understood that this was grief, fail-

ure, ruin: the blue jacket had gone out of fashion, floating by
Valery; like a rosy morning cloud, an ephemeral vision, cranes
flying overhead, or an angel in the lunar heights, the jacket
sailed off—it had beckoned, agitated, clouded his soul, entered
his dreams, and passed, just as the luxurious, colorful, spicy
empires of the East had passed, resounding and shining. Having cried his fill, Valery wiped his rigid Komsomol face with
a red hand, and we went on, hushed and sad, and parted at
the vegetable store on the corner, never to meet again.

Neither was Garik, a spiritual man, a suitable fiancé. Not
that the constant searches of his kennel bothered me: the government kept attacking Garik, confiscating his spiritual papers
and pictures, taking away his favorite books, and sometime
picking up Garik himself. It's not that I was scared off by his
six children from his former wife—Garik was a kind, loving,
sweet, and unusually resourceful young man: he managed to
feed the children, and indefatigably bustling about, he somehow quickly resurrected the papers at the same time. But I
got sort of bored listening to him—everything was "vineyards"
and more "vineyards," and paths, and quests, and bliss, and
the sweetest and not of this world, and yet life went on—a
bad life, but the only one around, and his den was full of
rubbish, rags, dust, and glue bottles on the windowsills, and
meatless porridge in a burned pot, and tatters on a wobbly
nail . . . and could it really be that this, this puny, ugly world,
was the one whispered about and promised, proclaimed and
presaged when everything began, when the unseen gates
opened and the inaudible gong sounded?

To tell the truth, love was what I wanted, and it was there
too, because love is always there, right here inside you, only
you don't know whom to share it with, whom you can entrust
with carrying such a marvelous, heavy burden—this one's a
bit weak, and that one will tire quickly, and those—you should
run from as fast as you can, before they've grabbed you like

a jam roll on sale near the store Children's World, slapping down a coin and wrapping up their catch in oiled paper.

Yes, I wanted something . . . something that would be heavier than Valery's weights and lighter than Garik's homespun wings. I wanted to travel or just leave, or talk for a long, long time, and maybe listen, and I imagined an indistinct traveling companion, friend, passerby, and the road appeared dimly: a path at nighttime, the fusty scent of rot, drops from wet bushes, laughter in the dark and a light ahead, a wooden house and a washed floor, and a book in which everything was written—and the sound of the high, unseen trees all night long until morning.

And also . . . but it doesn't matter. There was reality: the kitchen, the shouts, the gray stubble of Spiridonov's beard diving into a glass of tea, the crowdedness and the two of them, this unnatural pair with far-flung plans. We closed the window tight, so as not to hear the distant, needle-sharp, endless, tormenting cry of Uncle Zhenya.

"You know what, old girl," Lyonechka hinted, "if the fate of Russian letters is dear to you, why not bring the cot out into the kitchen?"

I didn't want to sleep in the kitchen, or "go out for a walk," or spend a week in Friazino, and Spiridonov didn't want to either. But Lyonechka swore, fought, and cursed Spiridonov and me—both privately, as a matter of course, and in poems, for eternity—and bought us tickets to a double feature with newsreels.

Spring was in the air—cold, nocturnal. The wind already droned in the trees, and water flew in the wind, and birds, cawing, bunched in billows in transparent trees, on rusty domes; clear puddles trembled, reflecting the lights of stands selling dumplings, vodka, and meat pies; and alarm, life, and desire breathed, sailed, and ran in the air—common property, unclaimed, no one's. I shuffled arm in arm with the gloomy, foot-dragging invalid Spiridonov along the crooked lanes, under Moscow's Muslim moon, and his foot, laced up in a fourteen-ruble, thirty-kopeck shoe, traced a long, meandering line through Moscow, as if plowing the barren urban asphalt, as if preparing a furrow for unknowable industrial seeds. And then, hunkered down in our damp coats in the movie theater, the invalid and I sullenly watched some fleetingly glimpsed factories, pig iron, awkward heroes of labor, tempered iron beams, tractors, record-setting hogs, bald, well-fed people in tweed suits rubbing ears of wheat between their fingers; we watched the stream of ideologically consistent grain flood us; we watched, waiting submissively for the friendship of homeless people to gel somewhere out there in the form of the illegal infant Pushkin, our last hope.

By summer there was still no Pushkin, and my life had become completely unbearable: the international lovers had made themselves at home in my room, they ate noodles straight from the pot, played the zurna, walked around naked, and even tried to start a campfire on the floor on a sheet of metal; for scientific entertainment Lyonechka bought Judy some white mice and a white tomcat; being a convinced pacifist, Lyonechka imposed his views on the cat—he developed a system of enlightening lectures and conducted practical seminars on restraint from mouse eating.

The Hannibals were always short of money. Lyonechka got a half-time job for a while working on a women's daybook calendar as an ethnic cuisine columnist. But here, too, love of truth did him poor service, because no one at the calendar wanted base truths, critical harping, and exposés, they didn't want the recipe for May salad to start with the words: "Let's be frank—there ain't nothin' to eat." They didn't want missives and sermons like: "Ladies, if you can afford to buy tomatoes at the market, stop and ask yourselves: Have you been living the right life? Where did you sin? When did you take the wrong step, turning from the narrow path of virtue onto the

beaten track of temptation? . . ." And he was fired again, and
again he was proud and indignant and immediately picked up
a couple of friends, or rather pupils and followers: bearded
guys dressed in rumpled clothes, draped with crosses and bells,
with wandering smiles and aloof, bovine gazes, and, inviting
them home—to my place, that is—he gave them edifying lectures, taught them to choose the unfalse path, and produced
as a living visual aid the cat, who, having experienced the power
of the True Word, had already become the most perfect
Buddhist and had transcended all earthly, ephemeral, and scur-
rying things.

A warm summer, an emptied, Sunday city—I would go out
to wander the side streets, choosing the old, dark corners where
it smells of beer spilled in the dust, of cheap stucco, of the
wood fences of construction sites, places where shingles stick
out of the walls of buildings, and dandelions—no matter how
you trample them—innocently and stupidly sprout at the foot
of sheds and temples from the time of Ivan Kalita. The grave
luster of a church dome in the distance, the meaningless, unceasing rustle of already darkening leaves, fleet coins of sun,
rags, and reek around garages, grass in linden shadow and bald
earth patches in the courtyards where laundry hangs to dry—
this was where I was to live and die, not meeting a soul, not
speaking a word to anyone.

Maybe there actually was a certain someone in another city
. . . but who cares, what does it matter if nothing came of it,
and now, after so many years, I'll sit alone and drink a glass
of rowanberry cordial to the memory of Judy's soul, and I'll
look into the candle's flame for a long time, and won't see
anything in it except a shining petal with a white core, except
for emptiness burning in emptiness.

Farewell, Judy, I'll say to her, you're not the only one who
didn't make it. I'm done for, too, all the beasts of my breed
have scattered to the four winds—they've gone beyond the
green waters of the Lethe, beyond the glass wall of the ocean,

which won't part to allow passage; those who didn't pay close attention were shot and wounded, the hunters had a glorious hunt, their mustaches are bloody, and fresh feathers have stuck to their teeth; and the ones who bounded off in all directions in the desperate hope of surviving hastily changed into alien clothes, adjusted their horns and tails in shards of mirror, pulled on gloves with claws, and now you can't tear off the dead, fake fur. I run into them sometimes, and we look at each other turbidly, as if from underwater, and I should probably say something, but there's no point in talking. It's like when someone is seeing you off on a trip and you stand inside the train car behind the unwashed double glass, and he stands on the platform in gusts of night rain, and you're both smiling tensely; everything has already been said, but you can't leave, and you nod and draw waves on your palm: "write," and he nods too: I get it, got it, I'll write. But he won't write, and you both know this, and the train keeps standing there, it won't budge, none of it will start—the jolts of movement, the sheets, the rubles, the neighbors' chatter, the dark, sickly sweet tea and oiled paper, the dull flash of lampposts on an empty railway platform, the blazing, beaded gold of raindrops in dotted lines on the glass, the sinful, sidelong glance of a soldier, the swaying crush of bodies in the corridor, the shameless cold of the john where the rumble of the wheels is stronger and more demeaning, and your own reflection stares at you from the murky half-dark, close and unflattering, your own reflection—humiliation—destruction . . . But this is all to come: right now the train is still standing and hasn't moved, and your smile is strained and ready to slip, to drift into a tear; and in anticipation of the jolt, the end, the last wave of the hand, you move your lips, whispering senseless words; eighty-seven, seventy-eight; seventy-eight, eighty-seven—and on the other side of this deafness he also moves his lips and lies with relief: "Definitely."

It was then that Spiridonov, who had ruined his teeth on

cheap crackers and the damaging effects of the hot water he drank every evening, was obliged to order himself new crowns. The scatterbrained invalid supposed that he was having gold ones put in, but his very mouth was ripped off for a pretty sum as it turned out later. However, the variety of metals in his middle-aged mouth created a rare but marvelous effect: Spiridonov himself began to receive radio broadcasts without any supplementary appliances. Soft tangos floated out from him, distant foreign voices and prayers, soccer matches howled, raging who knows where. He usually worked on shortwave and turned on in the evenings. In the early hours he transmitted all kinds of rubbish, "For all you inquisitive people out there," or a concert of machine operators' requests, but the thicker the darkness grew, the more mysteriously the world muttered and laughed, and lights escaped from the gloom, and there were colored lanterns and drums . . . and water ran somewhere, full of lights. What kind of water and what kind of lights, and what the drums were saying—how could we possibly know? . . . And at midnight the invalid broadcast in Portuguese, I think. Maybe it wasn't Portuguese, how would we know? But oh, what a beautiful language! A taut, flat ocean rhythmically beat at the shore in a wave as long as a whip, colorful sails entered the harbor, and stone steps descended to the water, and there was the smell of seashells and boiled rice, and under red roofs stern women sang loudly of flowers, murders, vessels freighted with burlap and lacquered boxes, birds and beads, purple silk and fragrant pepper. Perhaps it wasn't like that at all—but how could we possibly know if we had never seen it and would never, never, never see it—never, to our dying day, to the squeak of the cheap, painted coffin of wet pine slabs lowered on a hairy rope in jolts, spurts, and last earthly lengths into the sandy autumn soil, loam, red earth . . . to the last aster, the royal flower, stamped into the November earth, its head bitten off by the heel of a purple-faced, hurried grave-digger? Never, never, sang Spiridonov; never, I sobbed; never, shouted Lyonechka. Time has stopped, space has dried up, people have hidden in the cracks, the domes have rusted and the fences are wrapped round with bindweed; you yell—and can't be heard, you look—and can't lift your sleepy eyelids, there's dust as high as the clouds, and Pushkin's grave is grown over with thick goosefoot! cried Lyonechka. O'er summer's thickened goosefoot dragon-geese go flocking by. Like beasts at first they'll howl, or stamp their feathery feet and cry. A lonely maid is frightened—bearded dragon-geese fly by, Is that you Ivan Susanin? See me home, dear, or I'll cry. To our plans there are no limits, the whole nation reaches high; blackened crabs have picked the flesh off of a dead and bloated thigh. Peter's pinching peppered pickles, pinching pecks of parsnips too; slews of Slavs have sharpened sickles, but can't figure what to do. Beyond the gates the cold winds blow—the nightingale its teeth has bared; the fiend, sweet home's ferocious foe, refuses to be spared! The night bird croaks upon his bough, beneath him breaks the cradle slim; and cock-a-doodle-do bewails aloud the six-winged seraphim. God's little birdie knows no mercy—neither knows he shame; he'll tear your heart out, eat it whole, and gaily seek his fame. Midst foggy mist a string resounds—the road is all in dust; if life should e'er deceive you, then it's homeward that you must.

But Spiridonov, deaf to Lyonechka's decadent poetry, dreamed his own dreams, and his plans were grandiose: some sort of antennas, amplifiers, coils of wire, radio vacuum tubes, musical light shows. Ha! What light shows; he already planned to wire entire imaginary dance halls and stadiums for sound; he fantasized television images, festivals, cross-country friendship races, the investiture of Olympic medals, the erection of congratulatory statues in the motherland—marble to the neck, bronze to the nipple, a full five stories of granite with sword in hand; he was already razing mountains and excavating tunnels, damming rivers, and redrawing the borders of republics, he was already traveling into outer space and from there, his fake gold caps twinkling, his telescopic eyes rolling, huge as King Kong, he would knock down ballistic missiles and establish eternal peace throughout the whole world.

And there was still no Pushkin.

Then the vigilant comrades from the house management committee visited the apartment, led by old man Dushkin, who, if he slipped on the street or the sour cream had turned, never wrote to any less an authority than the Politburo. The comrades wanted to know: Why all the noise and music, and why did the lights burn at night? Your documents, please. Spiridonov took the blame on himself: he was an inventor, he worked at night, the sounds of the zurna and drums stimulated him. He brought out his eighth-grade achievement certificate from boy's school #415 of the Red Guard region, a publication from *Science and Life*, "MAKE a handy new MOP from old TOOTHBRUSHES," and a museum curio: the text of Lenin's "How We Should Reorganize the Worker-Peasant Inspectorate," reproduced in encrusted fish bones on a walrus tusk by an unknown folk master. If it's not allowed, said Spiridonov, then he wouldn't do it anymore, but his documents were in order, we know the residence rules. We, thank God, aren't children, we know that everything's forbidden: we mustn't stand at night on the side of the Moscow Ring Road, operate without support, pull except in case of emergency, lean over the driver's cabin, take more than six hundred grams per person, tamper with the packaging, bring a bottle for consumption on the premises, place objects on the handrails, peddle without a license, open before coming to a complete stop, walk without a muzzle, transport foul-smelling, poisonous, or oversized items, talk more than three minutes, descend and walk along the rails, stick our heads out, climb up, photograph, offer resistance, croak, whistle, shout thrice in the dawn like a basilisk, or engage in the sawing of firewood after eleven o'clock at night local time.

It was better not to joke with the comrades from the house

management committee. I kicked out Lyonechka's pupils; the white cat left on his own, having talked the mice into voyaging with him—and that autumn, by the way, they were seen in the upper regions of the Volga; the cat walked, leaning on a staff in a garland of forget-me-nots, aloof; the mice, six of them, ran behind carrying their tiny belongings, salt and matches—I'm afraid that they lit campfires in inappropriate places, and we were to blame; and to add to it all, Uncle Zhenya—who had arrived at his appointed place, and had already strolled through the official rooms of his new dwelling, yanked on the windows, doors, locks, and blinds, checking for sturdiness, unpacked his suitcases with striped ties, checked ties, and peacock feather ties, explained to Aunt Zina how to use the air conditioner ("Zhenya! Hey, Zhenya! I don't quite . . . I can't figure it out!")—Uncle Zhenya did not relax his vigilance for a second and sent Lyonechka a letter by diplomatic mail with a copy to Lyonechka's parents, warning that Lyonechka should stop it (he knew what Uncle Zhenya was talking about) and shouldn't even think of doing any such thing; that someone had already been warned and would follow through strictly, for he had been empowered to do so; and if Lyonechka didn't turn over a new leaf, Uncle Zhenya would let it be known in certain quarters and then he'd really catch it. And Lyonechka shouldn't think that just because Uncle Zhenya is in certain places he doesn't give a hoot. No, it's all very serious, because—you understand yourself, and especially now, when . . . well, precisely. There you have it.

Poor Uncle Zhenya—he wrote, he thought hard, and chose subtleties of meaning, but his death had already left the distant forests and, sniffing around, was running to meet him on soft paws, flexing its muscles. Uncle Zhenya finished writing, drank the coffee that was now available, and looked into the empty cup—and all the coffee grinds of the world, all the daisies, palm lines, pictures in distant stars and packs of cards with frowning kings and arrogant knaves had already fallen into the simple contour of a tombstone, trustingly revealing to Uncle Zhenya his imminent fate, but he couldn't read it, for this knowledge was not given to him. And Uncle Zhenya sealed the envelope and daydreamed of the future's fruits, of swimming in the sea, of new spare tires for a new car, of official reports and labyrinths of intrigue—he became lost in sweet thoughts of things that eventually came to pass, of course, but that no longer had the slightest relationship to him. It's strange to think that he died almost at the same time as Judy, and that as he pierced the metaphysical heights, he may perchance have bumped into her in the gray light of otherworldly bodies and not recognized her.

Uncle Zhenya wasn't joking: he pushed the buttons available to him, and in October—I remember the day: panic, Lyonechka's shouts, Judy's tears, and in the southern side of the sky that night, the distant, trembling dawn of Uncle Zhenya's malicious delight—in October Judy was summoned to a certain unpleasant place, an official building, and it was suggested that she be so kind as to get the hell out, go wherever she liked, only get lost. Obviously, we didn't sleep all night: Lyonechka gave Decembrist speeches, his sister Svetlana, in tight ringlets and heavily made up, ran back and forth from us to her parents (Mama was a real cow, and Papa was even more uncouth) despite the late hour (who knows, what if love were suddenly waiting around the corner) conveying, on the one hand, her brother's radical plans: to marry, emigrate, leave for the north, for the south, for Mars, contrive an act of self-immolation on Pushkin Square, and so forth; and on the other hand—everything that one expects in such circumstances. When Svetlana informed us toward dawn that a telephone call had been placed to the Southern Hemisphere (they announced that "Lyonia something or other," and he replied "call so-and-so") all of us—lovers, Spiridonov, Svetlana, and I—took off in an undisclosed direction, as they say, and fought along the way. Svetlana wanted to head for the sea, since she really liked sailors and the gifts they bring to girls of Svetlana's life-style; I proposed Friazino, where Mama had a little house, planted around with black currants and lupine; Lyonechka was attracted by the taiga (as usual, for ideological reasons); and as a result Spiridonov won, carrying us off to the town of R., where his sister Antonina Sergeevna was a bigwig in the city government.

Although the authorities in the town of R. lived better than simple people, as the authorities always do—for the May holidays they could sign up to buy marshmallows, Chinese towels, and even *Stories of Burma* in a colorful binding, and for the November holidays they got to stand on a heated tribune, sincerely waving their mittened hands to the freezing masses —and many simple people dream of such a life while tossing in their beds at night—still, the authorities have their dramas, too, and it seems to me that there's no point in maligning or envying them from the word go. Antonina Sergeevna, who sheltered us, had to answer somewhere high up in her empyrean for the hot-water pipes, and when the asphalt in the town of R. began collapsing and people started falling irretrievably into the boiling water underground, the empyrean raised the question of Antonina Sergeevna's responsibility for this unplanned broth. But, after all, the asphalt itself wasn't under her jurisdiction, it was under the jurisdiction of Vasily Paramonovich, and a stern warning should be issued to him, claimed the angered Antonina Sergeevna, slapping her palm on the light-colored, polished table in the office, and on the dark one at home. When the people collapsed, Vasily Paramonovich was absent, however—a general had invited him to Naryan-Mar to hunt the kolkhoz deer from a helicopter—and he most decidedly did not care to be sternly warned. He drew Antonina Sergeevna's attention to his friendship with the general as if it added a lily-white cast to the pure pallor of his nomenclatural raiment; he hinted at such and such and also at this and that, and, deftly summarizing, juggling and shuffling everything, emphasized the fact that had Antonina Sergeevna's pipes not rusted, the water would not have eroded Vasily Paramonovich's asphalt. Correct? Correct. While this mutual bickering continued, the water undermined Akhmed Khasianovich's trees, which fell over and squashed a couple of homeless dogs belonging to Olga Khristoforovna, for whom it was already time to retire on her special pension. Naturally, it was she who bore the brunt of responsibility in the end, since, as she was reminded, the department under her jurisdiction hadn't shot its quota of ownerless dogs, and during that fiscal period these dogs had insulted the dignity of our people in the public squares and children's playgrounds, and the dignity of our people is a golden, unchangeable currency, the pledge and guarantee of our continual, unquestioned success, our pride and joy, for it is better to die standing in boiling water than to live on our knees, picking up all kinds of I don't even want to say *what* after her undisciplined dogs—mongrels, it must be stressed—and besides, it's not altogether impossible that it was in fact her dogs that toppled the trees, dug up the asphalt, and gnawed through the hot pipes, which is what led to fourteen people boiling in our dear native earth—not an inch of which will we yield—moreover the Western radio programs are slanderously claiming that it was fifteen, but, ladies and gentlemen, they miscalculated—as always for that matter—since the fifteenth recovered and joined the work brigade of the blind workers' cooperative that produces Flycatcher sticky tape, and the spurious slander of overseas stooges and the hysterics and yes-men of the right-wing émigrés are only fit for the "Gotcha" column of the regional newspaper.

Thus was the true face of Olga Khristoforovna revealed, and without a second thought she ran off on her special pension, in order to resolutely write her battle memoirs, for in her time she had galloped with a cavalry squadron, had known Commander Shchors, and even been awarded an engraved sword, which still hung across the raspberry-colored wall rug with blue zigzags that had been given to her by a Dagestan delegation, and under which, on the narrow bed, covered with an army blanket, her unclaimed spinsterhood languished at night.

By the way, I'd like to note—for the sake of fairness and the bigger picture—that though Antonina Sergeevna acted faintheartedly, sloughing off her guilt in the affair of the boiled citizens of R. (and who wouldn't have acted faintheartedly?), all in all she remained on top of the situation: she thoroughly understood and appreciated Olga Khristoforovna's role and her contribution to our successes, to our lofty today, as she liked to say; and although she certainly could have, she didn't cross Olga Khristoforovna off the Timur Scout's list of old people, but every October sent her two transitional age adolescents with an axe to chop firewood for the winter. In turn, Olga Khristoforovna tactfully refrained from pointing out that her building had long since switched to central heating and that she didn't need firewood; she didn't shoo away the adolescents, but gave them tea with quince jam and showed them how to handle a sword, without a thought to sparing the white geraniums on her windowsill; as a gesture of friendship she even sent them to get cigarettes—she was an inveterate smoker—at a nearby kiosk, which the adolescents then chopped open with the axe around New Year, carrying off four kilos of hard candies and two packs each of cheap macaroni for Mama and Grandma. At the trial they referred to Prudhomme, who taught that all property is theft, and likewise manifested a good knowledge of Bakunin's works; leaving for the camp, they promised upon their return to apply to the philosophy department, and waved their prison handkerchiefs at a sobbing Olga Khristoforovna.

As a matter of fact, Antonina Sergeevna was a great gal, even though she wasn't one of us; she had steel teeth, a head of curls, and the nape of her neck was shaved high. "Girls!" she would say to us. "You don't know how to work, oh, go jump in a creek, the lot of you, what am I going to do with you?" Her jacket was official and inflexible: under it in a rose blouse resided her warm, unembraceable, already rather elderly expanses; she wore a wooden brooch at her throat, and her lipstick was bright, Parisian, and poisonous—we all had a taste of it ourselves when Antonina Sergeevna would suddenly jump up from behind the bountiful table ("the tomatoes! set out the tomatoes!") and press our heads to her stomach with emotion, kissing us with unabated strength.

Antonina Sergeevna took our motley crew in stride, said that she was very, very, very glad we had come—there was much ado, a lot of work, and we, of course, would help her. R. was preparing for a holiday: they were expecting guests from the Greater Tulumbass tribe, which was a collective sister region of the whole R. region. A three-day friendship festival was planned and the authorities were beside themselves. The undertaking was ambitious: to create all the necessary conditions for the Tulumbasses to feel at home. Plywood mountains and ravines were urgently erected, the string factory wove lianas, and in order to be stained black, a color closer to the heart of the sister region, the pigs were forced to wade twice across the Unka River, which had been noted in a chronicle of the eleventh century ("And the Prince came on the Unka River. And it was wide and terrifying"), but had since lost its strategic significance.

Pushing aside the plates, Antonina Sergeevna immediately laid papers out on the table, and waving away the clothes moths, acquainted us with the heart of the leadership's arguments. She herself proposed a thorough, comprehensive plan: an international scramble up a smooth pole; a sauna for the chief; a visit to the embroidery factory with gifts of dust ruffles and embroidered towels; a sight-seeing excursion around the city to include the ruins of the nunnery, the house where legend had it another house had stood, and the bakery that was being built; the placing of earth at a friendship tree; the signing of

joint protests against international tensions here and there; and
tea in the foyer of the House of Culture. Vasily Paramonovich
made a counterproposal: a meeting with Party activists; an
excursion to the acid guild of a chemical factory; a concert of
the voluntary militia choir; the presentation of memorial envelopes, the signing of a proposal to name one of the Tulumbasses an honorary member of the cosmonaut detachment;
and a picnic on the banks of the Unka with campfires and
fishing. For the dust ruffles he proposed substituting the Urdu
language edition of South Seas explorer and ethnographer
Miklukho-Maklai's collected works, which had appeared recently in local stores in unlimited quantities. Akhmed Khasianovich reproached his colleagues with a lack of imagination:
all this had been done, he said, when they received the delegation of Vaka-Vaka Indians. Fresh ideas were needed: a mass
swim across the river, a parachute jump, or on the contrary,
an excursion down into the local limestone caves, but a friendly
two-week trek across the desert or the tundra would be best
of all; however they'd have to agree on the route immediately
and set up stands with lemonade and sour-cream buns along
the way. The best gift of all would be a copy of the famous
painting *The Poet Musa Jalil in the Moabit Prison*, since it had
everything one could want in a painting: ethnicity, folk ele-
ments, protest, and optimism, expressed in the rays of light
pouring through the barred window. Antonina Sergeevna ob-
jected that, as far as she could recall, there weren't any windows
in the painting, and even if she were mistaken, the prison is
depicted from the inside, which could be depressing, and
wouldn't the painting *Life Is Everywhere*, in which the prison
is seen from the outside, be better? The sweet faces of children
peer out of the windows in that one, which inspires warm
feelings even in unprepared viewers. Vasily Paramonovich,
who was not strong on art, said in a conciliatory fashion that
the safest thing would be the poster "With Every Year—Our
Step Grows Wider," there are several hundred rolls in the

warehouse, we could give a copy to each of the Tulumbasses. They had decided on the poster, but now Antonina Sergeevna wanted to know our opinion, as people more in touch with the capital.

Antonina Sergeevna has to be given credit: Judy's past, present, and future, her looks, name, bad pronunciation, and clothes, which in their abundance and quality reminded one of the increased production at the Three Mountain Manufacturing plant at the end of the year, utterly failed to rattle her: Spiridonov knew where he was taking us. Judy was Judy, the Tulumbasses were Tulumbasses, five guests or twenty-five guests—it was all the same to Antonina Sergeevna, a woman who thought in categories and documents.

Twilight was already upon us and distant islands awoke in Spiridonov: the ocean seethed, Trinidad and Tobago stirred, a little wind played in the tops of the palms, a coconut fell, the blind coral threw out a new prickly arrow, and seashells opened their gates in the warm murk of the lagoon; and in the smoky dream of a pearl oyster what must have been Paris floated by—in a gray rain, in grape cluster of lights, quivering, Paris floated by like a sweet intimation of existence beyond the grave. Violins squealed like the brakes of heavenly chariots.

"Keep it down, Kuzma," remarked Antonina Sergeevna, raising her head from the papers and unseeingly glancing over the top of her glasses. "So then, Vasily Paramonovich wants to call in the blimps—he has good connections—and stretch a holiday banner between them—a few sickles, golden ears of wheat as symbols of peaceful labor—the sketch has already been approved by the censors. In this regard, a question for you Moscow comrades: Do we need a little slogan or two for the ears, what do you think?"

At the word "slogan," Lyonechka became politically aroused with dangerous speed, and, noticing the negative symptoms (sweat, trembling, electrical lightning storms of protest in his eyes), we all retreated quietly to the porch.

Early autumn had already crawled into the town of R. and
showed itself here and there—sometimes in brown bushes,
sometimes in bald patches on the foliage of subdued trees.
The air smelled of chickens, the john, and wet grass, the moon
rose so coppery and enormous that it was as if the end of the
world had already come; Spiridonov smoked and the music
of other worlds issued from his mouth, mingled with the
smoke; unshaven and lame, elderly and not too swift, he had
been chosen by someone to give witness to another life—
distant, impossible, unattainable—the kind in which there was
no place for any of us. The town of R. was our place, it was
as familiar as the back of our hands, known by heart, inside
out, whether you went to the right or the left or down into
the basement or up to the rooftop and, held up by your slipping
feet on the rusty tin and clasping the warm, potato-smelling
pipe, cried out to the whole world: to the thinning forests, to
the dark blue fog in the cold cleared fields, to the drunken
tractor drivers crawling into the tractor furrows and to the
wolves gnawing at the drivers' trousers and neck, and to the
tiny country store where there's nothing but packets of gelatin
and rubber boots, to the sleeping beetles and cranes overhead,
to the black, lonely old ladies who've forgotten how they trembled before their wedding and wailed at coffin's side; go on,
cry out—everything's known ahead of time, everything's been
trampled, verified, searched, settled, shaken out, there's no
exit, the exits have been sealed, every house, window, attic,
and cellar has been explored through and through, examined
thoroughly. They've touched every barrel, tugged on the
latches, driven in or pulled out bent nails, rummaged in the
basement corners that are either slippery from mold or dried
up, they've picked at the window frames, peeled off the brown
paint, hung and torn down locks, moved piles of loose, dis-
carded paper; there's not a single empty, somehow accidentally
forgotten room, corner, or hallway; there's not a chair that
hasn't been sat on; not a single stuffy-smelling copper door

handle that hasn't been handled, a catch or bolt that hasn't been drawn; there's no exit, but there's no guard either—leaving just isn't in the cards.

But the people who sing noisily in the fire and smoke in the invalid's illegal mouth—aren't they also searching for a way out of their own universe, diving, jumping, dancing, glancing from under their hands toward the ocean horizon, seeing off and meeting the ships: Hello, sailors, what have you brought us—rugs? plague? earrings? herring? Tell us quickly, is there another life, and which way should we run to seize its gilded edges?

Svetlana sighed heavily. She suffered because all over the world there were men, unattainable and magnificent, in the mines and in airplanes, in restaurants and on prison bunks, on night watch and under festive white sails, men whom she'd never meet: small ones and big ones, with mustaches and automobiles, ties and bald spots, long underwear and gold signet rings, with pockets full of money and a passionate desire to spend this money on Svetlana—who's right here on the evening porch, all curls and powder, ready to fall deeply in love with each and every one who asks.

Blending with the darkness, Judy sat silently, like everyone else. She hadn't said anything in a long time, but only now, when Spiridonov played a solo on his horn, could one suddenly hear how deep, powerless, and black her silence was; it was like the lonely obedient silence of a beast—that fantastic beast she wanted to nurse without knowing or seeing who beckoned with a hoof or claw; wrapping herself in scarves and shawls, she boldly set off into the distance, beyond the seas and mountains in search of that beast, in search of a warm, quiet, useful friend with soft wool, with silly dark eyes, with sparse hair on its face and a secret emptiness blowing from the pitted, rosy cartilage of its ear canals, with milk in its satiny stomach or a column of transparent seed in the curly caches of its loins; a beast with long, spiral horns and a tail resembling a geisha's hair in the morning, with a silver chain on its neck and a daisy in its carefree mouth, an affectionate, loyal, make-believe beast, imagined in dreams.

I wanted to hug her, to stroke her fuzzy head, and say: Now now, what do you want from us, foolish woman, how can we help you if we ourselves don't know whom to call, where to run, what to look for and from whom to hide? We're all running in different directions: I am, and you are, and so is Antonina Sergeevna, who sweats from her immense government responsibilities, and so is Uncle Zhenya, who's already far away, southern, almost otherworldly, comfortably wriggling his toes in his brand-new inexpensive sandals, ready to set out on the walk from which he won't return; and so is the maiden-knight Olga Khristoforovna, who wanted to do what was best, but was cut down by colleagues who wanted to do even better—the moon rises and torments Olga Khristoforovna with forgotten dreams, forgotten fields torn up by the cavalry's hooves, the hiss of transparent sabers, the smoke of soundless gunshot, the smell of porridge from the collective pots, the smell of sheepskin, blood, youth, and unreceived kisses. Look around, listen carefully, or even open a book. Everyone's running, running away from himself or in search of himself: Odysseus runs endlessly, spinning and marking time in the small bowl of the Mediterranean Sea; the three sisters are running to Moscow, motionlessly and eternally, like in a nightmare, moving their six legs, running in place; Doctor Doolittle who, rather like you, got lost in dreams of sick, overseas animals, is also running—"and Doctor Doolittle ran all that day, and only one word would he say: Limpopo, Limpopo, Limpopo!" Moscow, Limpopo, the town of R., or the island of Ithaca—isn't it all the same?

But I didn't say any of this, because at that moment the gate jingled and from the dew-befogged hawthorn bushes emerged Vasily Paramonovich, the devotee of the airways, white in his embroidered shirt, arm in arm with Perkhushkov, the regional ideological dragon.

"Who's there?" Vasily Paramonovich hooted, cheerful and alert, from the twilight. "I've come to work things out, I've got new plans with me, and then I hear: someone's misbehaving with music. And is this none other than Antonina Sergeevna's brother come to pay a visit? Welcome home!"

"What's that?" said Perkhushkov, roused, sensing Judy's darkness in the dark. "Don't tell me the foreign comrades have already arrived? The reservations aren't till the twentieth."

And he returned us to the house, where the sight and effect of tomatoes and cognac revived dim historical memories of the Battle of Borodino. "We're expecting the air squadron by morning," said Vasily Paramonovich. "Oh, what a celebration it'll be!"

"But where will they land?" said Antonina Sergeevna, surprised.

"Oh, they won't land anywhere: they don't have a permit," replied Vasily Paramonovich, casting a sidelong glance at Perkhushkov. Perkhushkov nodded. "They're going to circle and make figures. Tomorrow they'll rehearse, and then when our sister-regional comrades get here, they'll give them a real show."

"Couldn't we throw red carnations from the fighter planes? Paper ones?" asked Antonina Sergeevna.

"We used up our quota of paper way back in June! Now, then, Antonina, just what we need, more paper."

"What if we get the private sector in, the ones who knit flowers for the cemetery?"

"Under no circumstances! They knit roses, not carnations, and roses are apolitical," interrupted Perkhushkov. "You have to understand the difference. In fact, the cemetery is one of our sorest spots and a source of consternation," said Perkhushkov sadly, "a neglected plot of ideological work, I have to admit. It has a despondent, depressed spirit and a touch of mysticism uncharacteristic of our society: crosses, crypts, and some people even allow themselves to carve pessimistic inscriptions or erect cement angels, which are essentially unmasked subversions of materialism and empiriocriticism. And just think, on the tombstones and gravestones they carve— completely irresponsibly—not only the date of birth, but the date of so-called death, and most of the time neither have been cleared with the proper authorities. It's just plain cosmopolitanism. That's why there's a move now to enter stern reprimands—stern, mind you!—in the dossiers of deceased comrades if mystical figures and unauthorized dates appear on their graves—after all, we can't allow the Three Sources and Three Spare Parts of Marxism to be obstructed and squandered by a bunch of little cherubims introduced from the outside. And take other problem spots. No need to go far— why right over here, two blocks away, in the old-age home, what goes on there if you just scratch beneath the surface. Gaidukov, Andrei Borisovich: an Honored Worker, medals from armpit to armpit, so many of them that at last November's holidays they had to add panels to his jacket, thrice laureate of the Blue Sword. He's completely forgotten himself, hunts rabbits under his bed, shames the authorities. Boiko, Raisa Nikolaevna: you'd think that all the necessary conditions had been provided, they brought her to the political seminars on a hospital bed, camphor—be our guest, an IV—to your health, an oxygen pillow—our pleasure, everything's right at hand. And then she goes and confuses Jaspers with Kierkegaard, can't name the seventeen reasons of gradual transformation, and insists that Martin Luther King nailed the April theses to the Berlin Wall! What is this? And Ivanova, Sulamif Semyonovna? Quite understandable if she'd had a bad class origin, but no, she's a first-generation member of the intelligentsia, a doctoral candidate and everything, and at one time she even invented some kind of syrup for calming the nerves that was very popular at the end of the thirties, so popular that Mikhail Ivanovich Kalinin himself congratulated her, stuck a medal on her chest, embraced and kissed her, shook her hands, feet, neck, everything—he greeted her very warmly. This Sulamif became horribly senile—though I suspect it's not senility but a diversion—and pretends she's a young, capricious girl, moreover of the most vulgar sort: give her some bouquets of lilac, she says, she'll wallow around in them, and she wants elves with feather fans to blow zephyrs on her, for example, or—horrors!—siroccos. Can you imagine? This is one of our own Soviet old ladies—and to make such a political error. Friends, honestly now, how could there be siroccos in our country?"

Perkhushkov burst into tears, shaking his head, and Svetlana, drawn to male secretions—even if only tears—like a snake to heat, nestled up against the weakened commissar and set about drying all forty of his eyes with her fair locks, which she had dipped in sugar water for strength and set in strips of the newspaper *Red Star* the evening before.

And on the whole, said Perkhushkov, plunging into melancholy, how frightening and difficult it is to live on this earth, my friends. What dramas, collisions, hurricanes, tempests, tornadoes, cyclones, anticyclones, typhoons, tsunamis, mistrals, barguzins, khamsins, and North Winds, not to mention shaitans, occur at every step of our spiritual life. O! Literally this summer, just this August, this very August, Perkhushkov lived through a drama that no pen would dare take up—the Homer has not yet been blinded who could tackle this theme. Hell—Perkhushkov recounted bitterly—was nothing but a party with girls, just an amusement park, to put it mildly, compared to what he went through. That universal fool Dante, who supposedly roamed around the circles of hell with his pal Virgil, would have hanged himself on the spot if he'd had to go through anything like this; he wouldn't have bothered suffering. From the first to the fourteenth of August—days of mourning, weeks of woe—Perkhushkov suffered the hell of

separation from his homeland. Yes. He went to Italy. Yes. He
went there in an airplane, and came back—to increase his
torment—by train. The result: he went gray overnight (Perkhushkov moved Svetlana aside and showed his gray hair), and
bitter wrinkles sprouted over his entire face, ears, and even
the nape of his neck.

How to describe it?—after all, Perkhushkov isn't Homer or
Lope de Vega, or even the Pleiades poets. How to describe
the loneliness, the feeling of breakdown, the profound, interminable depression? And the oppression which seemed to
suffuse the very air? In Italy there's always a gray, gray sky,
Perkhushkov related, low, leaden clouds gather over the flat
roofs and press on you heavily, crushing you. The howling
wind only slightly enlivens the empty, pitiful streets. Bent low,
an old lady will hobble past, a beggar will crawl by waving the
bloody stump of a limb wrapped in filthy rags, and then silence
descends once again. An occasional snowflake, swirling slowly,
falls in the horrifying, stifling atmosphere. Industrial smoke
covers the crooked lanes of the cities in black billows so thick
that you can't see farther than your outstretched arm—and
there's nothing to look at anyway. The Italians are a gloomy,
morose people, hunchbacked from centuries of excessive labor; they have sunken, consumptive chests and are constantly
hawking blood, so that the streets are entirely covered with
bloody tubercular spittle. Rarely, oh, so rarely, a weak smile
illuminates the pale, haggard face of an Italian, exposing his
bloodless, toothless gums—and this happens only if he en-
counters one of us, a Soviet citizen; then the Italian will stretch
out his thin, rag-covered arms and quietly wheeze: "Comrade!
Kremlin!"—and again let his weakened limbs fall powerlessly
to his side.

In the middle of Italy rises a black, gloomy fortress—the
Vatican. A horrible, foul-smelling moat surrounds the fortress
on all sides, and only once a year a squeaking drawbridge
lowers its rusty chains to let in trucks full of gold. Crows circle

the Vatican cawing ominously, and higher up helicopters zoom around, and even higher—Pershing missiles. Once in a while a wheezing laugh sounds from within the fortress walls—it's the pope of Rome, a dreary old man whom no one has ever seen. He's well-fed and rich, of course; he has his own fields and flocks, so he eats sausage, fat, and dumplings every day, and pizza on holidays. In the Vatican cellar there's a harem: hundreds of magnificent girls languish there, including some of our Soviet girls who traded their native expanses for a pottage of lentils. Well, they miscalculated—they're only given lentils once a year, on International Women's Day, most of the time they only get gruel. And the piss pots aren't even emptied every day.

The Vatican guards are terrifying—whoever approaches is shot without warning. A step to the left or right is considered an attempt on the pope's life. That's why no one can do anything with him. Well-trained German shepherds and electrified barbed wire complete the oppressive effect.

Rats dart about Italy in such numbers that cars can hardly get through. And anyway, who has the money for cars? Perkhushkov cried bitterly. Only fat cats and the rich! They ride around happy as clams in linguini, drinking wine day and night in luxurious palaces and cathedrals and laughing loudly at simple Italians, who can only clench their gaunt fists powerlessly. The shelves in the stores are empty, and often, constantly even, you see little children—every last one of whom is on crutches, by the way—fighting in the garbage over a piece of bread.

"Who throws away bread, if there's nothing in the stores?" said Antonina Sergeevna, starting up in horror.

"The Mafia," Perkhushkov said sternly. "The Mafia throws bread away."

"My G-o-d . . ."

"Yes. And I can say this out loud to you, because you and I have nothing to fear, but for exposing this secret the Mafia killed all the police commissars, all the republic's prosecutors, all the carabinieri, and now it's holding the members of their families—including great aunts—hostage to unceasing terror. And the Mafia itself lives in luxurious palaces and cathedrals and laughs loudly."

Perkhushkov was so upset by the sight of the luxurious palaces and cathedrals built with loathing by the simple oppressed medieval masses that he couldn't even look at these odious edifices, which were barely perceptible through the smoke, and so covered his eyes with his hands; in fact, the entire Soviet delegation walked along with their eyes shut tight. A completely different, noble feeling seized him at the sight of the dilapidated hovels of simple Italians, and it was with particular warmth and tenderness that his eyes followed simple unemployed folk and the simple oppressed masses crawling by on crutches, and he even caught up with one of them and gave him a ruble with Lomonosov's profile. If he ran into someone wealthier, Perkhushkov clenched his fists and ground his teeth in rage, and between his eyebrows a fierce fold appeared instantly, smoothing out for good only on the way home when the train switched wheels at the border in Chop. From the very beginning Perkhushkov was tormented by homesickness. He began pining and feeling uncomfortable while still waiting for his passport to be issued. Worse! As soon as the word "Italy" had been pronounced, Perkhushkov was pierced by such intolerable anguish that he flew out into the courtyard like a pterodactyl and embraced a birch tree planted recently during a voluntary labor day in such a death grip that he had to be torn off together with the leaves and bark: before parting he had wanted to at least drink his fill of birch sap. Sitting in the airplane he pined: he pressed greedily to the window and watched with swollen eyes as his homeland slipped back. When the airplane crossed the border, Perkhushkov felt as though he'd been pierced by a white-hot rod, he was overcome, stricken. He tore himself from his seat, knocking over the packets of sugar and salt, the plastic cup with mineral water, and the meat patty in tomato sauce—so beloved and familiar!—and dashed, sobbing, to the emergency exit to unclamp the locks. It was only with great difficulty that he was held back by two stewardesses, the flight engineer, and the second pilot, whose eyes were also swollen from tears and longing for our native buckwheat expanses. Similar attacks of nostalgia, ever more frequent, overwhelmed him in Italy as well: at night he tossed about and bit his clenched, whitened fists; and during the day he sat in his room on the bed with a lackluster gaze, his head lowered, his arms limp as seaweed at his side, and continually muttered: "There's no place like home, there's no place like home, there's no place like home, there's no place like home, there's no place like home, there's no place like home, there's no place like home, there's no place like home, there's no place like home, there's no place like home." His comrades invited him to go to dilapidated theaters, drink disagreeable wine, ride in a leaky gondola— how could he? So it's understandable that on encountering a compatriot—one of our guys, from Tver—Perkhushkov threw himself on the fellow and clutched him so powerfully that the guy suffocated in Perkhushkov's embrace, in connection with which there was even a bit of unpleasantness about the corpse, an explanatory note had to be written to the institution which had sent the deceased to the capitalist country and a little fuss made about a pension for the widow and orphans, but that's unimportant, what's important is the agonizing patriotic feeling which seized Perkhushkov on his return: a feeling of pride in his homeland, her skies and other analogous spaces, her majestic achievements, broad step, steady stride, and high dairy yield.

"The homeland," cried an agitated Perkhushkov, "oh, what could be dearer than the homeland in a world of Final Resolutions? Nothing! And indeed, how wise are the golden Final Resolutions with their piercing light, how timely and yet how unexpectedly they occur, with what profound heat they scorch our souls, even like unto a gleaming sword, double-edged, bilaterally sinuous, filled with untold radiance, indestructible, indivisible, invincible forever and ever more! And truly—how would we live without Resolutions, we, who are pitiful, white, naked, blind, and trembling, like the cold worms and legless water larvae? O, shall we be likened unto the transparent lice, who in dense ignorance and animal unbelief gnaw the green leaf; O, shall we be likened unto the simple insects, who throng unaware in a drop of well water? O, shall we be likened unto the undifferentiated amoebas thirsting and fearing the division of their very selves—and sinfully thirsting in vain, for nothing which divideth in itself will stand; O, how dark, empty, and fearful it would be for us without Resolutions, how timidly we crawl between the stony desert's mountain outcrops, starting in fear at the least flutter or squeak, how pitifully we whine, stretching our hands, tentacles, metameric segments, chewers, pincers, and cilia into the utter darkness, which giveth forth only cold and a fetid roar: enlighten us! O, enlighten us! And how dimly the chill, extinguished, *previous* Final Resolutions glimmer, as if coated with fog and rust, for they have lost their currency and topical interest, like a maid loseth the color of youth, like a rose—its springtime pollen . . .

"And behold, the hour chimeth, and it cannot be foreseen, a voice thundereth—and who would dare envision it? The heavens open wide and the shrouds are rent, and the hundred-eyed Beast, whose number is twelve, sort of all in purple and scarlet, revealeth himself in a terrible thunder, rolling his legs:

"—and a papakha hat of costly lamb's wool is his miter, and his clothes are of wool, the finest spun and the color of evening mists;

"—and his breast and his loins are of rubies and purest unpolluted gold, his shroud is double-breasted, and in number his snaps equal the sands of the seas;

"—at his head lies the star Saryn, a corpse lieth at his feet; girdled is he with inexpressible crenulations;

"—and, raising high a horn, with a voice like the sound of the waters he thrice exclaimeth: Behold, behold, behold the Final Resolutions!

"And with uncompared strength, and sound equally beyond compare, the Beast unfoldeth the list of Final Resolutions, and their light, my compatriots—their light was like unto the explosion of a thousand suns, and seeing it, all gloom, foulness, and filth ran, hiding from the face of the earth, letting forth a stream of helpless maledictions.

"So, describe this, my friend, my young poet," Perkhushkov asked Lyonechka, "describe it as a citizen, as a soldier, one of the ranks. And may this book be as sweet as honey on our tongues, in our belly let it be ever as bitter as the root of the wormwood of Kara Kum, as the medicinal resin of the Pamir caves, as the salt of the lakes of Elton and Baskunchak, may its effect be ever purifying as the Carlsbad salts."

Perkhushkov peeled off Svetlana, stood up, and straightened his shirt, vest, army jacket, overcoat, cloak, parka, shroud, and black cape with an azure lining—he straightened everything that he had on or imagined he wore.

"And as far as the homeland is concerned," he said from the threshold, piercing a terrified Judy with his forty eyes, "I've explained it. Whosoever abideth in it, he will abide. As for those who can't—we'll find the right abode for them." And, narrowing some of his eyes, he flashed his spurs and left.

"Well, now," sighed Antonina Sergeevna, "home is always best, who can argue? This year there was even butter in the stores, and in the work rations there's always butter for 3.50 a kilo."

"There was yeast," affirmed Vasily Paramonovich.

"Yeast there was. And there's always flour. I don't know what else one needs. Veterans get raisins. Live as you please. Who needs any old Italy?"

"But he doesn't travel of his own free will," noted Vasily Paramonovich. "It's for his job. And about writing that

story—he's right. That's good. You write, young man, and you
listen to me," he recommended to Lyonechka. "I'll give you
a story too. Now, let's say we take a certain comrade. A simple
lad, a Russian. Served at the front, for that matter. Two
wounds, but one of them's not really serious, well, in the soft
tissues, let's say, that's it. But the other's worse. Yes. The
second should be a bit more serious. But then, of course, that's
not the point, I leave that to your imagination. So he returns
from the front, straight to the factory as a wire maker, the girls
there are nice, there's one particularly spunky one . . . but
that's also up to your imagination. That's not the point. So,
the years pass. They elect him to management. And the years
pass. He's in management, I can't deny it. But! You see, the
plot is that, well, they won't move him up higher, not for
anything. He soft-soaps Kuznetsov and Agafonov—I'm just
giving an example—no soap. It's like he's caught his pants on
a nail, to use the vernacular. What's going on? he wonders.
What's going on? Yes . . . There's a story for you. From real
life. They're always writing a lot of stuff and nonsense. Kisses.
All beside the point. And when you're in Moscow, you publish
it—what I told you, this story. Those in the know—will be
downright horridified, I tell you. There might even be distur-
bances. They might even have to bring in the troops. So you
go easy on it, don't overdo it. Keep the brakes on. Okay?"

On the eve of the Tulumbasses' arrival, Olga Khristoforovna
galloped through the town of R. on the kolkhoz steed with a
black banner in her right hand and an ultimatum in her left.
She demanded the abolition of money, of privilege rations and
regular ration tickets, demanded the closing of special distri-
bution order desks, the cancellation of exams in schools and
universities, and proclaimed the emancipation of horses, dogs,
and parrots, if it should happen that such were to be found

in the personal use of the inhabitants of the town of R.; she demanded the destruction of fences, locks, keys, curtains, rugs, sheets, pillowcases with and without rickrack, pillows, featherbeds, house slippers, underwear, handkerchiefs, beads, earrings, rings, brooches and pendants, tablecloths, forks, spoons, tea and coffee china—with the exception of plain tea glasses —ties, hats, ladies' purses, woolens, silk, synthetics, viscose, and nylon. Olga Khristoforovna permitted the inhabitants of the town of R. to keep for their personal use no more than one table, two stools, one zinc bucket, tin cups with handles (three), folding knives (two), one Primus stove with monthly registration, and one and a half cubic meters of firewood per family; blankets—one per capita; cigarettes and lighters—ad libitum.

Moreover, Olga Khristoforovna declared that she had renamed nature once and for all, on a global basis, and that henceforth the town of R. and the rest of the world would be granted August Bebel Autumn Rains, Vera Slutskaya Foggy Dawns, Nogin Clouds, Uritsky Sunrises, and Red Banner Snowstorms named after the Awakening Women of the Trans-Caucasus.

In conclusion, Olga Khristoforovna certified that her teaching was correct, because it was right.

It was in connection with Olga Khristoforovna's dangerous behavior that a nearby military unit was called in to assist; this was made all the more necessary, Vasily Paramonovich explained, because in any event you could expect excesses on the part of the population: after all, there have been cases in which local hotheads have forced their way through to visiting sister regionals and demanded that they convey slander of one kind or another to the United Nations: whether it's that the wheat is infected with beetles, or that horned fish are being sold and that they're supposedly radioactive—whereas if the fish happen to have horns, then it's for completely different,

personal reasons known only to the fish—or that men's socks
end up in the margarine and it's hard to spread on bread,
which isn't true. It spreads beautifully.

The Tulumbasses began arriving from the south, and from
the north came an unlimited contingent of troops. Blimps
hovered on high, decorated with mustachioed ears of wheat
and a short accompanying text: "Oh, rye, rye!"—all the rest
had been crossed out by the censor. Between the south, north,
and on high, Olga Khristoforovna galloped like the spirit of
vengeance, and the underground caverns, roaring with liber-
ated hot water, sonorously responded to the blows of the
horses' hooves.

In anticipation of meeting the Tulumbasses the comrades
in charge ascended the hill and Antonina Sergeevna demanded
that we, as guests from the capital and partly relatives, also
stand on the hill with kerchiefs and bread and salt in outstretched hands. Vasily Paramonovich had donned his sturdiest
suit and his electronic watch; Akhmed Khasianovich had
shaved three times and now worriedly fingered the quickly
darkening bristle rushing to grow out again; Antonina Sergeevna looked as though she had recently died and been styl-
ishly, expensively mummified—the cold wind blew on her
curls, amongst which rollers, forgotten in her haste, could be
fleetingly glimpsed. Perkhushkov was also around somewhere
pretending to be either a boulder overgrown with late, frostbitten plantains, or maybe that dead branch over there. The
rowanberry blazed, promising a stormy winter soon to come,
and far off, as far as the eye could see, the distant woods were
already yellow and reddish brown, enveloped in an autumnal
haze.

And the gray vault of the heaven over us where the squadron
howled, racing by with no place to land, and the distant brown
forests, and the hill in the middle of the globe where we
stamped our feet in the wind that blew salt out of the carved
salt cellars, and the frozen earth, shuddering under the hooves

of the raven black steed, invisible from here—at that moment all this was our life, our one and only, full, hermetic, real, palpable life. This is what it was and nothing else. And there was only one way out of it.

"No, this is not life," Judy said suddenly in a loud voice, reading my thoughts, and everyone looked around in bewilderment. But she was wrong. This was life, life. This was it. Because life, as we were taught, is a form of existence of protein molecules, and anything else is just empty pretense, patterns on the water, pictures in smoke. All you have to do is accept this wise view and the heart won't hurt so much, "and if it should—then just a little bit," as the poet wrote. If only we dreamed a little less—life is cruel to dreamers. What had I done wrong? But I wasn't even the issue. What had Judy done wrong: Judy who caught a cold on the hill in the town of R. and died two weeks later of pneumonia, not having given birth to Pushkin for us after all, not having encountered a single sick animal, Judy who vanished in vain? To tell the truth, she died like a dog, in a strange country, amid strangers to whom—why beat around the bush?—she was nothing but a burden. You remember her once in a while and think: who was she, what did she want, and what was her real name after all? And what did she think about these odd people who surrounded her, hiding, shouting, fearing, and lying—people white as beetle grubs, fly larvae, raw dough, people who would start babbling and waving their arms frantically, or suddenly stand stock-still at the window in tears, as if it were they who had gone astray in life's thicket? And Uncle Zhenya—what had he done wrong, he who was torn into pieces, into basic protein molecules next to a waterfall in an alien land—a stick in his hand, an uneaten banana in his mouth, pain and bewilderment in his bulging diplomatic eyes? And truthfully, feeling a romantic kinship with him, I won't judge him, as I will judge neither Olga Khristoforovna with her nightly spinsterish dreams of sabers and smoke and dappled steeds, nor

Vasily Paramonovich, who was born to crawl, but flew with rapture like a child whenever possible, nor Svetlana, a simple Moscow girl with the appetite of a padishah.

Then the hawthorn bush shook, and coughing, Perkhushkov spoke up unseen from the bush:

"Oh damn! Mea culpa. You people will be the death of me. We didn't foresee possible currency operations."

"What currency operations?" said Akhmed Khasianovich, looking around with his mad, magnificent goat eyes. Svetlana glanced at Akhmed Khasianovich, fell in love with him to the grave, and pressed herself to his breast.

"What kind, what kind," came the shout from the bush, "forbidden ones, that's what kind! Don't you realize what awaits us? I sit on high, look far and wide, never close my eyes, I spy, I spy: our sister-region comrades pass through town and village, our sister-region comrades bear Tulumbass currency: its light is blinding, its quantity uncounted, in town and village they're buying up milk and cabbage, galoshes and caramels, undermining the allowable, violating the permissible. Soon the Tulumbass comrades will set foot in the town of R., which is entrusted to my care: pillars will collapse and roofs will crack, walls will sway and the earth will yawn, the savings banks will go up in black smoke and a heavenly fire will devour the housing offices and government insurance departments if the tiniest unit of currency touches the right hand of even our lowliest compatriot. Terror, noose, and pit!" shouted the bush.

And, as if in answer to his speech, down below, at the foot of the hill, a horn rang out: it was Olga Khristoforovna announcing the assembly of all the units, which, however, weren't there.

"There's bad luck for you . . ." whispered Vasily Paramonovich. "Or maybe it'll work out? It seems the central authorities informed us that their currency is shells on twine. Tiny little things, yellow, with spots. Shaped like a baby's privates. There were instructions."

"Maybe it will work out," the bush said, calming down. "And anyway, Akhmed Khasianovich is responsible."

"They're coming!" shouted Akhmed Khasianovich. The Tulumbasses walked on and on in an endless stream, breaking bushes and crushing trees.

"About five thousand," estimated Vasily Paramonovich, swearing as nastily as a soldier.

"Tartars through and through," said Antonina Sergeevna sadly in a very old-fashioned way, to which the Tartar Akhmed Khasianovich replied, "I beg your pardon?"

"Why are they armed?" cried the keen-eyed Perkhushkov. "I'm going to have to annihilate a few people with entries in their dossiers."

"That's the way he always is," said Antonina Sergeevna. "Tries to scare you, but he's really a kind soul. He also loves fowl. At home he's got baby chickens and ducklings and turkey chicks. He recognizes them all and knows them by name. Feeds them himself and eats them himself. And he always writes down which one he's eaten: Rainbow or Buck Buck or White Tail, and he pastes a photo in his album. Just like children, honestly."

The sun broke through the clouds and shone on the gun barrels of the approaching crowd.

"Hey, it's our guys! Soldiers!" Vasily Paramonovich laughed joyfully. "They got here on time. Bread and salt retreat! Those are our guys. There, the tanks have appeared. Lord, what a wonderful sight!"

And truly, they were our guys. They moved harmoniously, beautifully, leaving behind them an even swath, like a highway. They moved on foot and on motorcycles, on jeeps, and tanks, and Volgas, black and milk-colored, and one Mercedes, camouflaged as a train trackman's hut.

The hut turned its back to the forest, its face to us, and from the lacquered door Colonel Zmeev emerged, glowing with unbearable male beauty.

On seeing him, Svetlana even let out a cry.

"Heigh-ho!" Colonel Zmeev greeted our leadership in English. "To your health. How many magnificent multicolored women and stylish civilians. How marvelously the sun shines and the frosty wind refreshes. How symbolic are the generous gifts of our rich earth: bread, and likewise salt. But we're no slouches: allow me to thank you for your attention and hospitality and offer you these modest gifts, made or requisitioned by our departmental craftsmen in their rare hours of leisure. Amangeldyev! Hand out the modest gifts."

Amangeldyev, a soldier of medium height whose face expressed constant readiness either for fright or for immediate physical pleasure, offered the box with the modest gifts and spread out on the withered grass a fringed tablecloth which was somehow instantly and densely covered with bottles of cognac and cold fish snacks.

"To your arrival!" Vasily Paramonovich clinked glasses with the guests. "Thank God. You got here in time. We had already started to worry. The aviation up there—they didn't disappoint us, they've been around since morning. The sixth ocean! You get my meaning!"

"The wild blue yonder," agreed Akhmed Khasianovich, glancing jealously at the colonel, who was thrice entwined by Svetlana. "Heavenly eagles."

"Steel birds zoom in where tanks fear to crawl," said Vasily Paramonovich joyfully.

"It's not quite like that," smiled Colonel Zmeev. "With the help of contemporary technology we can crawl in where our grandfathers never dreamed. The song's outdated."

"Pickles! Help yourselves to pickles! Dig in!" bustled Antonina Sergeevna, treating the guests to their own goods.

"Oh, the eternally feminine," said Zmeev, approving Antonina Sergeevna's fussing, and Svetlana squeezed him even harder.

Lyonechka looked at Amangeldyev, who, as a representative

of a national minority and moreover a simple subordinate, had instantly endeared himself to the poet.

After a snack, the colonel distributed the gifts. Lyonechka was presented a length of green Syrian brocade 240 by 70 centimeters, which he gave straightaway to Amangeldyev for puttees. (Like a shout in the mountains, this act provoked an entire avalanche of events: Amangeldyev's grateful relatives sent Lyonechka's family monthly parcels of dried apricots, whetting stones, fake medicinal resin, and dark blue raisins for two years; since by that time Lyonechka had already disappeared, his flabbergasted family, suffocating under the landslide of gifts and not understanding what it owed to the unknown givers, scrupulously tried to stop this bounty with no return address. Then three of Amangeldyev's cousins descended, wanting to rent an apartment, sell melons, buy rugs, and enter law school to become prosecutors; greeted with insufficient affection, in their view, they burned down a cooperative garage, tore up a children's sandbox, and bent in half the linden saplings recently planted by Pioneer scouts; not having fully appreciated the effectiveness of Aunt Zina's old connections, however, they were captured in the Hunters' Café in the middle of bartering a suitcase full of turquoise for yellow-striped certificate rubles with a certain Gokht, for whom the police had long been searching, but this is all beside the point). Judy received dried fish, Svetlana a pen on a granite base, and I got a Warsaw Pact Armed Forces calendar of memorable dates.

Then from the town the horn sounded once again and Olga Khristoforovna could be heard shouting through the megaphone:

"Everyone lay down your weapons! I'll count to 3,864,881. One! Two! Three! Four! Five! Six! Seven! Eight! . . ."

"There's time," said Zmeev. "Another round of drinks— and then we'll start shooting."

"Shoot her, my dears, she sings songs," complained Vasily Paramonovich.

And sure enough, far below, Olga Khristoforovna, having counted to ninety-nine, interrupted her count and started singing:

> *"Like conscience to tyrants, the blackness of treason,*
> *The cold autumn night is now here!*
> *Much darker than night in the deadliest season,*
> *The desolate vision of prison is near!"*

"That's all right, she's singing about the Vatican," said Perkhushkov, listening closely. "That's allowed."

"You don't have to shoot her, just catch her," said Antonina Sergeevna sympathetically. "She's not so bad."

"What do you mean, not shoot her, when she's right out in the open?" said Zmeev in amazement. "Amangeldyev, give me the gun."

The colonel hoisted the gun on his shoulder and fired. Olga Khristoforovna fell from the horse.

"Now she's not singing," explained the colonel. "Let's have another drink. The pickles are good."

"What are you doing?" Lyonechka screamed. "Why are you shooting people?"

But no one listened to him.

"Shooting—is beautiful. It's moving," Zmeev told his drink-flushed comrades. "After all, what do we value in life—what pleasures, I mean? In pickles—we value the crunch, in kisses—the smack, and in gunshots—the loud, clear bang. Just now we were coming here through the woods, and suddenly from all sides—a bunch of Negroes. Like this little lady here," he said, pointing at Judy. "All painted white, feathers in their noses, feathers in their ears, even, forgive me, in front of the ladies I won't say where, but there were feathers there too. Superb targets, little toys. We had a good shoot."

"Was anyone left alive?" asked Akhmed Khasianovich.

"Not a one, I assure you. It was all clean."

"Well, all right, then. We'll call off the blimps. Retreat," sighed Akhmed Khasianovich.

"Let them stay!" cried the inebriated Vasily Paramonovich. "Aren't they beautiful? Just like silver pigeons. I remember when I was just a little tyke I used to keep pigeons. You wave your hand and they—frrrrr!—they fly off! And how they quiver, quiver, quiver! Ah!"

"Well, one last round—and we'll go for a ride," proposed the colonel. "What do you young people say? We'll look for mushrooms."

"Let's go, let's go," Svetlana begged, admiring the colonel. "I want mushrooms, mushrooms."

"Amangeldyev, Mush . . . rrrooooms!!!"

In the tipsiness and turmoil it was hard to say who sat, lay, or stood where, or who hung on whom, but, twining into a living lump, we were already racing in the Mercedes over hummocks and roots, and the pines zipped by, merging into a sturdy fence, and the wild raspberry whipped the windows, and Judy cheeped, pushing away the fat stomach of the sleeping Vasily Paramonovich, and Antonina Sergeevna bleated, and Spiridonov, squeezed in somewhere just under the roof, played someone's national anthem, and no one divided us into the clean and unclean, and the sunset that appeared out of nowhere blazed like the yawn of a scarlatina-infected th~oat, and it was too early to let the crow out of the ark, for it was farther than ever to firm ground.

"My little rifle!" said the colonel, tickling Svetlana.

"Are you married?" Svetlana asked her magnificent beloved.

"Yes, siree. I'm married."

"But it doesn't matter, does it?"

"No, siree, it doesn't matter."

"I want mushrooms right now," begged Svetlana.

"You'll have your mushrooms. I'll show you a toadstool you'll never forget," promised the colonel.

"Oh, the girl is going to get herself into trouble," whined

Spiridonov through his anthem, feasting his eyes on Svetlana. And she was something to look at—but Svetlana, shining with happiness, was not meant for the invalid—her hair glowed with its own light, her eyes had turned purple like a mermaid's, her powder had blown away and her makeup fallen off, and she was so beautiful that Spiridonov swore quietly and pledged that he would give away half a kingdom for a glance from her—half a kingdom with all its half-palaces, half-stables, half-barrels of kvass, with all its mushrooms, pearls, tin, and brocade, with its kulich and gingerbread dough, raisins, bridles, saffron, burlap mats, sickles, plows, and rubies, its wild turkeys, azure flowers, and morocco leather half-boots. Only he didn't have any of this.

The ark stopped, and Svetlana, arm in arm with Colonel Zmeev, walked into the forest on tiptoe.

"I'll hire myself out as a sailor, and carry you off to Bombay!" Spiridonov shouted after her like a fool. And he himself blushed.

"We, too, were young turks once upon a time," sighed Vasily Paramonovich who had awakened. "And what are you doing here?" he suddenly jumped on Judy. "What's she doing here?"

"I . . . animals . . . want to cure animals . . ." babbled Judy.

"She wants to cure animals. You should cure us, that's what," Vasily Paramonovich raged, suddenly angry for some unknown reason. "Any fool can cure animals! I soft-soaped Agafonov, I soft-soaped Kuznetsov, I worked hard at it, how much good I did for people—anyone else would have puked. Need cement—go to Vasily Paramonovich, need stucco—go to Vasily Paramonovich, but for promotions—go to someone else. That's the point, not curing animals. All they do is walk around and around, around and around."

"He's kind, very kind," explained Antonina Sergeevna. "The weather's affected him, but he's very kind. At home he's got canaries, ten of them, and in the morning as soon as he's up, he sings to them—cheep, cheep, cheep, and they already know him, they chirp. They can feel kindness. Well, now, where are our people?"

Straightening his military jacket, Colonel Zmeev came out of the forest.

"Everything's in order. Let's go have dinner."

"But where's Svetlana?"

"I accidentally killed her," laughed the colonel. "I was hugging her and hugging her, well and . . . I squashed her a little. You know how it happens. It's all right, I'll send a unit up later, they'll dig a hole. There's not much work there. It's army business. Well, let's go. Amangeldyev!"

It's strange now, after fifteen years have passed, to think that not one of us has remained—neither Svetlana, who died, one likes to think, of happiness; nor Judy—even her grave is gone now, replaced by a road; nor Lyonechka, who lost his reason after Judy's death and ran into the forest on all fours—though they do say that he's alive and that some frightened children saw him lapping water at a stream, and there's a group of engineers, aficionados of the mysterious, who organized a society for the capture of "the wild mid-Russian man," as they refer to him scientifically, and every summer they set up ambushes with strings, nets, and hooks and set out bait—cakes, Danish, rolls with marzipan—not understanding that Lyonechka, an exalted and poetic individual, will only fall for the spiritual. Spiridonov's gone, he ended his life quietly with a natural death at a venerable age, and had subsequently invented many interesting things: a talking teapot, and automatic slippers, and a cigarette case with an alarm clock. There's no one left, and you don't know whether to regret this, whether to grieve, or whether to bless the time, which took these unfit, unnecessary people back into its thick, impenetrable stream.

Well, at least they sank into it untouched, whole, but Uncle Zhenya was picked up in pieces, in fasciae, hairs, and tufts;

moreover they never did find one of his eyes, and he lay in his coffin with a black velvet patch on his face just like Moshe Dayan or Nelson, in a new striped suit borrowed from the embassy cook, to whom, by the way, they kept promising and promising but never did pay any compensation, which pushed him into counterfeiting invoices for marinated guava. And it's well known: once you start it's hard to stop; the cook got carried away, it turned his head, and although every day he promised himself he'd stop, the demon was stronger. Somehow a Rolls-Royce appeared, then a second, a third, a fourth; then, of course, he developed a passion for art and began to understand all the subtleties of the expensive contemporary avant-garde and didn't like politics anymore, the ambassador and certain of the embassy secretaries didn't suit him—careful, cook!—then came the connection with the local mafia, the racket and narcotics business, secret control over a network of banks and brothels, intrigues with the military, and plans for a widespread government coup.

So by the time the cook, exposed at last, once again found himself amid the whortleberry copses and cumulous clouds of the homeland, he had managed to complicate the international situation so thoroughly, to inflate the prices on natural resources so enormously, and to introduce such bedlam into the art market, that it's unlikely to be corrected by the end of the current millennium. The oil boom was also his doing, said the cook on visiting Aunt Zina at the May and November holidays. He'd already gone to pieces by this time, was unshaven and dressed in a quilted jacket; Aunt Zina spread a newspaper on the kitchen floor so that the cook wouldn't drip while he drank a few shots of vodka; "I'm not asking you for money for the suit," said the cook, "I understand you're a widow, I only ask respect for my services, because the oil boom—that was my doing; and I never tasted that guava in my life, and there's no cause to go dumping it all on me, only

honor and respect, I don't need any suits, and if I've got a real
head on my shoulders then you should appreciate it, and not
attack me—in another government I would have been oh so
useful, they'd have asked me to be president and everything.
They'd have said: Mikhail Ivanych, be our president, and you'll
be honored and respected, and the suit, a piece of junk, is
totally unnecessary, to hell with your suits. . . . Here's where
I had them all," said the cook, showing his fist, "this is where
they all were, and if need be I'll have them in the same place
again: all those kings and presidents and general-admirals and
all sorts of shahs. If you want to know the truth, I already had
Norodom Sihanouk on a hook, I'd call him on a direct line:
So, Norodom, how's it going, you still hanging in there?" "I'm
still hanging in, Mikhail Ivanych!" "Well, then, you just keep
on hanging. . . ." "What is it, what can I do for you, Mikhail
Ivanych?" "Nothing, I say to him, just checking. . . . Keep on
hanging, just don't let go. . . ." Or else the emperor of Japan
would call me on the direct line: Here I am, Mikhail Ivanych,
he'd say, I sat down to eat raw fish, but it's no fun without
you, why don't you fly over and keep us company; yeah, sure,
as if I hadn't ever eaten that fish of yours; no, he says, hee-
hee-hee, you haven't eaten this kind, only I eat this kind . . .
but everybody keeps on talking about this guava business,"
swore the cook, as Aunt Zina pushed him toward the door.
"Don't you touch me! You, there, don't grab my sleeve!" And
snatching a ruble or sometimes even three, he would tumble
noisily into the elevator, where he vomited the grated carrot
and beet stars of a recently eaten salad.

Having done the appropriate amount of crying and mourning, Aunt Zina had long since calmed down, and, seeing as
people are weak and vain, found satisfaction in calling herself
a social consultant on the capture of the wild mid-Russian
man. She emphasized proudly that he was a close relative, and
her neighbors envied her and even tried to arrange intrigues

to deny her relationship, but, of course, they were put to shame. "How proud Zhenya would be if he'd lived to see this," Aunt Zina repeated, her eyes shining like a young woman's.

Every year in the fall, regardless of the weather, I drop by to fetch her; she straightens the lace scarf on her head, takes my arm, and we walk—in no hurry, a step at a time, to visit Pushkin, to place flowers at his feet. "If they'd just made a little more effort—he would have been born," whispers Aunt Zina with love. She gazes up at his lowered, blind, greenish face, soiled to the ears by the doves of peace, gazes into his sorrowful chin, forever frozen to his unwarming, metallic foulard blanketed with Moscow's snows, as if expecting that he, hearing her through the cold and gloom of his new, commendatore-like countenance, would raise his head, reach his hand out from his bosom, and bless everyone: bless those near and far, crawling and flying, deceased and unborn, tender and scaly, bivalve and molluscan; bless those who sing in the groves and curl up under the bark of trees, who buzz amid the flowers and crowd in a column of light; bless those who vanished amid the feasts, in the sea of life, and in the dismal abysses of the earth.

"And the Slavs' proud grandson now grown wild . . ." Aunt Zina triumphantly whispers. "How does the rest of the poem go?"

"I don't remember," I say. "Let's leave, Aunt Zina, before the police chase us off."

And it's true, I don't remember another word.

VINTAGE INTERNATIONAL

VINTAGE INTERNATIONAL

VINTAGE INTERNATIONAL

VINTAGE INTERNATIONAL

VINTAGE INTERNATIONAL

___ By Grand Central Station I Sat Down and Wept	$10.00	0-679-73804-5
by Elizabeth Smart		
___ Ake: The Years of Childhood by Wole Soyinka	$11.00	0-679-72540-7
___ Ìsarà: A Voyage Around "Essay"	$9.95	0-679-73246-2
by Wole Soyinka		
___ Children of Light by Robert Stone	$10.00	0-679-73593-3
___ A Flag for Sunrise by Robert Stone	$12.00	0-679-73762-6
___ Confessions of Nat Turner by William Styron	$12.00	0-679-73663-8
___ Lie Down in Darkness by William Styron	$12.00	0-679-73597-6
___ The Long March and In the Clap Shack	$11.00	0-679-73675-1
by William Styron		
___ Set This House on Fire by William Styron	$12.00	0-679-73674-3
___ Sophie's Choice by William Styron	$13.00	0-679-73637-9
___ This Quiet Dust by William Styron	$12.00	0-679-73596-8
___ Confessions of Zeno by Italo Svevo	$12.00	0-679-72234-3
___ Ever After by Graham Swift	$11.00	0-679-74026-0
___ Learning to Swim by Graham Swift	$9.00	0-679-73978-5
___ Out of This World by Graham Swift	$10.00	0-679-74032-5
___ Shuttlecock by Graham Swift	$10.00	0-679-73933-5
___ The Sweet-Shop Owner by Graham Swift	$10.00	0-679-73980-7
___ Waterland by Graham Swift	$11.00	0-679-73979-3
___ The Beautiful Mrs. Seidenman	$9.95	0-679-73214-4
by Andrzej Szczypiorski		
___ Diary of a Mad Old Man by Junichiro Tanizaki	$10.00	0-679-73024-9
___ The Key by Junichiro Tanizaki	$10.00	0-679-73023-0
___ On the Golden Porch by Tatyana Tolstaya	$10.00	0-679-72843-0
___ The Eye of the Story by Eudora Welty	$8.95	0-679-73004-4
___ Losing Battles by Eudora Welty	$10.00	0-679-72882-1
___ The Optimist's Daughter by Eudora Welty	$9.00	0-679-72883-X
___ The Passion by Jeanette Winterson	$10.00	0-679-72437-0
___ Sexing the Cherry by Jeanette Winterson	$9.00	0-679-73316-7

Available at your bookstore or call toll-free to order: 1-800-733-3000.
Credit cards only. Prices subject to change.

VINTAGE   INTERNATIONAL

also by

TATYANA TOLSTAYA

ON THE GOLDEN PORCH
translated from the Russian by Antonina W. Bouis

In this collection of thirteen stories, Tatyana Tolstaya portrays
a world that is paradoxically cruel and beautiful. With these
tales of modest yet memorable people living on the periphery of
contemporary Soviet society, she renders all the stark details of
life—its sights and sounds, its pleasures and pangs—vivid and
palpably real, while at once transforming them into something
magical and dreamlike.

"The most original, tactile, and luminous voice in Russian prose
today."

—*Joseph Brodsky*

Fiction/Literature/0-679-72843-0/$10.00

....